OUT OF THIS WORLD

A BROWERTON UNIVERSITY BOOK

A.J. TRUMAN

OUT OF THIS WORLD

(formerly published as *The Token Yank*)

By A.J. Truman

❀ Created with Vellum

ACKNOWLEDGMENTS

Thank you to James at Go On Write for the cover (and Natasha Snow for the wonderful original). Thank you for Paula, Anita, and Andria for beta-reading and Lisa for British beta-ing. And thank you to all the readers who have read and reviewed my books and written me notes. I couldn't have done this without your enthusiasm and encouragement, Outsiders!

What's an Outsider, you say? Oh, just a cool club where you can be the first to know about my new books and receive exclusive content. Join the Outsiders today at www.a-jtruman.com/outsiders.

Chapter 1

R<small>AFE</small>

It was a truth universally acknowledged that Rafe would fuck any guy with a British accent. It didn't matter if the guy was short, fat, pasty, or forty. There was something about the British accent that overrode normal conventions of beauty. Maybe it was a lingering evolutionary thread leftover from the British imperial era, and it helped explain how such a little country could've dominated most of the world. Who would've been able to resist a guy who sounded like he was forever reciting Shakespeare? Even a stuttering Colin Firth in *The King's Speech* was eminently fuckable.

Rafe's ears perked up in the airport as he listened to the dignified-sounding chatter around him. A British man in a suit (double sexy!) talked on his cell phone about work files. He had the dirty blonde hair and big eyes that reminded Rafe of Jude Law, the *Talented Mr. Ripley* era. *Excuse me, would you mind escorting me to the men's room and shagging my brains out?*

"Rafe, do you have your passport?" his dad asked him. Rafe looked up, and the British guy in a suit was gone.

"Yes." Rafe patted the front pocket of his backpack. "I am ready to get stamped!" He silently congratulated himself on the unintentional double entendre.

"Why is it in your backpack, sweetheart?" His mom looked at his dad in shock. The three of them all had the same lean figure and wild brown curls. It would be adorable if it weren't so embarrassing.

"Please don't keep it in your backpack." His dad half-closed his eyes and exhaled a breath. "Rafe, your passport is the most important document you have in your possession. You need to keep it in your front pants pocket. When it's in your backpack like that, it can easily be stolen."

"Sorry."

"Just be careful, okay?"

"I will." He put his passport in the special carrier his parents had gotten him and nestled it deep inside his pants pocket.

The three of them sat at a table outside a coffee stand before the security gate. Rafe saw other kids with their parents, and he wondered which ones would be in his study abroad program. It was rare for a sophomore to be going abroad for fall semester, but Rafe was compelled not to wait. He was in desperate need of adventure.

"You're going to have a wonderful time." His mom rubbed his hand. He wondered if she was going to tear up like when they finished unpacking his dorm room freshman year. "I loved studying abroad. I studied in Paris. You can go into any hole-in-the-wall place and have the best meal of your life." She stared wistfully at the table for a second. "Just be careful if you go to Paris. In any major European city, pick-pocketing is big there."

"I know you like to wear your wallet in your back pocket, but I think you should wear it in front," his dad said.

Rafe stood up and made a small production of putting his wallet in his front pocket for his parents, cramming it next to his passport. His dad winked at him and rubbed his head. Kids in college loved to complain about their parents, but Rafe stayed silent in those conversations. They loved him and meant well. He believed his coming out in eighth grade, and their instant acceptance and support, gelled them into a tight unit.

"And you checked with Verizon, and you'll have international service on your phone?" his mom asked.

"Yep!"

"And you have your credit card?"

"Yep again." Rafe patted his wallet, in his front pocket.

"So when you land, how will you get to the school?" His dad stood up to throw out his coffee cup.

"The study abroad program arranged it. The bus will take me."

"And what's this school's meal plan like?"

"Good. Dining hall food. There'll be lots of fish and chips." Rafe hoped his smile satisfied them.

"I'm just checking," his dad said, defensiveness in his voice.

"Rafe, you wanted to be in charge of arranging your study abroad trip, which we respect," his mom said. She and his dad seemed to be forever in sync. They've finished each other sentences, usually when those sentences were asking Rafe about his life. "You're an adult. It's your right. But we want to make sure we have all the details, so that we know you're safe and taken care of over there. It's not the same as you being in Pennsylvania at college. You will be an ocean away."

"I know. It's fine. I took care of everything. I adulted real hard when I planned this semester abroad. Don't worry!"

"We're your parents. It's our job to worry about you, Rafey." His dad rubbed his hair again. "We're going to miss you."

"You, too."

They sat there a few more minutes, until it was time for Rafe to go. His parents each hugged him twice. They walked with him to the security checkpoint, basically handing him off to the TSA agent, who could care less.

"I know it's a foreign country, but don't be scared. You're going to have the best time," his mom said as she pulled him into her chest.

"I love you." Rafe hugged each of them tight. He wasn't going to tell them that the only thing he was scared about was coming back to the states in December still a virgin.

———

RAFE DIDN'T SLEEP on the plane. He took advantage of the free movies and TV and made conversation with other American students in his program. But it was a long flight, the longest flight he'd ever been on, and so he had plenty of time to think.

He thought about sex.

Sex with hot British guys with hot British accents.

Most people he met were amazed that Rafe had come out at thirteen. He thanked his lucky stars for having loving parents and friends who supported him. But most people would probably be flabbergasted that despite being out and proud for six years, Rafe had never had a boyfriend. And he only managed to touch one other dick. There were guys deep in the closet who'd had more romantic experience than he. It wasn't for lack of trying, though. He performed many grand romantic gestures to win the hearts of guys, but every time, he came up empty. That's why Rafe nicknamed his study abroad semester Operation: Slut. He might fail at relationships, but by golly, he was going to succeed at sex! At least with fucking, there was no rejection. Nobody pulled out halfway through and said, "You're a really nice guy, but I'm just not feeling it."

And there was no reason why Operation: Slut couldn't start now. Rafe made eyes at a pale-skinned British hottie waiting to use the bathroom. Or loo, in this case.

Maybe we could join the mile high club together.

Once upon a time, Rafe believed in grand romantic gestures. Back at Browerton, he was always trying to win guys over with pre-planned romantic gestures that always seemed to work in movies but never real life. Except when his best friend Coop took over the library PA system to win over his now-boyfriend Matty last year. He would have to tweak his usual course of action now that he was in Operation: Slut mode. *Grand Buttsexing Gestures?*

Pale-skinned British hottie looked back at him! Rafe tried to contain his excitement, tried not to let the heat of their eye contact set him on fire. *It's on. I am going to lose my virginity on Virgin Airlines.* It seemed right.

He joined the hottie in line. He smelled so good, a mix of cologne and hand cream, like the men's department of Macy's.

"Hey. Good flight so far?" Rafe asked.

"Yeah." The guy checked his phone, which make eye contact difficult.

"Where in England are you going?"

"London."

"Cool. *London Calling*, right?"

The guy continued checking his phone, which struck Rafe as odd considering he didn't get service at 35,000 feet.

He heard the whoosh of the toilet flushing. It was now or never, and this trip and operation were all about the now.

"Do they have the mile high club in the U.K.? Or is it the kilometer high club? I'm down with the metric system," Rafe said as suavely as possible. If only the guy would look up from his phone, then they could give each other sex eyes to confirm how on this would be.

But instead, as soon as the lavatory door opened, the Brit swooped in and slammed it shut. His hottie turned cold. Not the most auspicious start to his trip. Rafe returned to his seat and hoped that this was not a sign of things to come. Or things that won't come, in his case.

———

WHEN THEY LANDED, the first thing he noticed was that London didn't look all that different from Virginia. Same landing strip, same air traffic guys with the wands, same trees and grass. Even the terminal wasn't too different from the airport in D.C. Until he noticed the exit sign.

Way Out, it said.

He spotted an arrow pointing to the Underground.

Ads dotted the wall for products he'd never heard of. Their prices were in pounds, and phone numbers were an odd jumble of numbers, and websites ended in co.uk. It really hit Rafe. *Toto, we are definitely not in America anymore.*

People buzzed around him. He was in a swirl of British accents. Guy after guy had one. *I'll bang you and you and you and you.*

He followed the other kids in his study abroad program to the customs line. "So what school are you studying at?" one of the girls asked him.

"Stroude University," Rafe said with an uncontrollable yawn. "You?"

"UCL," she answered in her American accent, which felt extra loud. University College London. Rafe heard that UCL was mostly Americans studying abroad. He wanted the real British college experience.

"Me, too," the girl behind them said. "I can't wait to be right in the heart of London."

"I'll be right outside London, so I'll definitely be frequenting."

"You guys are going to UCL, too?" A guy on the other side of the railing in their crisscrossing line leaned over into their conversation. "Nice!"

Rafe asked the other kids around him. They were all UCL, and two Oxfords. Showoffs. Rafe got a sinking feeling weighing him down, or maybe that was the jetlag.

"Is everyone going to UCL?" he asked, almost in desperation.

"Looks like it." The girl shrugged. "But you'll get a really authentic experience in...what school are you studying at?"

———

RAFE COULDN'T DODGE the sinking feeling that he'd made some big mistake. It followed him through customs, where the agent chastised him for not having his passport out and ready. It continued at baggage claim, where the other Americans in his program squealed about being in London and discussed bars to go to. Some kids didn't wait and picked up drinks at the airport bar. The legal drinking age in England was eighteen, not twenty-one. But not even that could erase the anxiety roiling around in Rafe.

Outside, busses were lined up waiting for all the

students. The names of the colleges were on signs in the front window. Rafe didn't even marvel at the bus drivers sitting on the passenger side. Most kids piled into the UCL bus. Rafe walked to the end of the waiting area, past the coach busses, to a white van with a sign reading Stroude scratched in bad penmanship.

"Going to Stroude?" The driver asked, almost surprised. He had a thick accent, choked with phlegm and cigarette smoke. The first non-sexy accent Rafe had encountered. "You..." He checked his list. "Rafe?"

"Yes."

"Fantastic." The driver loaded his suitcases in the trunk. "We are all set."

"What about the others?"

He rechecked his list. "There are no others, mate. Just you."

Rafe wanted to talk to someone in his program, a group leader, but the two women in charge were ensconced with the UCL students. Rafe unleashed another yawn that ripped through his lungs, but he wasn't tired. Exhaustion weighed down his body, but adrenaline kept him wired. He was in a new world, and he had no idea what was going on.

"You ready to go?" the driver asked.

"I guess so."

"Did you use the loo?"

"What?"

"The *bathroom*." The driver laughed to himself. "You Yanks are so formal. You should use the toilet. It's a bit of a drive there."

"I thought it was only a few miles outside London."

"Maybe on a map, but with traffic, it'll take about an hour."

I have made a big mistake.

"Don't be nervous. You'll have a good time over here," the driver said, seeming to sense his mood. "We Brits will treat you well."

"Thanks." Even though this driver didn't know him, it didn't sound like an empty promise. Rafe leaned forward in his seat. "What's your name?"

"Joseph."

"It's nice to meet you, Joseph. You're officially my favorite British person I've met so far."

Joseph gave him tips of things to eat and see in London. They were mostly things Rafe had already heard about through his research and general British knowledge, but he appreciated them nonetheless. Rafe wound up giving Joseph advice for asking out this woman he liked. Rafe might have had no need for grand romantic gestures this semester, but that didn't mean he couldn't pass on some tips.

Through his car window, Rafe watched the skyline of London get smaller in his rear window. The busyness of Heathrow Airport gave way to highway, then to rolling hills. This is what he'd told himself he wanted. An authentic study abroad experience. But the dreamy ideal gave way to the stark reality of being in the middle of nowhere in a foreign country surrounded by strangers. Any romanticism in that scenario quickly faded.

That is, until they entered the imposing, yet welcoming gates of Stroude College. A large castle, an actual castle made of stone and having castle towers, greeted them once inside the campus. Rafe's college back home, Browerton University, had ivy, but nothing compared to this. This was real history. The castle was probably older than Rafe's home country.

"Whoa!" Rafe gawked out the van window.

"This is a beautiful campus, mate. You're going to love it. How long are you here for?"

"Just until mid-December. So a little over three months."

"That's nothing. It's going to go like that." Joseph snapped his fingers. "So make the most of it."

"I will. Good luck with Janine! Remember what I told you. Stand in a heart made of candles and rose petals outside her balcony. Balconies are inherently romantic. Make sure the candles are unscented. She will be swoon central."

"Thanks, mate!"

Joseph dropped him off at the castle. A study abroad liaison waved Rafe over and led him to an orientation room with about a dozen other Americans, all wearing red Cornell T-shirts, and all just as sleep-deprived. They took up an entire row in the front.

"Welcome to Stroude!"

Rafe meant to say something back, but yawned instead. "Sorry!"

"Don't be. It's the jetlag. It'll wipe you out for a good two days. Just whatever you do, resist the urge to go to sleep this afternoon." The woman pointed him to a seat.

The thing with a British accent is that while it can be sexy, it can also lull someone to sleep. It's consistent and modulated like a metronome. She went over life at Stroude, the school's history and academic system. Rafe had picked out his courses before he arrived, and he looked up where they were on the campus map. But eyes had trouble focusing, and all they wanted to do was close. They drooped and drooped and the room went black.

"And don't you dare try to sneak a fag in your room."

His eyes bolted open. "What?" he yelled maybe too loudly.

"Rafe?" the liaison asked.

"That seems a little discriminatory."

"All rooms in Sweeney Hall have smoke detectors. If you try to disable yours, you will receive a fine."

"Wait, what?"

"That's why we don't want you smoking in your room."

"But you said…"

"Apologies." She blushed. "Fag means cigarette."

"Oh."

"I'm sure you will have many instances like this during these next three months. Culture shock!"

The kids up front laughed amongst each other, turned around to look at him, then laughed some more. He could tell they had all the friends they needed, and Rafe would not be one of them.

The liaison went on a few more minutes about life on campus, and when it was over, Rafe walked up to her with a question. She tensed up, seemingly anticipating another awkward moment.

"You didn't say anything about the meal plan. Or maybe I missed it." He bonked his head. "Jetlag."

"I'm not sure I know to what you're referring."

Even in his tired, anxious state, Rafe marveled at how eloquent Brits were off the cuff. An American would've just asked *Huh?*

"Meal plan. Where do students eat on campus? Dining halls?"

"There are none."

"What?" Rafe yelled.

"All dormitory flats are equipped with full kitchens. So you have the luxury of keeping and making your own food."

"The luxury," Rafe repeated. "Was this stated anywhere? This is the first I'm hearing about it."

"I believe the information was included on the website. In the program cost, meals were not part of the package." Her voice trailed up, like a question. *Are you really asking me this?*

Rafe's stomach growled. "What if I don't have any food?"

"There's a café in the student union."

He imagined his parents shaking their heads at him. How could he sign up for a program and not look into the meal plan? He was expecting culture shock to be calling an elevator a lift, not attending a school without dining halls. *Maybe I should've thought about more than hot British accents.* Perhaps his reach for independence was a stretch too far.

He remembered pushing his parents away when they tried going over study abroad programs with him. He'd never been a bratty kid, and had always welcomed his parents' opinions. But study abroad stirred something within him. It was about being truly on his own, and the idea of that flashed strongly in his mind like an immigrant seeing the Statue of Liberty in the distance. He was an adult. He didn't want someone else booking and double-checking his adventure for him.

His stomach growled in dissent, this time loud enough for the program liaison to hear.

———

RAFE ROLLED his suitcase down a sloping road into a valley of newly constructed dorms. It was steeper than it looked, and he had to catch himself from slipping since it was slick from a recent rain. He maneuvered down sideways, holding his arms out for balance. His suitcase got caught in the downward velocity of the hill, a snowball gaining speed.

Bam! The suitcase knocked Rafe in the back of the knees

and sent him tumbling down the rest of the hill. He landed in a rain puddle, which seemed about right. *Is it too early to go home?*

He found Sweeney Hall, the second dorm in a block of buildings. Kids gave him side-eye for his wet, dirty appearance. Rafe swiped his key and lugged his suitcase to the staircase. With its fresh paint and bright blue carpet, Sweeney Hall had the feel of being untouched. There was nothing quaint about it like he'd imagined his British dorm room.

He swiped into his suite. It was a hallway with bedroom doors and a swinging door at the end that he assumed held the kitchen. Nothing very suite-like about it. More like a nunnery.

"Wow." It was the sliver of good news he needed. A bedroom all to himself with a brand new desk, a full-size bed, and his own bathroom. He'd hit the college dorm jackpot. Maybe his study abroad trip wasn't a complete disaster yet.

Rafe didn't even wait to put sheets or a duvet cover on his bed. As soon as he hit the mattress, he was out. It was two p.m. England time.

Moonlight sliced through his blinds when he was jolted out of sleep by a violent crash, followed by the sound of a man yelling.

Chapter 2

Rafe stayed by the door for a second, not sure about what he heard, still fighting out of his sleep. He reached in his suitcase for something to defend himself with and plucked out a rain boot. It was heavy enough. It could work.

He crept out of his room clutching his rain boot, not knowing what he was doing or what he would find, but finding the bravery to keep going. He heard another crash and someone cursing in the kitchen. He pressed his hand to the swinging door, clutched his rain boot, took a deep breath, and ventured to his potential death.

But there was no crime scene. Just some pots and pans on the floor, a broken glass bowl, and a guy crouched over it, surveying the mess. The back of his sweater lifted up and flashed Rafe a sliver of skin and the waistband of his underwear.

"Bloody hell!" The guy jumped back upon seeing Rafe. "You scared the shit out of me."

It wasn't until the guy stood up and Rafe was able to get a good look at him that he realized he was talking to the most attractive guy he'd ever seen. He had light skin and rusty brown hair with the slightest curl that flopped perfectly on his head. But those were only the first degree of his hotness. He had these blazing blue eyes, the kind that could challenge the sky for textbook definition of the color. And then there was the scruff, immaculately sprinkled over his chiseled jaw. Rafe positioned his rain boot over his crotch, just in case.

"I'm sorry. I heard..." Rafe pointed to the fracas at the guy's feet.

"Were you the wanker who stacked the pots, pans, and bowls in the cabinet? I was trying to make myself a cup of tea. I opened the door," he slapped the cabinet. "and everything fell out. Now we got some fucking glass on the floor."

His accent had a hard, raspy edge to it, basically the auditory equivalent to a quick and dirty fuck in the bathroom of a dive bar.

Rafe found the broom and dustpan next to the fridge. He got to work sweeping up the broken glass.

"You don't have to do that, mate." He plucked the broom from Rafe's hands. "This is my mess."

"I can hold the dustpan." Rafe crouched down as his flatmate swept up the detritus.

"Louisa is going to kill me. This is all her shit."

"I'm sorry."

"Why? It's not your fault."

Rafe agreed, but he was at a loss to say anything else. When he was in the presence of really attractive men, he either got super chatty or super quiet. He didn't know which Rafe was better. His flatmate put back all the pots and pans and shut the cabinet.

"Thanks for the help. I'm Eamonn." He pronounced it

"aim on." He shook Rafe's hand, and Rafe savored the warmth of his skin.

"Rafe. I just got here. I'm still working off the jetlag."

"You're American?" Eamonn's lips quirked up into a funny smile, as if Rafe was as exotic to him as he was to Rafe. Which was not at all equivalent. Nothing about America was exotic. "Where are you from?"

"Arlington, Virginia."

"East Coast."

"Technically, but East Coasters are mainly New Englanders, and New York and New Jersey. Virginia is mid-Atlantic, so we're more Southern, though not too Southern." And here was super chatty Rafe, just in time. "How do you know about the term East Coast?"

"Because I don't live in a bloody cave. We get all your movies and TV shows here. Did you dig your way here?" Eamonn nodded at Rafe's dirt-stained clothes.

Great. Nice first impression, Rafe.

He cut his eyes to the dining table, where it looked like Eamonn was in the middle of rolling a joint.

"There's no smoking in here. I just had a whole presentation on it. Is pot legal here?"

"It's not a spliff. I roll my own cigarettes, and I'm well aware of these buggers." Eamonn pointed up to the smoke detectors. "I almost burned down my hall last year."

Rafe should've hated that Eamonn smoked, but the whiff of cigarette smoke on him was like it's own cologne, only adding to his attraction.

"So are you here for the whole year?" Eamonn's eyes were in a perpetual squint, like he was always on the verge of calling bullshit.

"Just until mid-December." He thought about getting that tattooed on his forehead.

Eamonn nodded exaggeratedly, like there was something funny about that. "I can't believe we have a fucking American in our flat."

"I'm excited to be here." *Right here. Looking at you and your wondrous body and listening to your sexy accent.* "I've never been out of the country."

"Well, we should welcome you proper then. What are you up to tonight?"

"I, um..." Rafe considered making something up because he didn't want to seem like a loser who stayed in, but he didn't want to miss an opportunity. "Nothing."

"Then it's off to Apothecary. Though you might want to change first."

EAMONN

Another year, another bloody night at Apothecary. Eamonn had spent way too much of his time at uni in this pub, but since Stroude was nestled in a town where everything closed at five p.m., he had few options. His new American friend, though, gazed at the pub as if it were a holy temple.

"You have bars? On campus?" Rafe asked him in wide-eyed wonder. Eamonn got a kick out of his accent. He'd never heard one up close.

"Yeah. You don't?"

"The drinking age in the U.S. is twenty-one. There was a bar off campus that was known for letting underclassmen in, but of course like all good things, it was shut down."

"That's naff." Eamonn couldn't imagine waiting that long to go to a pub. Hell, he'd been sneaking into them since he was fourteen.

Apothecary was built during the pre-Y2K frenzy and

hadn't been updated. It was a bit ritzy with white, sleek, futuristic interior designs and green lights around the curved bar. It made Eamonn think of a spaceship. Eamonn breathed in the familiar musty smell of alcohol.

He walked through the crowd to a booth in the corner. Heath and Louisa sat across from each other and gave him a big welcome.

"It's about time!" Louisa had pitch black hair against pale white skin, and a trail of freckles crossed her nose and cheeks. "Who's your mate?"

"This is the fourth member of our flat, Rafe. He's our token Yank."

Rafe turned red at the name and waved hello.

"Hiya. I'm Louisa."

"Hiya, mate. I'm Heath."

"Hi! I mean, hiya!"

Eamonn found that hilarious, though he wasn't sure why. The guy was as bouncy as his damn hair.

"Louisa, I broke your glass serving bowl. It's not my fault! Your pots and pans and bowls are all balanced on each other like a cuntfaced circus act."

"I loved that bowl!"

"It loved you, too." Eamonn directed Rafe to sit next to Louisa. "Grab a seat. I'll get the next round."

Louisa scooted down her booth and made room for Rafe.

"Another snakebite for Heath. Another Midori sour for Miss Louisa. And what'll you have?" Eamonn asked.

"What's a Midori Sour?" Rafe asked.

"Oh, this is Rafe's first time at a bar," Eamonn told his friends. "Apparently in America, the legal drinking age is thirty-seven."

"Twenty-one!" Rafe said.

"Actually, there's an agreement between the U.S. and the U.K. not to allow Americans under twenty-one to drink while abroad," Heath said. "The bartender will ask to see your passport."

"Are you serious?" Rafe covered his mouth in shock. It was quite cute, and Eamonn let it go on for another second before playfully smacking his shoulder.

"He's joking with you. Arse," Eamonn said to Heath. He put a hand on Rafe's shoulder. "We like to take the piss out of each other. You'll get used to it."

"Don't be afraid to tell Heath to sod off," Louisa said.

"Okay. I'll have a Midori Sour then."

"They're really good. Sweet and sour." She sucked down the last drops of her drink, which matched the green décor.

"Louisa should know. She's had about four of them so far," Heath said with a raised eyebrow. She raised her eyebrow back and bit off the cherry in her drink.

Here we go again. Eamonn rolled his eyes. That whole Just Friends agreement was *really* working out for them.

Heath stood up and came with Eamonn to the bar. Eamonn never considered himself short unless he was standing next to his best mate. Heath didn't make matters better when he styled his shock of white blond hair to stick up like a wave about to crash on the shore. Heath might've been taller, but Eamonn was the enforcer of the two. Ever since the first month of uni, when some bloke grabbed Heath's wet clothes from the washer and threw them onto the floor and Eamonn subsequently threw said bloke on the ground, he'd had his friend's back.

And having a giraffe for a flatmate served him well on nights like these.

"Can you see what the hell is taking so long?" Eamonn asked.

Heath didn't even have to stretch. His eyes scanned the bar area. "They only have two bartenders working tonight."

"Bleeding hell."

"You really need three to handle this amount of traffic. About one for every ninety patrons." Leave it to Heath to make these kinds of snap calculations, which were always spot on.

"Or you need students to make up their fucking minds before they get up there."

Heath had his methodology, and Eamonn had his.

"What are you doing next Thursday night?" Heath asked.

Eamonn looked around at the pub. "Same as usual."

"Well, maybe before we come here, we can go into London. There's this massive job fair. I think over 100 companies will be represented there."

"And what are we supposed to do? Go from booth to booth begging for employment?"

"Precisely. With a C.V., too."

It was their last year of uni, and Eamonn knew what came next. He just preferred not to think about it. They still had months before they graduated. Eamonn hated the whole process. *Oh, here's three years of some classes. Now choose one thing you want to do for the rest of your life.*

"It's all bollocks."

"Right. Work is stupid," Heath deadpanned. "Why would Eamonn Charles ever consider something as asinine as that?"

"You can sod right the way off. I've had jobs ever since I was twelve. I delivered papers, mowed lawns, washed dishes." When Eamonn's dad left, he didn't leave a fat check on the kitchen table for him and his two younger sisters. If it weren't for Eamonn's Uncle George and his company's generous scholarship, he wouldn't even be at uni.

"Wait. How come you never washed the dishes in our kitchen? How come you leave all your shit there?"

"Because no one's paying me."

Heath whacked him in the chest.

"Oy," Eamonn said. "How would you like a smack in the balls, Big Ben?"

"If you want to wank me off, just ask. I'll say no, but still appreciate the gesture."

Sometimes Eamonn couldn't believe this sarcastic arse was the same shy roommate he met as a first-year. They'd come a long way.

"Seriously, mate. You should think about coming with me," Heath said, still on about that bloody job fair.

"Why are you even going? You want to be a barrister. End of story."

"There'll be some firms there. It'll be a good first impression." Heath shrugged.

"Only if they have a fucking stepladder."

They finally reached the bar and put in their orders. Eamonn laughed to himself when the bartender handed him two Midori Sours and Heath two snakebites. He nudged his human periscope friend in the ribs. "Hey mate, how are Louisa and the Yank doing?"

Heath easily glanced over the heads of everyone in there. Eamonn had told him that he should be a spy, until Heath reminded him that he would stick out.

"They're talking, probably about some crap American series. Why are you so curious?"

Eamonn shook off the question, since he didn't have an answer himself. "No reason."

———

HEATH HAD BEEN CORRECT. When they returned to the table, they interrupted a conversation about the American version of *The Office*.

"Have you ever been to Scranton?" Louisa asked. "I have to be honest. I find the Steve Carell version better than Ricky Gervais."

"That's it. You're being deported." Eamonn handed her and Rafe a Midori Sour. Rafe marveled at his green glowing drink. Eamonn tried to remember what he felt the first time he went to a pub. He probably just wanted to get drunk.

"What should we drink to?" Louisa asked.

"Living in a country where we don't have to wait until we're twenty-one to drink?" Heath said.

Eamonn raised his glass and looked directly at Rafe. "To the token Yank, our new flatmate."

Rafe blushed, and Eamonn loved how it darkened his cheeks.

"I was wondering who they'd find to fill our fourth room on such short notice," Louisa said.

"Short notice? Was someone else supposed to be here?" Rafe asked.

The question tugged at Eamonn's insides. More like threw those insides to the ground like they'd taken clothes out of the dryer.

"Did you scare some other Yank away?"

The silence at the table made this moment even more awkward. Heath's eyes flicked over to Eamonn, but Eamonn didn't need anyone checking up on him. Rafe covered his mouth.

"Oh no. They died, didn't they? I am so sorry." Rafe shook his head.

"Nobody died," Louisa said. "Nathan left school to shoot a film. Ow!" She looked under the table then glared at Heath. "What? I'm not even allowed to say his name?"

"He's directing a film?" Rafe asked.

Eamonn couldn't talk. He just drank and listened to his beer slide down his throat.

"He's an actor," she said to Rafe without talking her eyes off Heath.

"That's so cool!" Rafe looked at Eamonn and seemed to regret his response.

Eamonn chugged the last of his beer and slammed down the glass. "*It's totally cool, dude,*" he said in his best American accent. It broke the tension that had gripped the table.

"Who are you trying to sound like?" Rafe asked.

"*I'm like totally an American, man.*"

"You sound like a California surfer. That's not how Americans talk."

"*We're like so glad you're here,*" Heath said in a similar accent. "*Really, it's so awesome that like, you could take time from surfing and shopping at the mall to hang with us.*"

"Literally nobody in America talks like that." Rafe drank his Midori sour.

"*Yeah, like really guys. Like oh my god. Seriously,*" Louisa said in a pitch-perfect Kardashian voice.

"Nobody talks like...not everyone talks like that."

"*What're you talking about, dude?*" Eamonn did not give up the surfer accent, not when it was causing Rafe to become adorably flustered.

"You can stop now."

"*Stop what? I need to buy a hot dog and work on my tan, man.*"

"Two can play this game." Rafe quirked an eyebrow at

Eamonn and cleared his throat. "Oh, look at me, old chap. I'm British, mate, and I love shepherd's pie. It's time to go on holiday at Piccidilly Circus and hang out with the Queen and Govna'."

"I'm confused. What accent was that?" Louisa couldn't hold back hysterical laughter. Eamonn and Heath joined in.

"British!"

"Are you sure?" Eamonn traded looks with their flat-mates. "Because it sounded like a cat getting a prostate exam."

Chapter 3

RAFE

Two Midori sours later, Rafe was officially drunk. It was partially the jet lag, but those drinks were surprisingly strong. Louisa had four of them, and she was strolling like she was stone-cold sober. Eamonn and Heath kicked back five pints, and they seemed barely buzzed. It didn't make sense.

"It doesn't make sense," Rafe said aloud. The campus was quiet, except for wind rustling through the leaves. "How are y'all not shitfaced?"

"We only had a few drinks. Bleeding Christ, Yank, you are a lightweight." Eamonn's hearty laugh echoed off buildings. He lit a cigarette he had rolled in the bar. Rafe wasn't a fan of smoking, but there was something sexy about watching Eamonn roll it, watching those assured fingers do their work, and that tongue slick up the paper and seal it shut.

"We've been drinking for years," Heath said. "I've been having a pint with my mum and dad at dinner since I was fourteen. Just more of a tolerance."

"Heath obviously comes from a family of lushes," Louisa said.

"And Louisa is a bastion of temperance over here," he shot back. Rafe loved their repartee. He and his friends were way too nice to each other. "Don't forget. All the people who don't drink fled Britain and founded America. All the cool people stayed here."

Rafe couldn't argue with that logic. His brain couldn't really handle logic right now. And his body couldn't handle the dip into the valley of their dorms. He held his arms out to balance himself as they walked down the hill. He was not going to fall splat in front of his new friends. *Friends. Yes, they are my friends.*

"You are all my friends," Rafe proclaimed. "I love it here!"

He knew they were laughing at his drunken state, or with. He realized that getting made fun of was a sign of acceptance in this group.

Suddenly, Rafe felt sturdy hands on his sides and a warm cloud of cigarette smoke blow past his ears. "What are you doing?" he asked Eamonn.

"Making sure you don't fall on your arse," he said with a cigarette hanging from his mouth.

"I have it. I can work. I mean, walk."

"We all need a little help sometimes." Eamonn stomped out his cigarette and tossed it in a nearby trash. He wrapped an arm around Rafe's hips and guided him down the slippery slope. Rafe had no choice but to put his arm around the guy's shoulders.

"Poor Yank can't hold his liquor." Louisa laughed.

"You're one to talk, Louisa," Heath said. "I distinctly remember last year on a walk home from the pub, you chundered in every rubbish bin from here to the dorm."

"There we go." Eamonn's grip was tight and protective. Rafe thought he felt Eamonn's thumb massaging his side as they walked, but that was probably wishful thinking. Rafe couldn't get enough of the way his lingering smoke and cologne mixed together into a manly, almost forbidden scent.

"I said I have—" But Rafe so obviously didn't. The hill had more of an incline than he realized, and balance became a tricky thing. He stumbled forward, but Eamonn yanked him back like a great-smelling seatbelt. "I guess I don't have it."

When they reached the bottom, Rafe thought Eamonn would let go, but his hands remained solidly on his body. Eamonn directed them to Sweeney. Rafe wondered if he really was that drunk, or if there was something more to Eamonn's gentlemanly gesture. The British accent really messed with his gaydar. With the accent, all British guys sounded a little gay. It was the polished thing, and maybe Heath was right. All the uptight people left England. American guys were so scared of coming off the least bit homo that they made themselves sound like cavemen.

Heath held open the door to Sweeney for the three of them. Eamonn moved him and Rafe sideways to get inside.

"I'm fine. I can enter a door," Rafe said, before knocking his shoulder against the frame.

"Right." Eamonn didn't relinquish his hold on Rafe, not even as they walked up the stairs, which Rafe did not mind. It felt good to be taken care of, though he knew he shouldn't get attached. Eamonn was just being a nice guy and there was nothing more to read into it.

Nothing more.

"Which one is your room?" Rafe asked. Eamonn motioned for him to keep his voice down.

"You are perfectly pissed." Eamonn laughed.

Louisa hugged Rafe good night. "We're happy you're here, Rafe."

"Really?"

"Of course, mate." Heath clapped him on the shoulder. He looked over his head to Eamonn, and Rafe wondered they were saying telepathically to each other. *I say old chap, this stupid American can't hold his alcohol.*

"I'm happy I'm here, too!"

Heath and Louisa went back to their rooms, and Rafe stopped being drunk for a second and realized he was in Eamonn's room, inches from Eamonn's messy bed.

"Your room..."

"Looks just like your room," Eamonn said.

"...it has character." Band and soccer posters were thumbtacked to the walls. Books piled on his desk. "When did y'all move in?"

"Y'all?" Eamonn had a short burst of laughter. "Two days ago."

"It's funny when you say y'all in your accent. It makes it sound so serious."

Rafe wasn't sure what he was doing. Even though he knew nothing would happen, because Eamonn was most likely straight and Rafe just wasn't that lucky, he didn't want to go. He wanted to keep breathing the same air as this charming Brit.

"I love British music." Rafe studied the posters. There was one for this band Bloc Party, and one for the Rolling Stones. "Where's your Beatles poster? You can't call yourself a true Brit without one."

He seesawed his head. "The Beatles are rubbish."

Rafe looked around to make sure the British police

weren't going to bust in and arrest Eamonn right then and there. "You hate The Beatles?"

Eamonn nodded. Even his nodding was hot.

Rafe didn't know much about music, but this was like somebody telling him that continental drift never happened. "But *Hey Jude*...and other songs besides *Hey Jude*."

His mind went blank at the worst moments. This was why Rafe would never go on *Jeopardy!*

"My dad took off a few years ago to play in a Beatles cover band. He had to follow the music, he said. I think he's in Helsinki this month. We get postcards from him, but that's pretty much it. The Beatles were like my family's Yoko Ono." Eamonn's eyes darkened for a split-second, then he shook it off. "Sorry about that, mate. Not sure why I blurted that out."

Rafe didn't mind. He thought it was nice to be let in for a moment. "I'm sorry your dad ruined *Hey Jude* for you."

Silence crackled in the room, though maybe it was all in Rafe's head. He wasn't good in these moments, but he wasn't going to make an ass out of himself and throw himself at a straight guy on his first night in a new country. He wasn't born gay yesterday.

"I'm completely knackered. I'm going to turn in," Eamonn said.

Rafe stood there, not sure if that was a statement of fact or an invitation. This was a day of firsts. First time out of the country. First time at a bar. And now first time in a boy's room possibly being invited into the boy's bed.

"Sounds g—" Rafe began to sit on his bed.

"Let's get you back to your room."

"Yep." And he was back to standing.

Eamonn put a firm hand on Rafe's lower back, which

was a nice consolation prize. He walked Rafe across the hall to his room.

"I like what you've done with the place."

"I just got here!" Rafe plopped down on his desk chair. "You know, you guys are very sarcastic."

"Are we now?"

"I think y'all are just bitter about losing the war."

"The Revolutionary War?"

"Yes. You once ruled the world. Then we put a stop to it. And now we rule the world."

"And what a good job you Americans are doing. All those Big Macs and mass shootings."

"I don't even like McDonald's!" Rafe rolled his head back to gaze at the ceiling. "Well, I like their fries. Their fries are good. And I like their burgers. Just the regular cheeseburger. The Big Mac is too much. Too, too much. What were we talking about?"

Rafe blinked his eyes, and his bed was all made. The pillows in pillowcases, the sheets stretched out on the mattress, the duvet inside the duvet cover.

Eamonn stood over the finished product. He gave Rafe a squinty smile that he was sure to dream about. "Sweet dreams, Yank."

Chapter 4

RAFE

Rafe awoke the next morning with a pounding headache and a growling stomach. It was a bad combination of hunger and hungover. He thought sun was shining through the slats of his blinds, but it was an outdoor light. He looked for his phone on his nightstand, then realized it was still in his pocket. Because he was fully dressed, in a made bed. *That Eamonn made.*

Rafe smiled at the hazy memory because his head throbbed again. He pulled his phone from his pocket. It was just past three a.m., and he was wide awake. Damn blackout sleep, or jetlag, or both. He stared at the ceiling. *I am in a foreign country.* It was still cool to think about.

His stomach growled again. It was *angry*.

Rafe didn't know when breakfast was. *Wait, I don't have a meal plan.* He wasn't sure what he was going to do about that. He checked the café on campus, but it didn't open until six-thirty. After a little bit more laying there with his angry stomach and pounding head, Rafe decided to look for a vending machine. He wanted to take some Advil, but couldn't on an empty stomach. He needed food.

He crept out of his room so as not to wake his flatmates. Rafe searched Sweeney Hall and found a vending machine in the laundry room. *Thank goodness!*

Or not.

The vending machine was cash only. British cash only. Rafe didn't go to a currency exchange or a bank yesterday. He only had American dollars. George Washington gave him serious side-eye. He rested his head against the glass of the machine, willing a candy bar to drop.

Rafe had about three hours until the campus café would open. He told himself he could make it. His stomach growled back.

"Well, we don't have any other options," Rafe hissed at his stomach. Just walking up one floor drained him of his last reserves of energy. He returned to his flat, when he noticed a sleeve of English tea biscuits on the floor outside his door.

He must've walked over them when he left his room. Rafe didn't waste any time. He ripped open the packaging and jammed a biscuit inside his mouth. It had the carby sweet goodness of a graham cracker. He ate another one.

His eyes drifted to Eamonn's door. Without knowing, he just knew.

The door next to Eamonn's opened, startling Rafe. Heath stumbled out with messy hair, wearing his shirt from last night. His pants were draped over his shoulder. He jumped back when he saw Rafe. Rafe didn't want to seem like a creeper, so he waved hello and ate another biscuit.

"Morning," Heath said. He tried his best not to sound awkward. It was a valiant effort.

HOURS LATER, Rafe awoke for the second time, much more refreshed. He munched on another biscuit. The sleeve was half gone already.

Rafe splashed water on his face and ventured into the kitchen, where Louisa was fixing herself a cup of tea.

"Y'alright?" She asked.

"Better. Still recovering from last night."

"Would you like some tea?"

"Absolutely!"

Louisa grabbed two mugs from the cupboard above the sink.

"Did the three of you go in on the kitchen stuff?"

"It's a hodgepodge from our families, though mostly mine. We were so excited when we got placed in Sweeney. Most dormitories here are old and quite dodgy. The beds here are loads more comfortable."

Rafe smiled to himself, thinking about earlier this morning.

"Um, so I saw..." Rafe instantly regretted saying anything, like he was some gossip. "Never mind."

Louisa brought over two cups of tea to the table. "You saw Heath."

"I...yes. I wasn't stalking or anything." Rafe took a sip of his first-ever English tea. The warm, refreshing liquid soothed his throat and stomach. It was like a warm bath for his insides. "I didn't know you guys were dating."

"We're not," she said firmly. "It happens sometimes. Especially after a night at the pub. I mean, he's right there." She shrugged, totally casual about it. "You were really funny last night."

"I don't even want to know. If Eamonn wasn't there, I

probably would've rolled down the hill." Rafe shook his head, waves of embarrassment coming over him.

"Eamonn's the best."

"Yeah. He's cool." Rafe thought of how wonderful he was last night, of that squinty gaze focused on him.

Louisa pulled her chair closer. "Did you pull him last night?"

"Pull him where?"

"It's slang. It means pick someone up."

"Like hooking up?"

"I guess."

Rafe put down his teacup. "What? No. Why would you even—I mean...Eamonn's straight. Right?"

"Total puff."

Rafe didn't know much British slang, but there was one word he knew about well before his journey across the pond. He had to know what the word for gay man meant if he was going to be a gay man in England.

"Eamonn's gay?"

Louisa nodded yes. As if it were no big deal. She got up and took out a small skillet from the cabinet next to the fridge.

"Seriously?"

She nodded again and grabbed a loaf of bread from the counter.

"I didn't know. I mean, I wondered...it's the accent! The British accent is throwing off my gaydar. I'm gay. Did you know that?"

She nodded again and retrieved a block of cheese and butter from the fridge.

"Do you fancy him?" she asked.

"Eamonn? I just met him." Just knowing that Eamonn was gay got Rafe's head all dizzy and his mouth all dry. He thought about last night, if Eamonn might've been flirting with him. He was probably just being nice.

"I think you two would be quite cute together."

"I'm not looking for 'together.' I'm only here for a few months. I just want to have fun. Like you and Heath." Rafe had fallen for guys who'd been nice to him before. But the feelings had never been mutual. He would crush, then crash. Mistakes like that would not be made during Operation: Slut.

"Maybe it's for the best." Louisa buttered up the toast and cut slices of cheese.

"Are you making a grilled cheese?"

"What's that?"

Rafe pointed at the stove. "A grilled cheese sandwich."

Louisa giggled louder than Rafe expected. He didn't think he said anything funny. "*Grilled cheese*?" She stretched the words out. "That's what you call it?"

"Yeah. That's what it is."

"It's cheese on toast," she said.

"Cheese on toast?" That sounded a bit too formal to Rafe, as did everything British. "I mean, that's technically an accurate description of what you're eating, but you're missing the best part. That's it's grilled. Mmmm." Rafe couldn't resist the salty, grilled aroma filling up the kitchen.

"Grilled cheese sounds like you tossed a hunk of gouda on a barbeque."

They laughed at what that might look like. Louisa made him a sandwich, too.

"Let's compromise and call it a grilled cheese on toast," Rafe proposed.

"Deal."

The sandwich hit the spot more than the tea biscuits,

the biscuits that Eamonn presumably dropped off. *Just to be nice. Flatmates can be nice without it meaning anything more.*

"What did you mean before, Louisa, when you said 'maybe it's for the best?'"

"I reckon that Eamonn is still getting over him."

"Who?"

"Nathan."

"The actor?" Rafe asked, thinking of the awkward silence from last night. "Was it a bad break-up?"

Louisa shook her head yes. "It's why friends should never date. Only shag, like Heath and me." She wiped a stray piece of cheese from her lips. "But Eamonn isn't the casual type. He can be quite the romantic."

Like me, Rafe wanted to say. But it wouldn't be true.

Not on this continent.

Chapter 5

EAMONN

Even though Eamonn's hometown of Guildford was only a half-hour from Stroude, it was like two separate galaxies. His visits home usually coincided with handiwork needing to be done around the house. Eamonn stood at the top of a ladder changing outdoor light bulbs.

"You really don't need to do this." His mum watched from below. "I'm not made of glass. I can do this myself."

"I know you can, mum. But I can, too."

She was only in her forties and in good shape, but after waiting tables all day for years to put a roof over his and his sisters' heads, helping out around the house was the least he could do. This was supposed to be a job for his dad, if he hadn't skipped out on them years ago.

"Jesus, mum. How long has it been since you changed these things? Did you purposely want the house shrouded in darkness?" He unscrewed a bulb above the front door and put in a fresh one.

"Thank you."

Eamonn came down the ladder and discarded the dead

bulb in an old shopping bag. He moved the ladder to the side of the house, and his mum handed him a fresh light bulb. Back up he went.

"I was having a chat with your Uncle George the other day," he heard his mum say, and he already knew where this was going. "and he says he'd love to have you join him at his company when you graduate. They have a trainee program that's a fast track to management."

Eamonn rolled his eyes at the house, never at his mum. It seemed that the closer he got to graduation, the more people wanted to give him unsolicited advice.

For most of his summers and weekends going back to when he was barely a teen, Eamonn worked at his uncle's box factory. He would fold and pack boxes until his fingers chapped. He was proud of the work, and grateful for the chance to make extra money, but he always saw it as a means to an end. He didn't intend to build a name for himself in the box industry. He had been told by teachers to think outside the box, and he took the advice literally.

"Uncle George says you should give him a ring and discuss what you're interested in doing. The trainee program can lead to manager positions in marketing, accounting, manufacturing, product development."

"Product development? Are they creating an even boxier box?" Too bad Eamonn didn't know what he wanted to be doing for the rest of his life. He seemed to be the only uni student who didn't. Eamonn screwed in the new light bulb.

"You owe him a call," she said.

He came down the ladder, and in her eyes, he saw she wasn't going to let up.

"If it wasn't for him and his company's scholarship, you wouldn't even be at Stroude."

"I know."

"They have an annual all-hands meeting in Tahiti!" She was more excited by that than her son.

"That's not going to sway me."

"Right." She stopped herself. "You know, flying is actually the safest form of transportation in the world. I remember when we went on holiday to Greece all those years ago, you loved flying. They gave you little wings."

"That was a long time ago." Eamonn took down the ladder. He dropped the second dead bulb in the shopping bag without caring whether it broke.

"What changed?"

Eamonn grit his teeth. "I don't hate flying. I hate airports."

"I heard security checkpoints are bad, but it's a shared miserable experience for all travelers. And then you get to jet off to someplace new."

Watching his mum daydream about the magic of flying made his stomach twist into a tight knot. He carried the ladder around the house to the shed in the backyard. He shoved it against the wall a little too hard. The clanging echoed loudly in the shed.

"Eamonn." She jogged up to him. "What did I say?"

"Airports are where people go to walk away from those they love and never come back."

His mum's face flooded with concern, and an uncomfortable silence filled the space between them. She put a hand on his cheek. "Eamonn..."

"I'll call Uncle George. I promise." He kissed her hand before moving it off his face and leaving.

———

EAMONN RETURNED to campus and met Heath for a midday

pint. They settled into a booth at Apothecary. Eleven-thirty wasn't too early to start drinking.

His finger circled the rim of his glass. "So, what the fuck is going on with you and Louisa? Are you two shagging again?"

Heath looked away, but his red cheeks were always a dead giveaway. Eamonn remembered the time as a first-year when he walked in on Heath wanking off on his bed. All that week, whenever he saw Heath, the guy looked like someone smashed two cherries on his cheeks.

"You two were being extra nasty to each other last night. I know it had to be shag central."

Heath beamed with his goofy smile.

"We haven't seen each other all summer. We were just catching up."

"Well, that's a new euphemism."

"We are still broken up. Just friends."

There it was again. *Just Friends.*

"I know what you're thinking." Heath tried to sound adamant, God bless him. "I don't want to get sucked into all that drama again."

"Riiiight." Eamonn had heard it all over the past two years. Just friends would turn into shagging friends, then into a relationship, then a fight, then a break-up, and finally back to just friends again. Living in a flat with them was like living with a roller coaster.

"It's true. Louisa is impetuous and flighty and loud. I can't believe she brought up Nathan last night."

Eamonn's chest tightened. He hated that just his name could do that to him.

"It's fine," he said. "Rafe asked about the fourth person in the flat. She had to give him an answer."

"She didn't have to start talking about his bloody acting career."

Eamonn had encouraged Nathan to try out for a play as a first-year. He couldn't forget the look of pure joy on Nathan's face when he got the lead. He reaped what he sowed.

"He's your mate, too," Eamonn said. "It was always the four of us. Nathan and I just couldn't do the just friends thing like you two."

Heath squirmed in his seat, which made his long torso rock back and forth like a skyscraper in an earthquake.

"What?" Eamonn asked.

"Nothing says you two can't get back together." Heath shrugged.

"Oh, come the fuck on."

"What? Nathan only broke up with you because he got cast in that film. He didn't drop out of uni. He's just taking a semester off while they shoot."

"He's not coming back. He's going to be a movie star. Why would he come back for a stupid degree after acting opposite Helen Mirren and Hugh Grant?"

Heath tipped his glass at Eamonn. "For you."

Eamonn rolled his eyes. "Trust me, mate. That's not happening."

He got up and walked to the toilet. People had written their names and messages all over the walls. It was a mishmash of scribble and color, and for a moment, it allowed Eamonn to block out the memories. But only for a moment. Then he vividly remembered the night Nathan told the three of them together over drinks that he was leaving school to take the part. He said it so coldly, as if he were telling someone on the Tube. "Sure, I'll miss you guys," Nathan said matter-of-factly.

Eamonn watched him pack up his room a week later, completely calm. In his mind, he was already on set. "What about us?" Eamonn asked, his heart beating wildly in his chest.

"We should just call it quits now. No sense in dragging this out," Nathan said while folding his shirts.

"I'll come visit you."

"I don't think that'd be a good idea, E." Nathan looked up at him with his big green eyes, those same eyes that had been Midori sour green during sex and cloudy gray in the morning when they woke up. But that night, they were two vacant lots. "I don't know where this will take me, but I'm going to see it through. I don't want to be held back. And this comes at a good time because let's be honest, things were petering out between us, don't you think?"

That was news to Eamonn. He had fallen hard for Nathan and hadn't stopped for almost two years. This person in front of him wasn't the same man he had given his heart to.

Nathan balled up his socks and shoved them into his suitcase. Eamonn grabbed his hand.

"I love you," he creaked out.

"I appreciate that. But we both knew this wasn't going to last forever." Nathan took back his hand. "I really need to finish packing."

Eamonn stared at himself in the bathroom mirror. He didn't want to think about what happened next. He felt empty all over again. He had given his heart to Nathan, and he stomped on it, tore it into scraps, set it on fire, and pissed on the ashes. Eamonn wasn't going to let that happen again.

He drove his fist into the wall of scribble and color as hard as he could, then returned back to Heath.

Chapter 6

After another day, the fog of jetlag was beginning to lift. No longer did Rafe wake up in the middle of the night full of energy. That was one problem down. And the campus café had a decent selection of breakfast foods and sandwiches. Rafe could live off of sandwiches for a few months. He had walked into town, but the only place that sold food was a dingy corner store where expiration dates only seemed to be a suggestion.

Rafe had to remember the study part of studying abroad. He wasn't just in England to legally drink in bars. He had to go to class, too. He had signed up for a quartet of courses on sedimentology, medieval history, physics, and Shakespeare.

The sedimentology and physics courses didn't seem like they would be as rigorous as the comparable courses Rafe took back at Browerton, which he didn't mind. He didn't want to spend his entire semester abroad in a library.

He was a geology major and had his sights set on getting into BISHoP, the Browerton Integrated Sciences Honors

Program. It was a competitive two-year program starting junior year that provided research funding and specialized classes. BISHoP was one of the big reasons Rafe applied to Browerton. Part of the reason he was studying abroad as a sophomore was because as a requirement of the program, he had to be on campus for his final two years.

Today was his Shakespeare course, which he was most excited for. What better place to study the bard?

He took a seat in the middle of the room. He soaked in the accents. That aside, it wasn't much different than a class back home at Browerton. Notebooks, chatter, desks.

"Y'alright?" The lecturer, a woman with short hair and wearing a pantsuit, asked the classroom. "Welcome back to uni."

She had everyone go around the class and state their name and where they were from. Most kids were from somewhere in England, usually London or just outside. Rafe was looking forward to it being his turn. For the first time, he had a different story.

"I'm Rafe. I'm studying abroad at Stroude this semester. I'm originally from America. Virginia specifically, right outside Washington D.C. I'm excited to study Shakespeare. I love *Empire*. It's this show that's *King Lear* set in the rap world."

"We have *Empire* here, too," said a cute Indian classmate in the front row. Rafe instantly noticed his bright brown eyes hidden behind thick glasses. The rest of the class laughed. Rafe could've sworn the guy's eyes stayed on him for an extra second.

And he wasn't the only one. Two other gay guys in class (Rafe's gaydar wasn't completely off) checked him out. Rafe smiled to himself about the attention. It wasn't something he was used to at Browerton. He remembered classes at home when there'd be a foreign student. No matter where he or she was from, the student always came off as exotic. It made them interesting. Maybe, just maybe, Rafe's American accent was as attractive to these guys as their British accents were to him.

For the first day of class, the lecturer went over the list of titles they would be reading. Rafe's focus, though, pinballed between the three guys in his class who had checked him out. Perhaps he would be lucky to hook up with one of them. Or all of them. At the same time. That was what Operation: Slut was all about.

When class was over, Rafe did a hair check to ensure his curls weren't out of control. He walked over to Arjun, the cute Indian classmate, who was typing out a text.

"What's done is done," Rafe said.

"Excuse me?" Arjun asked.

"That's the only line I remember from *Macbeth*. That and 'out, out brief candle,' or something like that."

"That's more than me."

"I saw that *Twelfth Night* is on the list. There's this Amanda Bynes movie *She's the Man* which is a modern-day retelling of it. So in case you fall behind, just watch it."

"Thanks."

"It's a classic. Kind of a classic. I'm really happy that she's getting her life back on track. It's on Netflix. Maybe, you know, we could watch it sometime." Rafe resisted using the term "Netflix and Chill."

"Thanks, mate. I'll have to check it out." Arjun held up his phone. "I have to go meet my boyfriend. See you around."

Arjun left. Rafe tapped his fingers on his desk. He wished his gaydar came with singledar.

ON HIS FIFTH day in a new land, Rafe called his parents to check in. He gave them the rundown of his classes and dorm. He told them about going to pubs with his new friends and made sure to point out that this was a normal part of British social life, like happy hour.

"Rafe, we're glad you're having a good time, but we're a little concerned," his dad said. "You've been going through your money at a fast clip. I see on your credit card all these charges to a campus café."

"Oh." He sat down on a bench just outside the café, feeling extra busted. Since his dad paid his credit card bills, he had access to Rafe's account, which Rafe never had a problem with until now, when he had something to hide.

"That's a lot of eating out. With the exchange rate, that's almost forty dollars a day."

"Is there a reason you're not eating at the dining hall?" his mom asked.

Shit. Rafe was not one to lie to his parents, but he couldn't deal with admitting a massive screw-up with his study abroad trip. He didn't need to hear his dad do one of his audible exhales and get this pinched tone in his voice.

"I am eating in the dining hall. But my friends and I have also been eating out. We're into snacks. I didn't think about the exchange rate." He really hadn't, and he felt a wave of embarrassment come over him for being so careless. "I'll be more mindful in the future."

"Is everything okay there?" his mom asked in her soothing voice, the voice that made everything better when he was a child. "Are you having some fun culture shock moments?"

"Kind of."

"Has anyone been mean to you?" His dad got very serious. "Have you been harassed?"

"No." Rafe looked up at the kids walking past him, all in their friend groups. They'd had years to get to know each other. They had history.

"It hasn't even been a week," his dad said. "You're still adjusting. This is only just the start."

"I hope so."

"Just try to be more careful with the eating out."

EAMONN

When he was done with classes for the day, Eamonn strolled over to the campus café for some afternoon tea. He spotted Rafe at a table in the window with his laptop open. Seeing Rafe made his spirits brighten. There was something buoyant about him that drew in Eamonn, like he was the hook of a pop song come to life.

"Hello, stranger." He knocked on his table. "How was the first week of classes?"

"Interesting."

Eamonn's back straightened up, as it usually did whenever he sensed trouble for his friends. "Did someone say something to you?"

"A kid in my physics class said that Americans like me are ruining the planet. I told him everyone in my family drives a Prius. It's fine. My country kind of deserves it." Rafe picked apart pieces of his blueberry muffin and plopped them into his mouth one by one. "I forgot to thank you for the tea biscuits. They really hit the spot that morning."

"Of course. Had you ever had them before?"

"No. I loved them!" Rafe went back to looking at his computer screen. His smile dropped.

"What's wrong?"

"Nothing."

"You sure? *What about if I asked you like this, dude*?" Eamonn asked in his best California surfer accent.

"You see this muffin?" Rafe pointed at the remaining pieces on his plate. "This is my dinner. And it will be my dinner for this entire semester."

"That's a pretty dodgy diet."

"I don't have enough money to eat food for the semester. I thought there was a meal plan, but there's not."

"Well, there's a grocery store one town over."

"I looked it up. It's expensive. If I put sizable weekly grocery charges on my card, they'll see and they'll know I fucked up, and then I'll get another lecture."

"From who?"

"My parents. They can see what I spend."

Eamonn couldn't wrap his head around that. His mum had never intruded on his financial situation and combed through his expenses, although that was because hers wasn't that much better. Was this *1984*? Big Brother was watching Rafe's bank account?

Rafe shut his computer and dragged his hands through his hair. "I can't believe I let this happen. Maybe I should've let my parents help me plan this trip."

"That's bollocks. Sandra fucking bollocks. When life kicks you in the balls, you don't run back to Mum and Dad." A brilliant idea came to Eamonn, and he rubbed his hands together. "Asda."

"Beg your pardon?"

"You need cheap food. Asda has it."

"What's Asda?" Rafe asked.

"Figures you Yanks don't have Asda back home. It's the best food you can get for the lowest price. And it's a huge store with lots of different departments, so your folks will never know you're buying food. There's one in Clapham Junction. Let's go."

"Right now?"

"Didn't you say you were going to starve to death otherwise?"

"Okay." The relief washing over Rafe's face warmed Eamonn's chest. A determination took hold in Rafe's eyes that Eamonn found a bit sexy, much to his surprise. "We're going to Asda."

"Yes we bloody are. Now finish your fucking muffin."

————

IT WAS funny to watch Rafe stare in awe at everything around them. It was just a normal train platform with the regular maps and adverts, but judging by Rafe's reaction, Eamonn could've been living in Willy Wonka's factory or Emerald City this whole time.

"This is so cool," Rafe said once they got on the train. "I am on the Tube. In England."

"It's not the Tube. It's a commuter train that brings people to London where they can then take the Tube."

"Oh. Well, I'll just tell my friends I rode on the Tube."

Eamonn led them to a pair of empty seats. Rafe rubbed his hand over the seat fabric.

"You might not want to do that," Eamonn warned him. "These seats can be very dodgy."

"I am literally *The Girl on the Train.*"

Rafe stared at every nook and cranny of the tube car. He stared out the window at the suburban sprawl. He was like a dog wagging his tail with no end in sight. Eamonn would've found it annoying if there wasn't something charming about this optimism, about the way the glaring fluorescent light reflected in his brown eyes.

He found himself laughing. "What are you doing? They don't have automobiles and roads and handrails back in America?"

"I know," Rafe said. "I know I'm probably being ridiculous right now, and I'm making a big deal out of everything, but I'm just this kid from Arlington, Virginia. Just this ordinary kid who lived this ordinary life in this random town. And now I'm on another continent, in another culture, thousands of miles from home. It may be cars and roads, but it's part of this amazing journey, this *adventure*, when you think about it.

"Think about you and me. We grew up an ocean apart, in separate worlds basically. Complete and total strangers. And now we're on this train together. *Connected.* It's...I don't know if I'm explaining it correctly, but it hit me, this sense of how large the world is."

Rafe's eyes were wide and expressive. Eamonn wished he could understand what Rafe was trying to articulate. He'd never traveled a distance like Rafe had. But he got swept up in Rafe's passion. He got it without actually getting it. It was rare for someone to open up to you, and you had to grab those moments, even if you weren't quite sure what was happening.

Clapham Junction was announced over the speaker.

"That's our stop, right?" Rafe asked.

Eamonn broke away from Rafe's gaze. He cleared his throat and nodded.

Mind the gap, the announcer said.

"Mind the gap. I love that!"

Chapter 7

R<small>AFE</small>

R<small>AFE</small>

"It's Wal-mart," Rafe said when they walked through the front doors. "Asda is Wal-mart."

Rafe couldn't believe there was a Wal-mart equivalent in England. It dulled some of the country's luster, like every time he saw an American chain store.

Except for now.

Asda was the savior Rafe needed. He'd never been so happy to see discounted goods. Eamonn grabbed a cart and followed him to the food section.

"What do you want to make for your meals?" Eamonn asked.

Rafe hadn't given that much thought on the train ride. He'd been transfixed by the British landscape, and he found that being in such proximity to Eamonn scrambled his circuits. It was like when two walkie-talkies were held up to each other and let out a high-pitched noise. And one of those walkie-talkies had scintillating blue eyes. After his talk with Louisa about Eamonn and his ex-boyfriend though, Rafe realized that the guy needed space. He was still healing. So he would keep his scrambling circuits to himself.

"I can get cereal for one pound!" Rafe threw four boxes of Cheerio's in the shopping cart.

"You can't just eat cereal every day. What do you want for lunch?"

Rafe stopped in the aisle, catching stolen glances at all the cheap food. He came to a realization he was afraid to say out loud.

"What do you usually make?" Eamonn asked. Rafe didn't respond and looked at the floor. "Have you ever made yourself a meal?"

"Outside the dining hall?"

"Are you serious? Are you actually a real person, or are you a toddler full-grown like that Brad Pitt movie?" Even Eamonn's scruff gawked at him.

"At home, my mom made all of my meals. She did all the cooking."

"You've never cooked a meal in your bloody life?"

Saying it out loud made it sound ridiculous, but it made sense to Rafe. This was how he grew up, as did most of his friends. When he awoke for school, there would be a bowl of cereal and a cut up banana waiting for him on the kitchen table. His mom would hand him his lunch or his dad would give him lunch money. And in evenings, when he was up in his room doing homework, or pretending to do homework, he would eventually smell the beginnings of a savory aroma brewing in the kitchen. It would get stronger, setting his stomach to rumble mode as he waited in anticipation for what would be in store downstairs. That's just how it was in his house. In college, he remembered the surge of freedom he felt when he got to choose his own meals in the dining hall, a fact he would not repeat to

Eamonn. He didn't want to hear the sarcastic response to that tidbit.

"I'm assuming you've cooked all your meals ever since you walked out of the womb."

"Most of them," Eamonn said with a smile that threatened to scramble more of Rafe's circuits. "Mum's a great cook, but her hours at the restaurant were a bit naff, so I wound up making dinner for me and my sisters. It was nothing revolutionary. I'd heat up some chicken in the oven and zap a bag of frozen vegetables in the microwave."

Rafe imagined Eamonn wearing an apron preparing a home-cooked meal. He was probably adorable with his sisters. Teasing, yet fiercely protective.

Eamonn's face softened, and he gave Rafe a nudge with his elbow. "Well, there's a first for everything. It's all part of that global adventure you were discussing. Just think, somewhere in Zimbabwe, there's a boy also learning how to cook." He interlocked his fingers. "Connected."

"Funny."

Eamonn wheeled the cart through the maze of aisles. Rafe loved seeing all the pound and pence signs in the prices. He was probably the only one in Asda who appreciated them.

"So what's the best meal you've ever made?" Rafe asked.

"Chateaubriand steak. It's this meat you have to get just right. I made it for my first anniversary with…"

"Nathan?"

Eamonn nodded yes.

"I'm sorry for asking about him at Apothecary the other night. I feel like a *prize idiot*." Rafe said that last in his best cockney accent. That got a smile out of Eamonn, which could have illuminated all of Asda. "Nathan also sounds like a prize idiot, too."

Eamonn's non-response told Rafe that he was a lot worse. Louisa was right. He did not seem like a guy who did the casual thing.

"What about you? Do you have a boyfriend back home? A Chad or Skip?"

"Is your knowledge of America based solely on Eighties teen movies?" Rafe knew Eamonn didn't mean any harm, but his question still stung. "There is no Chad or Skip waiting for me. There, uh, never was."

"Well, that's bollocks. American men sure have their heads up their arses."

"I usually found myself in the Baxter role."

Eamonn pointed them to the dairy aisle. "Yogurt?"

"It's only sixty pence? Sure!"

Eamonn tossed yogurt cups in their basket. "What's a Baxter?"

"It's this term from a movie I once saw. He's the nice guy who gets dumped in romantic comedies so the two leads can get together. Think Bill Pullman in *Sleepless in Seattle*, if you've seen it.

"In high school, there was this guy I liked, and I thought we were hitting it off at a party until he asked if my friend was single. Then last year, I started dating this guy, until he dumped me for his closeted fuckbuddy. I don't know. I've gone on lots of first and second dates, but I just can't seem to score a run. That was a baseball metaphor."

"I know."

"Do they play baseball here?"

"No, but I still know what baseball is."

"Right." Rafe didn't know what made him open up about this. Perhaps it was the magic of Asda.

"I stand by my original statement. It's bollocks and

American men are prize idiots, *dude*," he added with his American accent.

He knew Eamonn was just saying that to make him feel better, but it worked. "Relationships. Who needs 'em?"

"Precisely."

In a way, Rafe was glad that Eamonn didn't do casual and was his flatmate. They were two strikes against Rafe trying to pursue him for Operation: Slut. It would only end in disaster, and Rafe liked having him as a friend.

Eamonn leaned over the shopping cart. "We have breakfast covered. What do you like to eat for lunch?"

"Sandwiches. I like sandwiches."

"Alright then! Well, for that, you will need bread and lunch meat." Eamonn clapped his hands together, and Rafe had this spark of knowing things would be okay.

"To the bread aisle!" Rafe yelled.

"To the bread aisle!" Eamonn called out like he was Buzz Lightyear. He put his feet on the bottom of the cart and zoomed down the main aisle. Rafe ran alongside him.

"You don't have to go so fast."

"Yes, we do. No adventures start with walking." Eamonn's smile and arched eyebrow sent a wave of heat rolling through Rafe. He would have to get used Eamonn's facial expressions giving him that reaction. Like the rest of his British culture shock, he assumed it would subside eventually.

But for now, to the bread aisle!

———

RAFE DIDN'T KNOW how much time passed in Asda. It was like a Vegas casino. No clocks. No sense of hours and minutes. He and Eamonn zipped through the aisles like they were on supermarket sweep. Each choice of food emboldened Rafe and demystified cooking for him. He grabbed whole wheat bread, peppercorn-flavored turkey meat, Dijon mustard. He even bought a head of lettuce, not the pre-mixed bag. He was ready to live dangerously.

Rafe nearly jumped for joy when he saw how cheap Asda-branded canned food was. Only fifty pence apiece for off-brand Chef Boyardee and Campbell's soup.

"Wait a tick," Eamonn said. "Those are condensed soups."

"What does that mean?"

Eamonn laughed and shook his head, a normal occurrence this afternoon, but Rafe didn't care. He found himself saying things just to get a reaction for Eamonn. He knew that there were different kinds of mustard. He knew that non-perishable food had expiration dates years in the future. He hadn't planned to play the role of dumb, gullible American, but he was addicted to Eamonn's reactions. In this instance, Rafe honestly didn't know about condensed soup.

"Condensed soups mean you have to add water. You pour the soup and a can full of water into the saucepan." Eamonn pointed to the directions on the can.

"And it doesn't taste watery?"

"No."

"Do I need a saucepan? Where do I pick one up?"

"They sell them here," Eamonn said. "Aisle seven I believe."

"Wow. Asda has everything!"

"You can spring for the better canned soup." Eamonn picked up a different can. "This one has chicken and wild rice."

Eamonn held it out to him.

"That one is double the price," Rafe said.

"One whole pound."

"It adds up!"

Another laugh and head shake from Eamonn. Another private swoon for Rafe.

Eamonn placed three cans of better soup in the cart. "These are on me."

"You don't have to do that."

"I insist. Condensed soup is honestly rubbish. It's watered-down shite."

"Thank you." A quiet suddenly came between them. It was too quiet. "They have canned ravioli?!"

Rafe sprinted down the aisle. He pointed the food out to Eamonn, and this time did an actual jump for joy. He put as many cans as could fit in his arms. His mom never made him this kind of food because of the salt content. But Rafe was in charge of his culinary destiny these next four months. And by George, he was going to eat ravioli!

When he turned around with his arms full of canned goods, there was Eamonn staring with a look that could burn a hole right through him. He wasn't smiling or laughing or shaking his head, but something was going through his mind. Nobody had ever looked at him this way, like he was someone worth taking notice of. It both unnerved Rafe and made his insides melt like a Klondike bar.

I need to get dessert, too.

"Do they have Klondike bars in England?"

"Yeah—yes," Eamonn croaked out, a little flustered. "I mean, of course we fucking do."

"Do you think they'll melt before we get back to campus?"

"Only one way to find out. It's all part of the adventure."

"Thanks for today." Rafe leaned against the front of the shopping cart. A part of him wondered if there was more to Eamonn's friendliness, or if it was all out of pity.

"Anytime."

"I didn't realize grocery shopping could be so fun!"

Rafe still detected a slight mood shift, like he wouldn't be getting anymore head shake reactions from Eamonn. "I think it's time to check out. We have to carry all this crap back to campus."

It was a fifteen-minute walk from their dorm to the train, something Rafe had not taken into consideration during his adventures in groceryland.

Eamonn put a guiding hand on Rafe's lower back and the other on the cart and led them to the checkout section. He knew how to get there, but he wasn't going to stop Eamonn. Even when they got in line, Eamonn's hand lingered on Rafe's back until they had to start emptying their cart. It was what he would remember most about his very first grocery trip, even if it was probably just him being nice.

EAMONN

Eamonn yawned as they got on the commuter train, hands full with Asda bags. The shopping trip wore him out. He stumbled to a seat, and Rafe pretty much fell into the seat beside him.

"I don't know how people work and grocery shop and then cook all of this!" Rafe said. "I need to call my mom and thank her for her superhuman endurance."

Eamonn smiled out the window. He lost track at how many times Rafe made him laugh today. He'd never had this much fun inside a bloody Asda. It really was a different world, like Rafe said. There was no Nathan and no bad memories inside the superstore.

"Is everything okay?" Rafe grinned up at him, and Eamonn had this impulse to wrap him in a tight hug, which he resisted. He couldn't try to start anything with him. Rafe was leaving in a few months. Starting anything with him was a one-way ticket to getting hurt, something Eamonn didn't want to go through again.

"Yeah."

Like they said in the dairy aisle, *relationships: who needs 'em?*

Eamonn watched the landscape change out the window. There was magic out there that only Rafe could see, he thought. He wondered what it was like to be so far away from home. Eamonn hadn't traveled in years, and he wasn't planning on doing so anytime soon. He had plenty of adventure in England. Still, seconds before the train lulled him to sleep, he imagined himself in America, staring up at the Statue of Liberty, Rafe at his side.

The conductor announced their stop.

Eamonn blinked to life. He saw that sometime during his nap, Rafe had fallen asleep against his shoulder, and Eamonn's arm was around him. It was one of those actions that seemed completely natural. Their bodies just fit together, like some kind of instinct Eamonn didn't know he had. He smelled the warm scent of Rafe and pulled him close for a second.

Rafe emerged from his nap, but not even he seemed surprised by the position he found himself in. "You have a very comfortable shoulder."

"And you snore like a foghorn."

He bolted up. "I do?"

"Just taking the piss out of you." Eamonn took back his arm and looped his hands through grocery bags.

"I didn't snore, right?"

"Right." That was a lie. The truth was that Rafe did snore a little on the trip, a quiet, steady drone. But there was a greater truth, that Eamonn had found it quite endearing.

Chapter 8

Rafe

"You guys are going to fa-reeeeeeak. This is going to be the dopest dinner you've ever had in your entire lives."

The flatmates sat around the table, while Rafe stood over the stove stirring. The sauce aroma fluttered up to his nose, and it reminded him of home for a second. Even though it was canned food, he believed his parents would be proud of him. More importantly, he was proud of him.

Rafe turned off the stove and carried the saucepan over to the table. "And...here...we...go," he said as he spooned ravioli onto everyone's plate. Some of the sauce burned and pieces of ravioli fused to the bottom of the pan, but his flatmates didn't need to peek behind that curtain.

"This looks amazing," Eamonn said.

"It's just canned ravioli, right?"

Eamonn thwacked Heath on the arm.

"I love ravioli," Louisa said, mostly to Heath. She ate her first piece. "This is delicious. The pasta part just melts in my mouth."

"Louisa moonlights as the chief food critic for *The*

London Times," Heath said. "She's going to write you a smashing review."

"Bugger off," she said to him in that way that meant anything but.

"It was incredible. Asda is so cheap. And there was all this food, just everything you could want," Rafe said, still on a high. "I can't wait to go back."

"You don't get out much, do you?"

Eamonn gave Heath another thwack on the arm.

"I'm just taking the piss out of you, mate," Heath said.

"And I'm going to put the piss back into you, with my sincere appreciation," Rafe said. The more sarcastic his friends would be, the more he played up his American perkiness. "That sounded better in my head."

"That's pretty gross, Rafe," Louisa said.

"Not dinner conversation. At least, not here in the U.K. Maybe in Arlington, Virginia." Eamonn used his fork as a spoon and scooped up a load of ravioli, cramming it into his mouth.

Why do I find that attractive? Rafe asked himself.

"Sounds like you had a great day." Louisa went to the fridge and got out a pitcher of water. *I forgot about drinks!*

"Yeah, it was a rollicking good time. Rafe learned what condensed soup was." Eamonn glanced at him from across the table, and goosebumps rolled across Rafe's lower back, right at the spot where Eamonn guided him. He'd had moments while cooking dinner where his mind would wander, and he'd think of being with Eamonn in the store, of that squinty-eyed smile fixed on him. It'd left him with butterflies swarming his stomach—and burned ravioli on his brand-new saucepan.

It's not going to happen, Rafe reminded himself. Eamonn was just being nice, and he obviously still had feelings for his ex-boyfriend. And more importantly, there were no butterflies allowed in Operation: Slut.

———

DINNER DIDN'T TAKE LONG. His flatmates cleaned up the dishes, and a few minutes later, they all headed out to Apothecary to drink. Going to the bar every night? Rafe could get used to this. It was so much cooler than a cramped party in some senior's apartment or playing games in the dorm.

They grabbed what Rafe deemed their usual table in the pub, with a view of everyone. He saw across the room the American students from his orientation, being just as anti-social as he remembered. They all crowded around one table, all looking at their cell phones, with no other British students. So much for the cultural experience.

"Do you know them?" Eamonn asked. This time, they were sitting next to each other in the booth rather than across. Rafe felt something heating up in the narrow space between their bodies.

"They're Americans," Rafe said with a tinge of disgust. He told them about how they didn't talk to him at orientation and made no effort to be friendly.

"Those cunts," Heath said.

"Massive cunts," Eamonn said.

"Tremendous cunts," Louisa added.

"I have to say something." Rafe took a swig of his Midori sour. "Why do you use that word? It's a really bad word."

"You mean cunt?" Heath asked, the word rolling off his tongue.

"Yes. That word."

"You don't use it back in the states?" Eamonn drank his pint.

"No! It's an incredibly offensive word. It's not like asshole or fuck or shit, which are more common." Rafe dropped his voice when he used those words. Old habits. "Why is the c-word your expletive of choice?"

"It just is," Eamonn said. "It's so versatile. You can use it for anything. Those Americans are cunts. The Budweiser beer they're drinking is a cunty choice of beverage."

"We're not getting drunk. We're getting cunted," Heath said.

"I love Jennifer Lawrence, but she's a tad cuntish," Louisa (*Louisa!*) said.

Eamonn: "Semi-cuntish."

Heath: "A solid two-point-seven on the Cunt Scale."

Eamonn: "And Prince William! He's just cunting all over the place."

Each use of the word was a tiny jab at Rafe's flesh. He couldn't help it. It was his American upbringing and feminist tendencies rejecting that word. When he was in sixth grade, a kid in his math class called a girl that, and he was suspended for three days. Here, he'd probably get extra credit.

"I'm glad y'all got that out of your system," Rafe said, trying to keep a straight face.

Eamonn let out a hearty, loud laugh that boomed above the din of the pub. He wrapped his arm around Rafe and pulled him closer. It was an "I'm just messin' with you" bro-ish hug, but Rafe liked it all the same.

A little while later, Heath and Eamonn darted over to an available snooker table, which was like pool but with different colored balls. Eamonn and Heath quickly got into the zone, and Rafe could admire Eamonn's serious game face all day. He could also watch Eamonn bend over to take a shot all day, too.

Louisa and Rafe enjoyed another round of Midori sours at the bar.

"So what's the deal with you and Heath?" Rafe asked.

"No deal, really."

It seemed like a dodge by Louisa. Heath scored a shot and talked smack to Eamonn. It naturally included the c-word, which Heath said at an extra-loud volume while looking at him. Louisa smiled a bit longer at his antics than Rafe, and it reminded him of the reaction of Eamonn to his naïve grocery comments at Asda.

"At the end of last year, we said we were just going to be friends. We've always worked better as friends," Louisa said. "And I don't know, I just don't think I'm the serious girl-friend type. So much seriousness at our age only leads to premature wrinkles."

Rafe nodded in agreement. Now was not the time in our lives to be so serious. Not while on an adventure.

"The other night just happened. I went into the kitchen to make myself a late night cup of tea, and he was there just finishing. I skipped the tea and brought him back to my room." Louisa shrugged. "We're still friends, but friends who shag."

"Friends with benefits."

"Like that Justin Timberlake movie!"

"I prefer the Natalie Portman version, *No Strings Attached*. It's highly underrated."

Rafe needed his own *No Strings Attached/Friends with Benefits* hookup, and not the kind like in those two movies where they eventually fall in love.

"Maybe you and Eamonn could have something simi-lar," Louisa said.

"What?" Rafe had reacted like she claimed the earth was flat. Not that it wasn't something Rafe thought about, usually when he was in the presence of those icy blue eyes. "Just because we're both gay and in the same flat?"

Louisa nodded yes, as if it were really that simple.

"He's getting over Nathan."

"And you could get under him in the meantime."

"That's a terrible idea." Rafe wasn't going to mess with a guy with a fragile heart. Eamonn was a genuinely good guy, not worth getting ensnared in Operation: Slut.

As if luck was shining down on him, a gay guy with a patch of freckles across his nose came up to the bar to order a drink. His body fit well in those tight jeans.

"I have a better idea. *Pardon e moi,*" he said to Louisa. He nudged his head slightly so she knew who he was talking about.

"He's cute!" She winked at him.

Rafe downed the rest of his drink and casually strolled over to Freckles, dragging his finger along the bar. He had this. He could do this. The nerves pouncing through his system would be channeled into witty banter.

"Hey," Rafe said. "I bet I can guess what you're going to order."

"You can?" Freckles asked, seemingly interested. He had lovely teeth. Rafe didn't get where the bad teeth stereotype came from, but it was seriously outdated.

"Give me three guesses. If I get it wrong, I'll buy you a drink. If I get it right, I'll buy you that drink and we'll keep talking."

"Fair enough."

"Hmmm..." Rafe rubbed his temples, pretending to be using psychic powers to determine the right answer. "You seem like a hard alcohol kind of guy. You don't mess around. So I am going to say...vodka cranberry."

"Wrong."

"That was just a warm up. I still have two more guesses, and I going to blow your mind." Rafe rubbed his temples again and closed his eyes. "The universe is telling me that you were about to order a...vodka soda."

"Wrong."

Freckles wasn't giving him much to work with. He was taking this way too literally. Rafe had one more guess, and the stakes never felt higher. His sexual viability hung in the balance.

"I think you're throwing me for a curveball and you really are a beer drinker. So that's why I'm positive...that you are ordering a Guinness!"

"Wrong." Freckles remained stubbornly monotone. The bartender came over. "I'll take a Pimm's Cup. He's paying." Freckles nodded his head at Rafe.

It was a sign of life that maybe Rafe had a chance.

"I'll take one, too," Rafe said. "So maybe I'm not psychic. But I have a very good memory, like Truman Capote. He could recall entire conversations, which is how he wrote *In Cold Blood*. Although there have been rumors that he fabricated events..." Rafe's fingers brushed along the edge of the guy's hand. It was a sly, stage-one flirting move. Low stakes but a potential gateway to more.

"Right, so I'm straight, actually," Freckles said.

"What? Why didn't you say anything?"

"I'm saying something now."

"After you let me buy you a drink."

"I thought you were just being friendly."

"But your jeans are really tight." Rafe pointed.

"I'm proud of my body."

The bartender returned with their drinks. He swiped his lightning fast.

"Thanks for the drink, mate." Freckles was gone, back to his friends at a high table.

EAMONN

"That's the third shot you missed. I knew we should've bet money on this game," Heath said. He surveyed the snooker table like a cat scoping out a mouse.

"Sod off," Eamonn said half-heartedly. The scene at the bar kept pulling his attention. More like yanking it by the collar. Why did he care who Rafe flirted with?

"Damn." Heath said. Eamonn watched his ball bounce off the side of the table. "It's your turn."

"Right." What was he doing? Did he have a headache? He couldn't understand why Rafe kept rubbing his temples.

"Where are you?" Heath asked.

"What?" Eamonn leaned down to take a shot. *So Rafe was trying to pull someone. Not my problem.* He hit the snooker ball with an extra gust of force. "Christ!" Heath yelled. The snooker slammed against the table and leapt onto the floor.

"Off night," Eamonn said. "I don't trust that guy talking to Rafe."

"Why?"

"I've seen him around. He's a bit dodgy."

"How so?" Heath folded his arms and arched an eyebrow. He would not be turning Apothecary into his courtroom.

"He just is."

Heath had a shit-eating grin on his lips. He found this all hilarious.

"What?" Eamonn asked.

"Nothing. Nothing at all."

Eamonn flicked his eyes back up at the bar, and the guy was gone. Rafe was not. He looked so alone. *What the hell was that wanker's problem?*

He put down his cue.

"You're quitting?" Heath asked.

"I'm letting you win for once." Eamonn joined Rafe at the bar, with Heath close behind. Rafe drank a Pimm's Cup, which he did not seem to enjoy.

"Y'alright?" Eamonn asked.

"What is your problem?" Rafe asked Heath. "Why don't straight guys announce they're straight right off the bat?"

"Sorry?" Heath shrugged his shoulders.

"The guy was a total cunt," Eamonn said. "I could tell."

"Eamonn was taking mental notes."

He elbowed Heath in the ribs.

"He made me order a Prick's Cock or whatever this is," Rafe said of his drink.

Eamonn took it and smelled. "You really wanted to pull a guy who ordered a Pimm's Cup? That should've been your first warning sign."

"If you're so eager for a shag, why don't you just use Grindr?" Heath asked. Eamonn wanted to elbow him much harder, even if he wasn't sure why.

"Grindr is scary. I downloaded it once and it was like a wall of torsos and dicks coming at me." Rafe shook off the memory. "I'm better in person. My witty banter doesn't translate to text." He turned to Eamonn. "Are there any gay bars around here?"

"There's one in Staines," he said. "I'll take you sometime."

"I've never been to a gay bar. I mean, I've been to plenty of eighteen-plus nights, but they never serve alcohol. Which means you have to pregame before going, which means your buzz wears off halfway through the night and by that point you've broken the seal...Anyway, thanks."

Rafe flashed him a smile that made Eamonn all fuzzy inside, even though Rafe made it clear that he was focused on finding other guys to pull who were most definitely not him.

"Where's Louisa?" Heath asked, and Eamonn was grateful for the new subject.

"She should be somewhere around here," Rafe said.

Heath's face dropped as soon as he got his answer. She was at the far end of the bar, busy talking with a guy who was in Eamonn's maths class last year. He heard her flirty giggle carry through the crowd.

Eamonn patted Heath on the back for support, but he pushed his hand off.

Chapter 9

RAFE

Zzzzzzzzzzz

Rafe's cell phone buzzed in his pants. He pulled his phone from his pocket.

Mom and Dad.

Fuck.

Usually, he liked talking to his parents. But that was before they chewed him out for his spending.

"Shit. I have to take this. I'm sorry." It was for the best, since Rafe's dick was on the verge of embarrassing him in front of his flatmate and the thought of being under him. Rafe had to get it together. Louisa said it as a joke. Her suggestion was not supposed to be taken seriously.

In the few seconds it took Rafe to take the call, his boner vanished, never to be heard from again.

"Hi," he said into the phone as soon as he got outside. Students smoked by the entrance.

"Hi," his mom said even louder. "Is everything okay?"

"Yes. What's up?"

"What are you up to tonight?" his dad asked.

"At a pub with some mates."

"You sound so British!" his mom said.

"Thanks." Rafe regretted not letting it roll to voicemail. He could give them a full report tomorrow.

"Rafe, we're a little worried," his dad said. "Something didn't add up from our last call, and I went online and researched Stroude. There's no meal plan."

"We looked at the fee breakout for the study abroad program, and meals are not included," his mom said. "We called up the Browerton study abroad office, and they confirmed that for your program at Stroude, students are living in suites with kitchens."

"We are. But it's fine," Rafe tried to assure them.

"Why didn't you tell us?" his dad asked. "Why did you say that there was a dining hall?"

Rafe hung his head. His parents were looking out for him, and he felt bad for lying to them. But at the same time, he wanted to tell them it was none of their business.

"It's okay. I got food at a grocery store. I'll make my meals."

"Rafe..." his mom began, her voice full of doubt. It had the same tone as when he pleaded with his parents to let him watch an R-rated movie in junior high. "Do you even know how to cook? I don't want you burning yourself."

"I'm not going to burn myself." He leaned against the brick wall and inhaled the smoke around him, which he promptly coughed out.

"What was that?" his mom asked.

"Nothing. You guys, I can make my own food."

"I can email him a list of healthy microwave dinners he can buy. Oh, and some vegetable steamers," his mom said.

"I just hope he isn't going to order pizza and takeout every night," his dad said to her.

"I didn't send him with any plates or utensils."

Rafe waited for his parents to finish their side conversation *about him*.

His dad exhaled a sigh. He could only imagine what they were going to say about this once they hung up. "Rafe, I'll put more money in your bank account, but I think you and Mom should have another call to discuss what you can make over there."

"I'll be fine. Seriously."

"We love you," his mom said. "This was just a surprise. Our son is an ocean away. I don't him starving to death."

"And everyone is still treating you well?" his dad threw in.

"Yes."

Rafe rested his head against the brick wall. He thought about his trip to Asda and Eamonn's jokes about his cluelessness. They were funny then, but they stung with truth now. It hit Rafe just how much control his parents had over his life.

"Don't worry, Mom and Dad."

"We're not worried anymore. We addressed the situation and have come up with a solution," his dad said. "Just remember that we want you to have a good time there. We're not yelling at you. This is your first time on a trip like this, so we want to make sure you're prepared."

"Thanks." But Rafe didn't feel any better. He had tasted freedom, and he wanted more.

EAMONN

His last class of the day, Humanitarian Policy, he had

chosen because it was closest to his hall, so he didn't need to walk far to get home. It turned out to hold his attention longer than any other class. Eamonn hated seeing people getting treated like shite, and he couldn't believe the atrocities that were still being committed. The professor brought up clean water initiatives and how one billion people in the world didn't have clean water.

Fuck. He thought of the water fight his hall had last spring when it got really hot out. They took that clean water for granted.

Eamonn returned to the flat and smelled the salty, processed aroma of ravioli. He felt a smile take over his face as he approached the kitchen.

"Look at you. Watch out, Jamie Oliver." Eamonn took a seat at the kitchen table and watched Rafe work his culinary magic at the stove.

"Do you want some?"

"Sure. I'll take a few squares."

"Nobody calls it that."

Eamonn shrugged. "I reckon that makes me the first."

Rafe dipped his finger in the sauce to check the temperature, then licked it off. Eamonn twitched in his trousers.

"How are things?" Eamonn asked, not sure how to touch on Rafe's 180 last night after his phone call. "Everything okay back home? Did they run out of McDonald's and pickup trucks?"

Rafe stirred the ravioli. His face clouded over with what had to be a memory of the call. "My parents are just worried about me and how much I'm spending and how I'm going to eat while I'm here."

"They've been snooping in your bank account again?" The anger rose inside him. "Your parents shouldn't be able to tell you what to do and where to spend your money."

"Their money."

"Well, that obviously needs to change." Eamonn had heard the term helicopter parents, especially in posh areas of London, but Rafe's mum and dad reminded him more of co-leaders in a totalitarian regime.

"I don't know if I can get a job here. I'm on a visa. Do you work?"

"Bet your ass I do." He listed off some of his former jobs. Through the tint of nostalgia, Eamonn looked at those experiences as character-building and fun memories, but he also remembered the slog of waking up early and delivering papers in the rain. "I just work summers now in my uncle's warehouse. I make enough money to last throughout the year."

"That sounds really awesome."

Eamonn detected jealousy in his voice. It made him think about people who drop fifty pounds on vintage clothing or sign up for expensive wilderness programs so they can pretend that they live off the land. "You need to start making your own money."

"Agreed. But I don't know how. I don't have a work visa, and I'm not eligible for work study."

"I will gladly pay you for sexual favors." Eamonn leaned back in the kitchen chair, pleased with making Rafe laugh.

"You're joking, right?" Rafe asked with some seriousness.

Eamonn nodded yes. *I am joking, I think.* "There has to be a way for you to make some money while you're here that doesn't involve putting some stranger's cock in your mouth."

"Let's hope."

"Have your parents always been like this?"

"Yes. They would always take care of things for me. I never knew it was something to notice until I got here. I did some thinking on this last night." It seemed like Rafe was still thinking about it. "I feel like it intensified when I came out to them. They became even more protective. They started wanting to drive me more places rather than me getting rides from others. They knew all of my teachers' names and the subjects they taught in high school. Even now, my dad always asks me if people are treating me well. I think they were worried for me—still worried—that the world would be much rougher for a gay teen."

"And so they kept you in a bubble."

"They mean well. All parents want their kids to be safe. It's biological."

"Did they ever teach you to stand up for yourself?"

"If there was ever a problem, I knew to identify a teacher or adult in charge."

"I'm talking about throwing a punch, duffing up some wanker who deserves it." Eamonn had gotten into a few scuffles in primary school, but soon, the other kids knew he was one puff not to fuck with.

"My school had a zero tolerance policy against bullying and violence."

"The world doesn't have a fucking zero tolerance policy." Eamonn walked up to the stove, dipped the wooden spoon in the sauce, and had a taste. "I think it's ready."

He dipped it again and this time held it to Rafe's mouth. The guy happily parted his pert lips, and Eamonn couldn't help being a little turned on. "Is this your family recipe?"

"Yes. Passed down over five generations. When my grandparents immigrated to America, they only had this ravioli recipe on them."

"Was that sarcasm, Rafe?"

"I believe it was."

"Well, holy baskets of cunts." Through the laughter,

their eyes met over the bubbling sauce. "Eat up, because we have work to do when you're done."

"We do?" Rafe asked.

"Tonight, I'm going to show you how to beat the shit of somebody."

Chapter 10

RAFE

Eamonn took Rafe to a soccer field across campus, which Eamonn called a football pitch. ("Because that's what it's called! Not *soccer field, dude*.") Rafe practiced making a fist on their way to the field, curling his fingers at his side while they walked. He looked back on his life, and he had never thrown a punch before. Well, there was one time he was stressed out about a test and punched his bedroom wall, but that hurt him more than the wall.

"Why are we going all the way here?" Rafe asked.

"We'll have space and some peace, so you won't feel embarrassed or have any onlookers. Most students don't come to this pitch since it's a bit of a walk. It's got a great view."

Rafe didn't mind the view right now, walking behind Eamonn, glimpsing his back muscles in his long sleeve T-shirt.

Eamonn pushed aside some tree branches and welcomed Rafe to the field—er, pitch. It was a perfectly mowed piece of land surrounded by woods, like a guy with a bald head and hair on the sides. The first amber flecks of sunset dashed across the sky, giving the grass and the goalposts a golden glow. They walked up to the goalie net, which Rafe marveled at for its size.

"You've never seen a goal?"

"I played soccer when I was a kid. I've never seen a professional game. This is an intense goal. You need two goalies to cover it."

"Nope. Just one."

Leaves fluttered in the breeze. It was just the two of them out there, and all they could hear was the faint sound of car engines in the distance.

"Make a fist," Eamonn said.

"We're starting now?"

"No. First it's tea time. Yes! Fist. Now."

Rafe held up the most non-intimidating fist in the world.

"You're not showing off a bloody wristwatch. Make it tight, like you actually want to scare someone."

Rafe hardened his fist and put on his best fighting scowl.

"Better. Keep your thumb on the outside of your fist or else you'll break it. Here." Eamonn moved Rafe's thumb in between his index and middle finger, just below where the fingers curl under. His fingers moved with determination, and they sent a buzz through Rafe's body. His hand lingered on Rafe for an extra second before pulling back. "That's much better."

You will not get hard during boxing practice. That is unsportsmanlike.

"And now I just..." Rafe flung out his fist, but it was more like a coordinated dance move than incitement of violence.

"When you punch, try to angle your wrist slightly, so that the flat middle part of your fingers are what makes contact first. And shoot out your arm so that it aligns with the direction you're punching. That will add maximum impact."

"Are guys really thinking about all this when they throw a punch? Aren't they usually drunk or just intent on causing damage?"

"Do you want to be smart about it or fight like a sodding drunkard?"

"I guess the former, although the latter sounds fun."

"Right." Eamonn's lips curled into a cheeky smile. "Wanker."

Rafe punched his chest, but his first merely bounced off Eamonn. The guy didn't even blink. Rafe had seen some definition under his shirts, but now he was certain Eamonn's chest must've been a fortress of muscle.

"Good start." Eamonn stood in front of him and held up his palms. "Do it again. Hit me."

Rafe lazily held up his fists and threw a punch, which grazed Eamonn's right palm.

"Come closer. You're too far away."

He took a step toward Eamonn, toward his scruff and chest of muscle.

"How exactly should I put up my dukes?" Rafe imitated a boxer with hands held in front of his face.

"You want to hold them comfortably." Eamonn stood behind Rafe and positioned his arms and fists to where they should be. *Concentrate. Don't be...unsportsmanlike.* But that was hard to do when Eamonn's scent of cologne with a hint of cigarette smoke took over Rafe's nasal passages.

Eamonn moved away from Rafe in an instant, seemingly flustered. *Crap. Was I smelling him?* Eamonn held up his fists to show Rafe. "You need to hold your fists tight, like you fucking mean it."

"Is violence really the answer? Maybe Gandhi was onto something."

Eamonn got right up to Rafe's face and jutted out his chin.

"Do you see this scar?" Eamonn asked. "This cunt named Daniel Washburn sucker punched me in the cafeteria because I was a puff. I was eating my sandwich, someone tapped me on the shoulder, and boom!"

Rafe jumped back.

"Did I run to a teacher? No, I got up, and I pasted him in his pretty mouth. He was the one who ran away crying. And from then on, the pricks at school let me eat my lunch in peace."

"Shit. I thought stuff like that only happened in movies."

"No. It's real fucking life. You got to be prepared. I don't want anything to happen to you." Eamonn glanced into the woods for a second. "I mean, let's give this another go."

He stepped back and held up his palms in front of Rafe's face. "Let's go. Give me one punch."

Rafe tightened his fist. He'd always been a bit of a teacher's pet, and he wanted to do right by this teacher. Eamonn cared about him and his wellbeing. He slammed his right fist into Eamonn's left palm.

"Nice!"

Rafe shook out his hand.

"Remember what I said. Thumb out and angle your wrist."

Rafe heeded his orders and punched his right palm, then left.

"Better!"

They went a few more rounds. Rafe's fists slapped against Eamonn's calloused palms, and the louder the slap, the more it motivated him.

"Harder," Eamonn said. "Don't go easy on me."

Rafe tightened his fists and shot them out with more strength.

"What was his name?" Eamonn asked.

"Whose name?" Rafe didn't stop punching.

"The kid who bullied you, who laughed at you."

There were too many to name. His school had a strict zero tolerance policy, but Rafe didn't get off scot-free. None of us did. Memories came back to him of kids snickering when he talked and imitating him when they thought he wasn't in earshot. Rafe felt his face crystallize into a scowl.

Eamonn shook out his red palms. "You're getting some good blows in, mate."

As soon as his hands were up, Rafe went back to punching. *Right, left, right, left.* He let out grunts with each swing, and he didn't care how they sounded. It was energy that had to be expounded.

He locked eyes with his sparring partner and slammed his fists into his hands. The setting sun bathed Eamonn in silhouette. Electricity crackled in the air between them, like the promise of lightning fizzing in a stormy sky. Heat burned in Rafe's hands and coursed into his chest. His grunting and the contact of his fist into Eamonn's palms filled the strangled silence between them.

The look Eamonn fixed on Rafe could strip the paint off a car. It made Rafe punch harder, punch faster.

Right, left, right, left.

Eamonn caught Rafe's fist and held onto it.

"What?" Rafe asked. His heart pounded in his ears.

But Eamonn didn't say anything. His blue eyes darkened. He tightened his grip on Rafe's fist.

"Eamonn."

He pulled Rafe to him and kissed him hard.

. . .

EAMONN

The animal look on Rafe's face. The masculine energy pouring from his fists. The fucking grunting.

Eamonn had to have him. He had to *consume* him.

They were bound together by some kind of gravitational force. Rafe wriggled his fist away and rubbed his hands on Eamonn's chest.

He clamped his hands on Rafe's lithe frame, down his torso. Rafe's erection dug into his leg, and Eamonn's cock was just as forceful. He ran his fingers through those unruly curls, loving the way they slipped over his hands. He smelled the light scent of sweat from their boxing session on Rafe's forehead and neck.

"Eamonn." He stopped Eamonn's hand from undoing his jeans. He remembered they were in the middle of a pitch. "Maybe we should wait until we get back to the dorm."

"I can't fucking wait." He said it as a raspy whisper. Lust choked his throat. Eamonn didn't care who walked by or who saw them. He couldn't move from this point. Not when he was enjoying the best snogging session of his fucking life.

He walked Rafe back against the goalpost, pushing netting off his shoulder. Rafe's hands were all over his body in an instant. Rafe was nearly clawing at his shirt. Rafe grunted out a moan that threatened to send Eamonn over the edge.

Eamonn slapped his American arse with one hand while the skated across Rafe's waistline and circled the button of his jeans. That hard cock pressed against his leg. He bit and sucked on Rafe's lower lip.

"Do you want me to stop?"

"No," Rafe whispered.

"Do you want me to put my hand on your cock?"

Rafe trembled under his fingers. "Yes."

Eamonn flicked open Rafe's jeans button while his tongue explored the insides of Rafe's mouth. Rafe exhaled a shaking breath. Eamonn unzipped his fly and reached inside. Rafe let out a huge moan that carried across the field. Eamonn's calloused hands rubbed themselves around Rafe's cock.

Rafe's teeth chattered as they kissed.

"Y'alright?" Eamonn asked.

Rafe nodded yes.

"Just cold?"

"No."

"I'll shut up." Eamonn nibbled at his bottom lip. He had a bad habit of getting chatty during sex, something Nathan tried to break him of.

"No. Keep talking. Your accent is so hot. Please keep talking."

Well, fuck Nathan.

"You like my hands on your cock?"

Rafe shook his head yes. He jutted out his hips to give Eamonn better leverage and gripped the netting behind him for support.

He pulled Rafe's cock fully out and began stroking it. Its heat burned into his hand. "You are so fucking hard."

Rafe unbuttoned Eamonn's jeans and let out another moan when he made contact with his dick. The cold of the air was negated by the heat just south.

"Grab that cock," Eamonn whispered into his ear. Rafe moaned in response.

Rafe's greedy hands dove into his pants, playing with his balls. And then they were out.

"What is it?" Eamonn asked when Rafe pulled his hands away.

"You're uncircumcised." Rafe said it almost like a question.

"Yeah...Is that a problem?" The quickest way to kill a guy's hard-on was to talk about it.

"No. I've just..."

"They don't have uncut cocks back in America?"

"I've never been with one. I'm not sure what to do. I don't want to hurt you." Rafe looked down, embarrassed. And now Eamonn felt bad for putting Rafe on the spot.

"It's the same as what you've got, just a little extra." He meant that in more ways than one since he noticed that he was thicker than Rafe. "I'll teach you."

If he could teach him to punch, he could show him this.

"Come here," Eamonn commanded. Rafe did as instructed, turning around and standing in front of Eamonn. "It's easier to demonstrate this way."

He took Rafe's hand and placed it back in his pants, where his uncut cock was already hard again. He had Rafe rub him softly, being sure not to pull on the extra skin.

"Just like that, mate." Since he was so close to Rafe's neck, he gave it some kisses just below his ear.

"Stroke it slowly. Up and down, just like that."

He could tell Rafe wanted to go faster, but Eamonn maintained a firm grip on his wrist. As like before, Rafe was a fast learner. Eamonn nibbled on his ear lobe. "This feels so fucking good," he whispered in his ear.

He fucked Rafe's hand and moaned into Rafe's neck. Then he reached around and slid his hand back into Rafe's jeans, where the Yank was already primed.

He stroked Rafe and Rafe stroked him. It was a perfect match.

"How am I doing?" Rafe asked.

"Fucking amazing. You're gonna make me come all over this pitch."

Birds chirped around them and a light breeze rustled the grass. Eamonn's cock was a fucking cannon. He tortured Rafe with a consistently slow and measured wank. Rafe turned his head for a kiss, and Eamonn's tongue dipped into his mouth while their hands beat each other off. Rafe was the first guy he'd been with since Nathan, and it was as if he was waking up from a long sleep and feeling the morning sunshine on his face.

"Since I'm such a fast learner, maybe you could teach me how to suck you off next."

Holy shit. "When is next?"

"Right now."

Eamonn didn't have to be asked twice. He lay on the ground inside the goal. His thick cock stuck straight up, his sensitive head red like a beacon. He motioned for Rafe to kneel beside him.

"Take that cock in your mouth." That was the extent of Eamonn's instruction, though. Once his dick entered Rafe, Eamonn lost the ability to give coherent thoughts. "Just like that, mate," he barely said.

Rafe's mouth was like a bloody five-star hotel for his dick. He took Eamonn slowly, making sure to be gentle to the head.

"Shove that cock in your mouth, mate."

Rafe complied. Eamonn grunted when his cock hit the back of Rafe's throat. Rafe gagged on it and had to take a second to catch his breath.

"You sure you're a beginner?"

"I'm an overachiever." Lust burned in Rafe's eyes, that

same intensity from when they were sparring. Eamonn had to catch his breath, too.

His cock disappeared into those pink lips. Eamonn grabbed his hair and pushed his head down, moaning for the whole pitch to hear.

Eamonn laid back and stared through the netting at the red and purple streaks flaring in the sky. "Fuck, mate, I'm gonna come."

But Rafe didn't move away from his cock. He continued to bob and down. "You're going take my load in my mouth?" Eamonn teased. *God, that would be so bloody hot.* "You're going to swallow my come?"

Rafe looked at him with a twinkle in his eye, something he would never forget for his entire life, a look that Eamonn felt in his heart as much as he did his cock.

"Fuck!" He jerked his hips up and drenched Rafe's mouth.

Rafe took every last drop. As Eamonn came back to earth, he heard Rafe grunt with orgasm. His leg got very warm all of a sudden.

Eamonn sat up. "Did you spunk on my trousers?"

"Sorry." Rafe tried to wipe it up with his hand, but he was making more of a mess.

"Forget it. Come over here." He patted the patch of grass. Rafe lay down beside him. He held him close and breathed him in. Before he realized it, he kissed Rafe on the forehead, then the lips. They watched the final seconds of the day slip behind the horizon. It was the ideal cap to the evening.

Chapter 11

So much for not hooking up with his broken-hearted flatmate. Rake awoke the next morning still buzzing from the night before. It wasn't just that he gave his first-ever blow job. That evening on the soccer field with Eamonn was more than the sum of its sexual parts. To call it a success for Operation: Slut would be to cheapen what happened between them, and what he felt brewing inside him, even if it probably shouldn't happen again.

Rafe texted his best friend and former roommate Coop to see if he was able to Facetime. It was two a.m. at Browerton, but Coop would be up, probably writing a paper or playing video games with other kids in the dorm. As he waited to hear from Coop, he put his ear to the door to listen for Eamonn out there. He wondered what Eamonn was thinking. Rafe believed he had done an adequate, if not superb, job yesterday.

His phone rang, and in seconds, Coop's face took over his screen. Coop was buff with a serious expression forever on his face, but Rafe knew he was a big softie at heart.

"Hey, what are you doing up so late?" Rafe asked.

"I was working on a new rap for Squadron." Coop fashioned himself the next Drake, and he liked to practice his material at this underground rap club that was a laundry room during the day.

"That's awesome! I'd love to hear it."

Coop cleared his throat.

"But not right now. Sorry. I have big news to share."

"How's England?"

"It's great. I'm taking a class on Shakespeare. I can drink legally. And I gave a blow job." Rafe's eyes darted to the door. He should probably keep his voice down.

"That all sounds very fun."

"Coop, the big question is how graphic should I get in my description?" Rafe sat on his desk.

"Not at all."

"If we were characters on *Girls*, you'd let me go into detail."

"Good for you, Rafe. Seriously. I'm glad you're having fun." Coop yawned, and it caused a chain reaction for Rafe. Rafe remembered talking to Coop as they fell asleep about the most random topics, like what if gyros were made with pizza as the pita. It was fun having a roommate.

"So, I'm not sure what to do now," Rafe said. "The guy I was with is my flatmate, and my friend."

"Were you drunk?"

"No."

"Was it awkward?"

"No. It was actually really nice," Rafe said wistfully.

"Do you want it to happen again?"

"I...I don't know. Eamonn, the guy, he's one of my only friends here, and he doesn't do casual hookups. I don't want to make things weird since I'm only here for a few months."

Rafe knew of plenty of gay guys who hooked up with each other yet remained friends like it was no big deal. That's what Louisa and Heath did. He didn't know if he was capable of that with Eamonn, though.

"Then leave it alone," Coop said. "Acknowledge what happened, then move on and go back to being friends."

"Right. You know best, Coop." Deep down, Rafe had hoped for a different answer, but this one was the wisest. It was the answer that would ensure he wouldn't mess this friendship up.

Coop yawned again.

"You should get to bed. Hey Coop! I'm technically calling you from the future!"

"Don't ruin the surprise." Coop cracked one more smile before yawning again.

———

RAFE SPENT his day away from the dorm. He attended his sedimentology and physics classes, then did homework at the library. He was grateful for the chance to bury his head in schoolwork. It was dark by the time he left the library. On his walk back to the dorm, he went over things to say to Eamonn about what happened. Maybe some guys could just shrug it off, say "duuuuuude," and laugh about it. Rafe was not one of those guys.

"What happened was animal. Chemical," Rafe said to himself as he walked down the sloping hill. "I read this article that said guys are sexually attracted to the scent of each other's sweat. We were sweating. It makes perfect sense that this would happen. But it happened, and..." Here was where Rafe got stuck. *It happened now let's never speak of it again?* Too harsh. *It happened and now it will never happen again?* Too severe.

Rafe entered his flat and went to the kitchen for some tea. Eamonn sat at the kitchen table, hunched over his laptop.

"Hey." Rafe rushed to the tea kettle. The lines he had for this conversation vanished and left him with the verbal skills of a goldfish.

"Y'alright?" Eamonn mumbled, eyes focused on his screen.

"Yeah. You?"

"I bloody hate applications."

"What are you applying for?" Rafe filled the tea kettle and lit the stove.

"My uncle's company has a management trainee program, so I'm going to do that."

"That sounds great!"

Eamonn didn't seem to share Rafe's sentiment. "I have to fill out this application with past work experience and what I hope to accomplish."

"I hate those questions. I wish I could just say 'I like your company because you're hiring.' Don't you have a résumé or C.V. to go off of for the first part?"

Eamonn blinked at him like a deer in the headlights. "You don't need a C.V. to work in a warehouse or run a paper route. I have no relevant experience. I'm wasting my time." Eamonn pushed his computer back.

"You're in luck then." Rafe took a seat next to him. "I am the résumé whisperer. I've applied for summer programs, research programs, internships, externships, and college, obviously. I am a master at spinning nothing into gold."

Rafe took Eamonn's computer and looked at what he had already. He'd been a dishwasher, box folder, and paper

delivery boy. All great and noble positions that unfortunately carried little weight in the professional world.

"You have ample experience, but you're problem is
you're being too honest," Rafe said. "You need to give the
people what they want."

"I've never worked in an office. It looks rather boring."

"Don't put that down on this. First, we should make your
C.V., in case there are other jobs you want to apply for." Rafe
logged onto his email and pulled up one of his old résumés
and copied the formatting.

"You've done a lot!" Eamonn said.

"That's just how it seems." Rafe had never worked hard
like Eamonn had at his old jobs. His responsibilities had
included making copies, fetching coffee, transcribing interviews, and lots of data entry.

Eamonn shuffled closer to Rafe, his familiar combo of
cigs and cologne commingling in Rafe's nose. Rafe tried to
ignore how close his beautiful face was. They had a résumé
to create.

"Some people say you should have an objective at the
top of your résumé. I call bullshit. If you're applying for a
job, then they know what your objective is. That's just
wasted space. It looks like your most recent job was working
at the box factory warehouse." Rafe read what was on
Eamonn's application. "This is the same company with the
management program, yes?"

"Yes." Eamonn jumped up and took the screaming tea
kettle off the stove. "It's my uncle's."

Eamonn did not sound thrilled about benefitting from
nepotism. He poured them both a cup of tea. There was
something hot about a guy making himself tea. In America,
he would be looked down on for doing something so girly.
But when Eamonn did it, it was the perfect mix of

masculinity and vulnerability. Eamonn caught Rafe looking at him. He whipped his focus back to the laptop screen.

"Right. So you worked in the warehouse. What did you do?"

"I folded boxes. I carried bundles of boxes to storage. I helped fill orders for clients. I got to ride the forklift a few times."

"So you assembled merchandise, organized and maintained the inventory storage system, liaisoned with clients, and operated complex machinery to streamline distribution."

"Holy baskets of cunts. Did you just come up with that?" Eamonn's eyes bugged out wide in disbelief. Rafe wanted to swim laps in them.

"I told you I was the résumé whisperer."

"You're the résumé alchemist."

"That sounds much cooler. Okay, what's next?" Rafe skimmed Eamonn's application. "Dishwasher. What did you do?"

"I washed dishes?"

"And?" Rafe gestured for him to keep going.

"I soaked dishes in water and washed off food and rubbed them clean. There really isn't much to it."

"There had to have been other stuff you did. Think in terms of management and leadership."

"I trained this other dishwasher they hired."

"Perfect!" Rafe clapped his hands together. "And did you come up with any new methods or systems?"

"Well, I recommended they use a different dish soap because I reckon the one they had had a weird smell."

"Love it!" Rafe typed away on the computer. "Keep going."

"And around the holidays, I would save some food that

went uneaten and give it to these homeless kids who hung around by the dumpsters. I even got the chefs to cook them a meal to send over to their shelter."

"That's really nice," Rafe said, genuinely touched. And he was staring at Eamonn again.

He snapped out of it.

"How does this sound: Developed three-step system for cleaning dishes, trained and supervised new employees, lobbied management for a greener, less-chemical-based soap which helped improve diners' experience, spear-headed partnership between restaurant and local shelter to feed homeless youth."

Eamonn sat up straight. "I reckon I'm quite impressive. I should be CEO."

Rafe and Eamonn worked on filling out his résumé with more jobs and other volunteer experiences. Eamonn found ways to help others no matter his job, whether that was feeding the homeless, donating extra newspapers to an old age home, and even bringing boxes to an animal shelter so cats should rest in them.

"Have you thought about applying for jobs in the non-profit sector?" Rafe asked him. "Your résumé has a very strong altruistic angle to it. There are non-profits that are working on things like homelessness and hunger on a global level. I think you would love working for one of them."

"I don't know how to even go about getting one of those jobs."

"I know people who intern for non-profits and government organizations and parlay that into full-time work."

"I can't afford to get an internship after I graduate."

Rafe pointed at the computer screen. "You have a great résumé. There are lots of organizations out there."

"I'll consider it." Eamonn cracked a smile. "Thanks for your help."

This time Rafe caught him staring, and it made his pants tighten.

Here would've been a good time to have The Talk about what happened, about how they should be friends and not let things get awkward. But there was this understanding in the air between them that didn't need to be verbalized.

Rafe helped him answer the rest of the questions for the box company's application. Eamonn poured them another cup of tea and broke out the tea biscuits. He challenged Rafe to come up with professional descriptions for the oddest of jobs. ("The guy who shovels elephant shit at the circus." "Leads waste management initiative.")

Eamonn got up from the table and swung open the kitchen door. "Hey." He held the door. "I'm glad we're friends."

Friends. The F word. Rafe didn't expect it to feel like the kick in the nuts it was.

"Me, too," Rafe said.

Chapter 12

The next week went by in a flash of classes as Eamonn's flatmates buckled down in their studies. They only went to the pub once and turned the kitchen table into a library. Eamonn didn't want to feel left out and joined them to do homework, though he didn't appreciate them wasting their final year of uni stuck in a book. Rafe turned out to be an academic renaissance man. He helped Eamonn with his maths homework and worked with him to craft an essay for his business ethics class. Eamonn resisted the urge to play footsie with him under the table or kiss his shoulder when he leaned close.

Eamonn was grateful that what had happened on the football pitch hadn't made things weird between them. That hadn't stopped him from thinking about that evening, though. He found himself dreaming of Rafe's lithe body bouncing up and down on his cock and then waking up with a massive erection. And the only way to take care of that was to wank off while picturing fucking Rafe's brains out. He kept this to himself, though. Rafe was his friend, and he didn't want to risk mucking that up any further by attacking him with his lips again. Plus, Rafe was making no effort to snog or flirt with him, so Eamonn figured his attraction was one-sided.

On Friday evening, Eamonn came into the kitchen and found Heath and Rafe with their bloody textbooks open yet again. It was simply unacceptable.

"No. I can't let this happen." Eamonn shut both of their textbooks. "It is Friday night. You are not staying in to do work."

"I was just finishing up." Rafe scribbled a final note in the bottom corner of his pad.

"I expected more of you, Rafe. You're an American abroad. You should be binge drinking and consuming copious amounts of drugs and doing things that would get you extradited back to your home country," Eamonn said.

"The night is young."

"And you." Eamonn turned to Heath. "What happened to my mate who once wrote a ten-page essay while smoking a spliff and watching a marathon of *Black Mirror*?"

"Still here, wanker. Hoping to graduate."

"Hopeless." Eamonn turned back to Rafe. "Apothecary?"

"Didn't you tell Rafe you would take him to a gay bar?" Heath asked. "The Yank is here for new experiences."

Rafe pointed a pen at Heath. "I agree with Mount Everest."

"All right then. Laffly's it is."

Rafe nodded his head with excitement. "Maybe I'll have better luck off campus."

Eamonn deflated at the remark. "Maybe."

He caught Heath looking at him, and like any good mate, he seemed to get it instantly.

. . .

RAFE

They took a cab to Laffly's. For a second, Rafe worried that he wouldn't be allowed in because he was underage, but then he remembered where he was.

Eamonn wore a fitted, button-down shirt that pulled against his chest and flat stomach. His hair was properly mussed, up and out of his eyes. Rafe hoped Operation: Slut would be a success tonight. He hoped he could find a guy who'd make him forget about the one guy he wanted.

The cab drove down a cobblestone street with quaint cottages and storefronts. Everything was so old in England, like it was all a historical setpiece. This block alone was probably older than all of America.

"How old do you think those cottages are?" Rafe asked.

"I reckon about 300 years," the cab driver said.

Rafe took pictures with his phone, savoring the history around them. In his suburb, "old" meant 1970s. His town had been basically torn down and rebuilt for modern amenities. Ye Old Strip Mall didn't have the same ring.

They stopped at a light. He took pictures of Eamonn with an old cottage in the window.

"What are you doing?" Eamonn asked.

"Commemorating."

"Nothing says Jolly Old England like a picture of a house taken through an automobile window."

"Unless I get a shirt that says 'Jolly Old England.'"

"You're a bleeding piece of work."

Rafe took that as a compliment.

"Give me that." Eamonn yanked the phone from his hands and snapped pictures of Rafe. He pretended to be a fashion photographer. "Yeah. Just like this. Good. How do you like it? Oh, yeah. Give it to me."

Rafe's heart beat rapidly in his chest, and his dick hardened in seconds. He smiled uncontrollably, a mix of massive awkwardness and sexual desire trying to come together. Eamonn put the phone down and realized what the hell he was saying.

"Shit," he said.

Rafe didn't know what to say to next. Their shared this weird moment, reveled in it, bathed in it.

The cab screeched to a stop. "We're here," the driver said.

Thank goodness.

"Right." Eamonn fed him cash.

Rafe hopped out of the cab. Eamonn put his hand on Rafe's lower back, on that magical spot, and led them inside to the bar. Rafe ordered the first round.

"Are you sure?" Eamonn asked.

"Yes. You've been so generous ever since I got here. I haven't once paid for a round of drinks."

"What if your parents find out?"

The question was valid, but still stung Rafe. He'd never minded being open with his parents because he felt like he had nothing to hide. This wasn't anything to hide, either. He was openly gay, after all. But there was something about his life in England that he didn't want to be an open book. Adventures were meant to be experienced first-hand, not recounted in credit card receipts.

Rafe pulled out notes which he'd gotten from the on-campus ATM and slid them over the bar. Eamonn waved his hand to get the bartender's attention. He ordered them their usual drinks. The bar was packed and bodies mashed against them. The gay guys he saw weren't much different than the ones in America, minus the accents.

"Does a British accent do anything for you?" he asked Eamonn.

Eamonn shook his head no and handed him a pint glass.

"What's is this exactly? I always see you and Heath drinking them."

"It's called a snakebite and black. It's lager, cider, and a dash of black courant. I think you'll like it."

"It's like ombre in drink form." Rafe had a taste and was pleased by the dash of sweetness mixed with the hardness of the beer. And it definitely had a bite.

There were no booths or stools available, but Eamonn pushed through the crowd and found a space by the wall. "Well, this works."

"This is great!" Rafe yelled above the din.

They placed their drinks on the piece of wood sticking out from the wall. The glow of the lights bathed them in a dark yellow haze. Eamonn took a sip of his beer and set it down. Laffly's wasn't so different from Apothecary. It was a bar. People stood around and drank. They just happened to be gay.

"They have snooker here, too," Rafe said. A gaggle of gays parted, revealing the open table.

"And it's open. We should grab it," Eamonn said.

Or you can grab me. Rafe had to make sure not to drink too much lest he say those thoughts out loud. He had plenty of available guys here to choose from. Why was he still fixating on Eamonn?

Rafe followed him to the table. "I don't know how to play."

"Do you want to learn?"

He nodded yes.

Eamonn handed Rafe a pool cue. "Time to break you in then."

Rafe's head went dizzy at the other kinds of breaking in Eamonn could do with him.

. . .

EAMONN

Eamonn explained the rules of the game to Rafe, but judging by the deer-in-the-headlights reaction he was getting from the Yank, most of it didn't stick.

"Don't worry. You'll learn as we go. Just remember that you want to pot as many reds as you can."

"Pot?" Rafe asked.

"Get balls in the hole."

Eamonn felt his cheeks heat up. Like his photographer impression in the cab, he had to watch what he said. He got into position and nailed the white ball straight into the pyramid of reds. They scattered in all directions like a flock of pidgeons.

He surveyed the table, devising a strategy in his head. He glanced over at Rafe, who was trying to do the same thing. Rafe squeezed the pool cue in his hands as he studied the table. It made his arm muscles tense. Eamonn noticed the definition hiding under his T-shirt, and it sent blood rushing to his own pool cue.

"Damn," Eamonn said after his shot. One of the reds bounced off the edge of the pocket.

"Don't go easy on me," Rafe said.

"I'm not." *I just got a little distracted.*

Rafe leaned down and pointed his cue haphazardly at a ball that he'd never get in. He might have been good at maths, but Eamonn doubted he could translate it here on the first try.

"Let's have this be an open game," Eamonn said. "It'll be practice. I'll help you."

He signaled for Rafe to come to his side of the table. He got close and whispered into Rafe's ear, "Aim for that red into the side pocket. You have a better shot of making it. You don't want to leave any balls that your opponent could easily get in."

Eamonn realized he didn't need to whisper any of this since it was obvious to anyone playing that this was a no-brainer shot. He did like getting a whiff of Rafe's musk, at least.

"Leave no balls hanging. Got it." Rafe bent over the table and got his cue into position behind the white ball. Eamonn might've checked his arse out—to make sure the cue was lined up correctly, of course. And what a pert, round arse it was.

"Yes!" Rafe yelled as the red slid into the pocket.

"That was knees up, mate!" Eamonn patted him on the bum without thinking. Rafe did a double take at the area of impact. *Shit.*

"Which ball next?" Rafe didn't seem offended, but that was probably his friendly American instincts, and he was most likely inwardly recoiling.

Eamonn put his focus back on the table. He found the yellow ball in close proximity to a corner hole.

"I got this," Rafe said.

"A bit cocky, aren't we?"

"A bit nervous, aren't we?"

Rafe studied the shot one more time before bending over the table. Eamonn sneaked one quick peek, just to make sure his cue was placed correctly. And then the guy gave his arse a little wiggle to get into position, and Eamonn nearly poked a bloody hole in his trousers. *Bleeding Christ.*

"That's two in a row!" Rafe straightened himself and hi-fived Eamonn. And even with that, Eamonn's hand still felt compelled to pat him on the bum!

Eamonn told himself to get it together and ignore the need to touch Rafe's body.

When Rafe whiffed his next shot, Eamonn set his sights on a red ball at the far corner of the table. He focused on getting the shot lined up. Rafe stood over the corner pot where Eamonn wanted his ball to go. His crotch was literally in his eyeline.

"Can you move over?" Eamonn asked. He took a deep breath and got back into position. "Shit."

The red hit the pocket too hard and bounced away.

Rafe's shot improved throughout the game, and Eamonn made sure not to let his eyes drift down to his arse again. Instead, he liked to watch how his eyebrows seemed to knit together as he concentrated, and how Rafe looked to his reaction as soon as he hit a ball.

"One ball left," Rafe announced a little while later. It was the blue ball. Appropriate. He had a look of hope in his deep, brown eyes. "It'd be a shame if you missed it."

"Are you trashtalking me?"

"Maybe."

Eamonn's cock jutted to attention. He gripped his cue hard, like he wanted to hold Rafe. He bent down to line up his shot. At the last second, a guy came up to Rafe and said something about seeing him around campus. Eamonn's cue only scraped the edge of the ball.

"Tough break," Rafe said. Eamonn wasn't laughing, though.

"We're in the middle of a game, mate," Eamonn said. He stared the guy down until he backed away.

"Do you want anything to drink?" the fucking wanker asked Rafe.

"He has a drink," Eamonn said. He didn't know this guy, but he hated him.

The guy flipped him the bird, which in England was the index and middle finger together, then disappeared back into the crowd.

"Did you know him?" Rafe asked.

"I...you have to be careful about guys buying you drinks. He could slip you something." Eamonn didn't know what came over him. Rafe wasn't his, but he couldn't watch him become someone else's right in front of his eyes.

Rafe didn't put up a fight. He studied Eamonn for a moment before turning his attention to the snooker table. "I can't make this shot."

And true, it was a doozy. The ball was at the far end of the table, due south from the white. To make it, he'd have to hit it on its right side at just the proper angle to get it to scoot inside the pocket.

"You can do it, mate. *You have this, dude.*"

Rafe got into position. Eamonn kept his eyes above the waist, even though he could sense a butt wiggle in his periphery vision.

"You want to move over a little so your cue hits the white at the right spot."

"Like this?" Rafe shifted over.

"Too far."

"How's this?" Rafe's cue was held at too severe an angle.

"Here. Let me help." Eamonn bent over Rafe's body. His right hand slid down Rafe's arm, feeling the bumps of his triceps and forearm muscles. He manuevered Rafe's cue into the correct position. The heat of Rafe's body scorched through his clothes, and up close, he could smell the coconut scent of his shampoo and see the trail of freckles on his neck.

"H-how's this?" Rafe asked.

Oh Christ. Rafe wiggled his bloody bum against

Eamonn's crotch. His cock hardened and pressed against his pants.

"Ready?" Eamonn steadied his hand over Rafe's arm as Rafe pulled back the cue. The ball whizzed down the green, smacked the bluer-than-ever ball on its side, and sent it on a one-way trip into a pocket.

"We did it!" Rafe jumped up. He spun around and hugged Eamonn. He probably felt Eamonn's hard nob jutting into his thigh, but if he did, he didn't show it. Thank goodness.

They held each other's vision, and the crowd and noise vanished. Eamonn wanted to hold Rafe. As he extended his arms to wrap him in a hug, which if he wasn't careful could lead to other things, Rafe said, "Do you want a drink?"

There went the moment. Eamonn got the same answer again. They were just friends, nothing more.

"Sure."

"I'll get this round." Rafe went up to the bar.

Eamonn leaned against the wall where they had originally been. This was for the best. Rafe was leaving in a few weeks. He couldn't risk falling for him and getting his heart broken like Nathan had done last spring.

Rafe ran back to him, his eyes wide with panic.

"What's wrong?" Eamonn asked, instantly going into protective mode.

"My phone's gone."

Chapter 13

RAFE

Rafe went from worried to full-blown panic attack in their cab. He imagined several possibilities, none of them good, some of them ending up with him winding up in jail for some reason. He had Eamonn call his phone, but nobody picked up.

"Do you have a tracker on it?"

"No. Because I'm an idiot." Rafe smacked his head against the cab partition. "Someone has my phone. They're probably downloading all of my personal information, and they've probably stolen my identity as this point."

"Calm down. There is only one Rafe. I assure you of that." Eamonn rubbed his shoulder, which Rafe couldn't even enjoy at this moment.

"What am I going to do? Should I file a police report?"

"Are you sure you were pickpocketed?"

"Yes. That bar was packed. Someone in the crowd easily could've swiped it.'"

"We'll call the bar in the morning. Maybe you just dropped it is all."

Rafe didn't have as much faith as Eamonn, but he hoped he was right. Eamonn seemed to sense this, because he said next: "And if the bar doesn't have it, I guess we can file a police report."

"You guess?"

"It's not going to help."

"A crime was committed."

"Yes, because amid the murders, abuse, arson, hit-and-runs, and armed robbery, Scotland Yard will dedicate a full team of constables to your case." Eamonn softened. "Sorry. Wrong time for sarcasm. The police have bigger cases. They'll take down your information, but they won't do anything about it."

Rafe didn't say anything for the rest of the cab ride. He was thinking. Thinking of what to do next. He honestly had no idea, which upset him as much as the pickpocketing. What did one do when one needed a new phone? He was on a family plan with his parents. He had pointed out which iPhone he wanted, and they bought it. He hated that memory now. *I barely qualify as a fucking adult.*

When they arrived back at the dorm, he hugged Eamonn good night and went to his room. "You need help?" Eamonn asked.

"No. I have this." It was time to figure out shit on his own.

He Googled "what do I do if I lost my iPhone." It told him to go to the cloud to activate a lost iPhone app, which was supposed to lock his phone and emit a loud beeping sound until it was returned. It also disabled all credit card information on the phone. Rafe tried it and waited for a few minutes. Nothing happened. *Whoever pickpocketed me probably knows about this app and already has a workaround.*

"Okay, I also need a new phone," he said to himself,

working through the steps of his dilemma like it was a word problem. He went on Verizon's website to look at new iPhones, but immediately exed out. *No. If I do that, my parents will find out.* He couldn't let them know about this. He wasn't going to have them swoop in and save the day. He wasn't going to get a lecture about being careless.

Some further Googling pointed him to prepaid phones. He could get a new phone and pay for service as long as he wanted. He blanched at the price, until he scrolled past the nice smartphones and found the most basic models. *Okay, I can get by with just texting and calling for three months. Party like it's 2005.* He found a store in town that sold prepaid phones that allowed you to "top up." He nodded to himself in his window reflection. *You got this.*

Before he went to bed, he emailed his parents:

Dear Mom and Dad,

   England is wonderful! Unfortunately, it's so amazing that it fried my phone. It's been on the fritz, so to be safe, I'm getting a prepaid phone for the rest of my time here. We can talk via Skype and email, and I'll send you the new number when I get it. Just wanted to give you a heads up.

   Love,
   Rafe

RAFE FELT the pumping of endorphins bringing an excited smile to his face, like he just completed some massive class project. Tonight was not the end of the world as he knew it, and he felt fine.

. . .

EAMONN

Eamonn heard Rafe stirring in the kitchen the next morning. He thought about him last night, and not just when he wanked off before he went to sleep. He believed that underneath all the babying from his folks, there was someone wild waiting to get out, and Eamonn wanted to release him. He went into the kitchen, but it was Louisa he heard, not Rafe.

"Have you seen Rafe this morning?" he asked.

"Afternoon," she said. Eamonn checked the clock on the wall, and it was a quarter past noon. "I haven't."

Eamonn knocked on Rafe's door, but there was no answer. He returned to his room and found a sleeve of English tea biscuits next to the door with a note.

Thanks for your help last night. I really appreciate it. We'll talk later. I'm busy adulting!

He read the note in Rafe's excited voice, and it made him smile. The tea biscuits didn't hurt either.

It was Saturday, and Eamonn had nowhere to be. He strolled through campus on this brilliant day. A crisp breeze swept through campus, and red and orange leaves rustled on trees. Autumn snuck up on him like that.

"Eamonn!" Rafe called out from an outdoor table in the student union courtyard.

Something seemed different about Rafe. He had this blaze of confidence on his face.

"I need your digits." Rafe pulled out a new mobile.

"Is that a flip phone?"

"It is. I'm going totally Bush era. I bought a prepaid phone and topped it up at a corner store in town. It's also where I got you those tea biscuits."

They exchanged phone numbers. Rafe crossed something off a list in his notebook.

"You seem like a man on a mission."

"I am. I researched work options last night, and in the U.K., people on a student visa are allowed to work up to twenty hours per week. First thing this morning, I came to the student union and looked at job postings, and Apothecary is hiring for a runner. I interviewed about an hour ago and was hired on the spot. The manager said he'd never met someone so enthusiastic about picking up empty glasses and stocking the bar with ice."

Rafe could hardly contain himself. He was like a contestant on *The X Factor*.

"I'll make an hourly wage plus get some of the bartenders' tips!"

"That's brilliant!"

Rafe did a drum roll on the table, apropos of nothing, just pure adrenaline. "I can't believe this. This has been one of the best mornings of my life. I can do anything! I mean, my parents and teachers always told me growing up that if I put my mind to something, I can achieve it. But this is the first time where I truly believe it." Rafe exhaled and came down to earth, or closer to it. *This fucking guy.* Eamonn wanted to scoop him up in his arms.

"I'll finally have money of my own. I'm not even going to do direct deposit. I can get paper checks and just cash them so my parents won't know." Rafe put a hand on his arm, sending a pulse of heat to Eamonn's head. "Thank you, Eamonn. I don't think I would've done any of this if it weren't for you."

His sincerity, and the way his lips puckered, left Eamonn tripping over his words. "I did nothing. This is all you."

Rafe hopped up from the table. The warmth of his hand lingered on Eamonn's arm.

"I'm gonna go fill out paperwork. I'm so excited!"

Chapter 14

RAFE

On his first day of being a runner, Rafe didn't break any glasses, which he considered a great start to his life of employment. Then again, he didn't have much opportunity to break any glasses, as today's shift was just about showing him around.

His second shift two days later proved slightly more demanding, with what actual customers and all. His boss had him working the early afternoon shift, and the bar was mostly empty, but it did give him good practice picking up glasses, and restocking the bar. It was a different kind of work for Rafe, one that made him feel productive in a way that he hadn't when doing homework. When he looked out at a room where there were no empty glasses on tables, he smiled with pride.

His third shift the next afternoon was slightly more difficult, primarily because whenever he picked up an empty glass or brought out ice for the bartender, one table in the corner kept giving him a rousing round of applause.

"Brilliant! Just brilliant work!" Eamonn cheered. He and

Heath gave Rafe a standing ovation while he cleared off a table.

"Did you see that?" Heath asked, like a sports announcer. "How he swooped right in and took away those two pint glasses without interrupting the customers' conversation?"

"Rafe belongs in the pantheon of great runners."

"He brings tears to my eyes."

"Oh? What's this? Rafe is carrying a container of lime wedges and he...look at that! He refilled the garnish tray without a single wedge falling onto the bar."

"We are watching history being made," Heath said.

They burst into applause again. Louisa shielded her face.

"Can you take it down a notch?" Rafe approached their table. "Like 100 notches?"

"We are witnessing greatness, mate," Heath said.

"We're proud of you, Yank." Eamonn flashed him a smile that shot right to Rafe's core. He gave Rafe a surreptitious pat on the ass. Rafe had to step away because if Eamonn did that again, he was going to pitch a tent, like he did when they played snooker. He doubted that was acceptable employee behavior.

"You're doing a really good job." Louisa shook the last bits of alcohol from her drink into her mouth.

"What's this?" Heath pointed at Rafe, then at the glass. "Rafe, I will let you do the honors."

Rafe shook his head, half-embarrassed and half-loving the attention. "Louisa, are you finished with your glass?"

She gave him her glass, and as if on cue, Heath and Eamonn gave him another damn standing ovation. Rafe walked back to the bar, feeling heat on his cheeks. When Rafe got his first paycheck, he looked at it for a long while, thinking about whether to frame it or cash it. That decision only took a second. He cashed his check and earmarked most of it for groceries and social events. He went into the kitchen and waved a twenty-pound note in the air for his friends.

"Drinks are on me tonight."

———

RAFE LOVED GETTING to buy rounds at the bar for his friends. He could be the one to help others and take charge.

He brought a round of drinks to the table. Heath and Eamonn only gave him a short round of applause.

"You don't have to do that. I'm not working tonight." Rafe put the drinks on the table.

"We're just happy that we're getting pissed for free." Heath took his drink and slid Eamonn his pint. Louisa had to reach in and grab her drink. Heath always passed Louisa her drink. It was a subtle moment that Rafe picked up on and wondered if he was overthinking it.

Rafe sat next to Louisa, another change up. He wondered if he was the only one who noticed.

Eamonn raised his pint glass. "Cheers to Rafe. Runner extraordinaire."

They brought their glasses together to clink.

"I wonder if they'll ever let you tend bar one shift. Say it's your one wish before returning to America and not being allowed to drink."

"Are you bleeding serious, Louisa?" Heath asked with a mean spark in his eyes. "You think they're just going to throw him behind a bar without any experience? That's probably illegal. Don't be daft. Just drink your Midori sour."

Awkward silence hit the table. This was far from typical

Heath sarcasm. There was a noticeable chill in his voice that shut Louisa up well. The not-so-gentle giant took a gulp of his beer.

"Don't mind, Heath," Louisa said to Rafe for the whole table to hear. "He acts like a baby when he doesn't get his way."

"Only Louisa gets to have her way and fuck all to everyone else," he muttered.

Louisa got up so quickly that their glasses shook. She joined a group of girls she knew standing around a high top table.

"Mate," Eamonn said.

Heath raised his hands, not wanting a word of it. "I'm tired of her bloody games. I'm serious this time."

A little bit later, Rafe went up to the bar to get the next round of drinks. As he waited, he heard the distinct sounds of an American accent. He was almost nostalgic for it.

"I can barely understand anyone here, Mom. These accents are so thick," a girl with wavy blonde hair and red, puffy eyes said into her phone. "Okay, okay. We'll talk later. Call me when you get home from book club. I'll be just waking up."

"Hey. You were in my orientation." Rafe recognized her as one of the kids in red T-shirts up front. He thought they only traveled in packs avoiding all British students. "It's great running into other Yanks here."

They reintroduced themselves. Her name was Allison.

"What dorm are you in?" Allison asked.

"Sweeney."

"Oh. Those are nice. We're up in Jones."

Rafe had only passed by Jones once, when he and Eamonn went to the soccer field. They were on the opposite end of campus, which explained why he hadn't seen her around.

"So how are you liking it?" Rafe asked.

Allison shot him a look, as if to say "look at my face."

"Isn't there a whole group of you?"

"They're in Edinburgh this week."

"During the week? What about classes?"

"They pay kids to write their papers and attend classes for them. They try to spend as little time as possible here. Most nights, we go into London to party with UCL kids. I don't go to Cornell with them. I'm camp friends with one of the girls, and this was supposed to be our adventure in Europe. But then we got in a fight because this Dartmouth guy she likes at UCL hit on me, and it's my fault. So now they're all traveling in Ireland and Scotland, and she didn't invite me. Bitch." Allison dressed for Apothecary like she was going to 7-Eleven to pick up a carton of ice cream to bring home.

No wonder Rafe never saw those Americans around. He did not miss their presence, and he was ticked off that they just left their friend behind.

Rafe handed Allison a cocktail napkin.

"Thanks. I'm just a little homesick, too," Allison said, with a sniffle. "It just hit me how far away we are. And I miss Syracuse. The buildings back home are old on the outside, but at least they're updated inside. Everything here is so old and so much smaller."

That was part of the charm of being abroad. They were living in history. England wasn't bland and cookie-cutter.

"And I hate watching soccer and having to convert things to the metric system and using a power adapter to plug anything in. Why are plugs different? Could they really not be standardized?" Allison sniffled again.

"At least we can drink legally," Rafe said.

"It's not the same. There are no parties. Just going to the pub. It's just different here." She shrugged, like there was no other way to put it.

Rafe glanced around at the packed bar and his friends in their booth. It *was* different but in the best way.

"You seem to love it here," Allison said, a hint of jealousy in her voice.

"I do."

"That's so wonder—" Allison cried into her napkin.

"Do you want to come sit with me and my flatmates?"

"You're friends with your flatmates? That's so cute. No, I'm going back to my dorm room to binge-watch *Unbreakable Kimmy Schmidt*."

"If you ever want to talk to another American about malls or driving on the right side of the road, give me a call." He gave her his number.

He returned to his table with a huge smile on his face.

"Did you get a handy in the bathroom or something?" Heath asked.

"Better."

Eamonn looked the tiniest bit concerned, which Rafe took a moment to enjoy.

Chapter 15

EAMONN

Over the next week, Heath and Louisa didn't say a word to each other in the flat. That made the times when they were all in the kitchen very uncomfortable. At least Eamonn had Rafe to help relieve the tension with a joke.

October was in full fall mode. Eamonn smiled as he walked through piles of leaves to the gym. He had woken up early this Sunday morning, and instead of lying in bed, he decided to get some gym time in. As he lifted weights and jogged around the indoor track, he found himself thinking about Rafe. No one memory in particular, just a montage running in his head. Rafe smiling, Rafe cooking at the stove, Rafe lining up his snooker shot. He also realized that it'd been weeks since he thought of his ex-boyfriend. He hadn't even been tempted to check his Instagram feed to see what stars he'd taken selfies with. Those years with Nathan seemed to have happened another lifetime ago. With each loop around the track, he moved further away from that pain.

It was just before eight when Eamonn returned to

Sweeney Hall. He put on a fresh pot for tea. Nathan had preferred using the electric tea maker, but Eamonn would never convert. He heated his water the old-fashioned way in a kettle.

The door swung open. Rafe placed his backpack on the table. Since it was the first truly chilly day of autumn, he wore a corduroy jacket, and he looked damn good in it.

"You're up early," Rafe said.

"Likewise."

He filled up his water bottle at the sink.

"Going somewhere?" Eamonn asked.

"I'm going on a day trip to Stonehenge as part of an assignment for my sedimentology class." Rafe capped his bottle and placed it in the side sleeve of his backpack.

"Are you hiking there?" Eamonn nodded at his backpack, which was packed to the gills.

"There's this tour group. You go out to the site on a chartered bus, and the leader gives a guided tour. And they provide lunch."

"What do you need a guided tour of Stonehenge for?" Eamonn pointed at the fridge. "Here are old rocks." He pointed at the microwave. "Here are more old rocks. End of tour!"

"Stonehenge is one of the great geological and historical mysteries of our planet. I *think* it'll be a little more in-depth." Rafe opened one of the cupboards and retrieved a bag of trail mix. He brushed against Eamonn on his way back to the table, giving his body another morning workout. "Have you ever been?"

"In primary school, but I just remember being bored out of my bloody mind. When does the tour leave?"

"Not until eleven, but I want to give myself enough time to get to London on time."

"London?" The tea kettle screamed on the stove. Eamonn turned off the burner and moved the kettle off.

"That's where the tour leaves from." Rafe poured some trail mix into his hand and knocked it back like pills.

Eamonn pulled out a map of England on his phone. There was Stonehenge, there was Stroude, and then there was London completely in the opposite direction. He showed it to Rafe.

"You're going to travel all the way into London just to drive all the way to Stonehenge, then all the way back to London to come back here."

"That's where these tours leave from."

"And all this for what? Some tour guide to tell you something you could've read about online. And where's lunch coming from?"

"I think it's just sandwiches. What? It's not like there are tours leaving from Surrey. It all leaves from London."

"You are not a tourist. You came to England to get the real British experience. No real British person would be caught dead on one of those tour busses."

Rafe seemed to absorb what he was saying. "Well, I want to see Stonehenge. What other option do I have?" He checked the clock on the wall. "I need to get going."

"I'll take you," Eamonn said just as Rafe swung the door open.

Rafe came back inside. "Really?"

"Really." Stonehenge was only an hour drive. They could leave now, look at the rocks for a few minutes, and be back by lunchtime. Eamonn would finish his class assignments tonight. "Just give me a few minutes to shower. And you can leave that ghastly knapsack here."

"How are we going to get there?"

"You leave that to me." *Going to a tourist trap. What a way to spend a Sunday.* But when he saw Rafe's face light up, and he felt that light deep in his heart, he knew he'd made the right decision.

———

THEY TOOK the train to Guildford, and as they walked to Eamonn's house, he gave Rafe a guided walking tour of his hometown.

"That Tesco on the corner used to be this massive arcade. I would go there with mates everyday after school. My mum was pretty pissed when I'd spend half my news-paper route money there. They had this game where you could pretend to play football with Beckham and all these great players. You would stand in this booth and wear this boot, and it was just like being on the pitch with these greats."

"Sounds just like that."

"Sod off." Eamonn gave him a playful shove. "It felt real when I was eight."

Leaves blew in their path. Eamonn kicked them aside. They walked down the middle of the street through the main strip. Most stores were closed on Sundays, so the town was theirs. Eamonn had been down this street a million times, but Rafe soaked it all in with wide-eyed wonder.

"It's just stores," Eamonn said.

"But these buildings!" Rafe pointed to a two-story building with a barbershop on the bottom. "This one could've been the home of a Redcoat. He could've hugged his family goodbye when he was sent overseas to fight some obnoxious colonists. And that little cottage right next to it could've been where guilds met in the Middle Ages."

"That's where this girl Lisa Book lived. She had a fondness for kicking boys in the stones."

"We don't have this in America. It's just strip malls and maybe something from the Civil War that isn't shrouded in a Confederate Flag."

Eamonn wouldn't mind living in a city where buildings were modern and updated. Those only seemed to exist in London, and only for loads of money.

He had them turn down a side street that reminded Rafe of Privet Lane in Harry Potter.

"I knew you were going to say that," Eamonn said, a smile crossing his lips.

"No, you didn't."

"A Harry Potter reference. Very original."

Rafe went to push Eamonn, but Eamonn stopped his hand.

And held it.

Rafe's warm palm fit perfectly in his. He didn't try to pull away. As much as Eamonn's heart wanted to leap out of his chest, he remained outwardly calm.

"I'll bet you haven't even seen a single Harry Potter movie," Rafe said.

"Yes I did! Daniel Radcliffe is a good-looking mate."

They walked the rest of the way to his house hand-in-hand, as if it were the most natural thing in the world.

Rafe

Rafe took back his hand when they reached Eamonn's house. Not that he didn't love the contact. Oh, he did. Rafe could've floated down Privet Lane, but he didn't want Eamonn's family asking any questions.

A teenage girl with bright pink hair answered the door. "Eamonn!" She ran into his arms. He squeezed her tight.

"Well, this is a surprise." The girl's twin, whose hair was as reserved as her sister's was wild, came outside. They each had the same squinty blue eyes as their brother.

Eamonn hugged one sister in each arm. He was officially the best big brother Rafe had ever met, and it made him regret being an only child.

"Who are you?" The pink-haired sister asked.

"Liv! You're not interrogating him," Eamonn said.

"I'm Rafe. I'm a friend of your brother's."

"You're American?" Mary, the other sister, looked at Rafe like he was a science exhibit.

"Born and raised."

"That's so cool!" Mary and Olivia said. Rafe shrugged with fake modesty. He loved having this instant cache.

"We can't stay," Eamonn said. "Just here to borrow mum's car for the morning."

"We're going to Stonehenge," Rafe said.

Olivia and Mary seemed as excited by that as their brother did. Rafe supposed it was like someone wanting to go to the Washington Monument. He did that years ago, and it was just a lot of waiting to go up a small elevator and stare out on more monuments for a few minutes.

"Let me save you some time. It's rocks," Olivia said.

"Like brother, like sister." Rafe smiled at Eamonn.

"It's going to be interesting and educational," Eamonn said.

"Two of your favorite things," Mary said. "We were just about to eat breakfast."

"Stay for breakfast," Olivia pleaded with her brother.

"Mum's making eggs," Mary said.

"We want to get going and take advantage of the nice

weather," Eamonn said. There was not a cloud in the sky, and with the sun out, the temperature had the perfect fall crisp. This was a day not to be wasted. Rafe imagined Stonehenge would be packed.

"We can eat in the backyard," Mary said.

"It's just rocks. They're not going anywhere." Olivia crossed her arms, underlining her argument.

Eamonn looked back at Rafe for his opinion. Breakfast al fresco actually sounded nice, and he was getting a kick out of this sibling dynamic. Rafe gave him a thumbs-up. The girls cheered.

"It's going to be a quick breakfast," Eamonn said.

"Our mum makes really good eggs and bacon," Mary said to Rafe.

"We can't wait to hear all about Eamonn's new boyfriend!" Olivia exclaimed.

"Boyfriend?" Eamonn's mom came to the door. She kissed her son on the cheek.

Eamonn's cheek went from zero to blush central in seconds. "What? Uh, no."

"No, I'm not—we're not boyfriends." Rafe found himself stammering, too.

"We're flatmates at Stroude."

"I'm his flatmate."

His mom nodded, but she didn't seem convinced. The sisters burst out giggling.

"I'm Anna, his mum." She shook Rafe's hand.

"Rafe."

"Nice to meet you, Eamonn's *flatmate*," Olivia said. She and Mary traded knowing looks.

"Right. Listen up." Eamonn held up his hands. "I have two tickle monsters here, and I know how to use them." He blew at them like gun barrels. The girls screamed and ran inside. Eamonn put his hands back down. "Works like a charm."

———————

RAFE PUT his newfound culinary skills to use helping out Anna, Mary, and Olivia in the kitchen. The girls were on toast duty at the kitchen table, Anna manned the stove, and Rafe was in charge of chopping up potatoes and vegetables for something called bubble and squeak. Eamonn was supposed to be setting the patio table, but he kept walking up and down the wooden steps to the lawn.

"What are you doing?" Rafe called from the kitchen.

"I think one of these steps is loose."

"It's fine!" Mary called to him.

Eamonn squatted down and checked out the middle step.

"Eamonn, it's fine!" Anna said.

"It's fine if you want to fall on your arse!" Eamonn marched over to the shed.

"He still likes to be the man of the house and take care of everything." She scrambled up the eggs in her frying pan with a wooden spoon. Rafe noticed that the lawn was recently mowed and the bushes around the perimeter were nice and trimmed.

"He cares," Rafe said.

"He really does. He gives people his whole heart, that's for sure." There was a serious undercurrent in her words, almost like they were a warning.

Anna got out another frying pan for him. She had him fry the carrots, peas, and cabbage he finished chopping.

"He really stepped up when his dad left."

Eamonn left the shed waving a screwdriver in his hand. "The steps just have a few loose screws."

"Takes one to know one!" Mary said. Eamonn stuck his tongue out at her.

Rafe smiled to himself. He was home. It wasn't even his home, but he felt that warm feeling of home, the kind that wraps you in a blanket on the couch.

"Did you know his previous boyfriend Nathan?" Anna asked.

"No, but I've heard about him. He's going to be in a movie."

"I won't be seeing it." She stirred the eggs, maybe a little too hard. "A mother never forgets."

Rafe gulped back a lump in his throat. He tried to tread lightly while also satisfying his own curiosity. "I heard Nathan broke up with him to be a movie star or something like that."

"Eamonn tried to stay together with him. He was in love, and my son falls hard. The night Nathan was set to leave, he borrowed the car and made a mad dash to Heathrow Airport. He bought a ticket so he could get into the terminal. It cost him most of the bloody money he made that month. When he told me what he was doing, I thought he was telling me the plot of some romantic comedy."

"It's like *The Wedding Singer* meets *Love, Actually.*"

"If only." She stared at the eggs with this intense gaze that was like a carbon copy of her son. Her blue eyes went dark. "He got to the gate, and Nathan was snogging someone else. When Nathan saw him, Eamonn said he just shrugged and boarded the plane."

Rafe's heart broke for Eamonn in that moment. He jabbed at the vegetables a little too hard. He wished Nathan was here right now. He'd punch him in the face.

Hissing and sizzling came from Rafe's frying pan. He went to shut off the burner, when Anna stopped him.

"That's the cabbage. It's bubbling and squeaking."

"I'm making a traditional English dish!" The sounds of his food frying were like a symphony. He took a picture of his bubble and squeak.

"You still have to add in the potatoes."

Rafe did as Eamonn's mom commanded. The potatoes mashed with the vegetables into something resembling a quiche. Rafe took another picture.

"What made you decide to go to school in Britain?" Anna asked.

"I'm just studying abroad for the semester. It's an immersion program, so I can get a taste of life in another country. I, uh, go back in December." Rafe glanced outside. Eamonn hammered in extra nails to the middle step. He smiled at Rafe in a way that went straight to his heart.

Eamonn stood up. He pulled at the middle step. "There! All better. Nice and tight!" He jumped onto the step to return to the kitchen, when it snapped it half, sending his foot to the grass below. "Cunt shit bugger fuck!"

The step was only a few inches off the ground. The real victim here was his pride.

Mary and Olivia burst out laughing. Rafe tried to resist joining in. He failed miserably.

Eamonn gave him the finger.

"I was just telling your mate how handy you were," Anna said. "Maybe I spoke too soon."

Chapter 16

EAMONN

It was early afternoon by the time they finished breakfast. The five of them enjoyed a leisurely meal under the canopy of trees blocking out the sunshine, complete with stories about how little Eamonn liked to urinate in the backyard.

"Particularly when we had guests over," his mum added.

Eamonn couldn't leave without replacing the now-broken middle step. He had wood in the shed to cut a new step from. Then of course, because *that* wasn't embarrassed enough, while he put in a new step, his sisters showed Rafe old pictures of naked little Eamonn running around the house.

"We really should get going." Eamonn shut the photo album and placed it back on the shelf.

"But we haven't even showed Rafe your old One Direction pillowcases!" Olivia pouted.

"Oh, I think there are pictures of Eamonn dressed up as Harry Styles," Mary said.

"For Halloween?" Rafe asked.

"No!" Mary said, and she and her demon twin exploded into giggles yet again. Eamonn wondered if his sisters spent their free time thinking of ways to torture him. As a big brother, that was *his* job.

"Rafe doesn't want to see any of that. If we don't get on the road, Stonehenge is going to crumble apart."

"Maybe next time," Rafe said. Eamonn cocked an eyebrow at him. *You're supposed to be on my team!*

"Eamonn, can I talk to you for a second?" His mum called from the kitchen.

He eyed his sisters. "Just so you know, I'm already thinking of ways to humiliate you in the future when you bring home boyfriends."

"I thought Rafe was just your flatmate?" Mary asked.

Bugger.

Eamonn clomped into the kitchen. His mum put away the last of the dishes.

"Do you need some help?" Eamonn grabbed the large skillet and placed it in the cabinet above the stove.

"I have it. You already washed all the dishes. Thank you." His mum kissed him on the cheek. "Uncle George called me to say how well-received your application was. The human resources director raved about it."

"Brilliant." Eamonn had Rafe to thank for that. He turned a shite C.V. into a work of literature.

"With such a strong application, and your uncle's push, you're a sure thing for the management trainee program. Congratulations!"

Eamonn managed a polite smile.

"You don't seem happy about it."

Eamonn looked out the window on the beautiful day he wanted to be enjoying with Rafe.

"It's a great company," she said. "He treats his employees well. He says they have a work hard, play hard policy."

"I'm grateful for the opportunity, but I don't know if I want to work there." He kept thinking of what Rafe said about non-profit work. He had done a little bit of research to see what was out there. He would have the chance to make a difference in people's lives, but the pay was awful or non-existent. It was an adventure, not a career.

"It's not glamorous, but it's a good place to be. What would you rather be doing?"

"I was hoping I had more time to figure it out."

"People who spend too much time figuring it out wind up lost. That's what happened to your dad. He's still finding himself in that stupid band of his."

Eamonn clenched his jaw. He wasn't going to be like him.

"I'm not saying you have to have your whole life pinned down, but you want to be going in a general direction. I haven't seen that with you." She smoothed down some of his hair in the back that liked to stick up. "Your classes have been all over the place. You can't make a career out of drinking with your friends at the pub and fixing things around your dear old mum's house."

"Did you know there are a billion people who lack access to clean water?"

"That's my son. Always caring about others. You can get involved with a charity on the side. Uncle George's company does a day of community service."

Eamonn nodded and acted respectfully, even though she was starting to sound like Rafe's parents.

"You're the first one in our family to go to university. You've been given this amazing gift. I just want you to make the most of it."

She kissed him and gave him a tight hug. He remembered the days when she'd completely envelop him with her arms. Now that was his job. "This was a great surprise." She peeked out the door. "I like him."

Eamonn's stomach twisted into a knot. "He's a good mate."

"Well, if he ever decides to be more, I would not be opposed to that."

RAFE

Rafe remembered traveling to Las Vegas years ago with his parents. All he saw out of his plane window was desert. Desert, desert, and then boom! Las Vegas. Here, it was countryside, countryside boom! Stonehenge. It was like the rocks appeared out of nowhere. Rafe didn't believe that aliens were responsible for building Stonehenge, but if that turned out to be the truth, he wouldn't be shocked.

"They're a lot bigger than I remember." Eamonn followed a few steps behind Rafe. He craned his neck up at the truly gargantuan rocks. Not even he could resist the awe of Stonehenge.

"Just try to imagine men thousands of years ago carrying these rocks hundreds of kilometers and placing them in this exact spot. The primitive engineering required to build this, and the sheer strength. It's unreal."

"Or maybe it was aliens."

Rafe shot him a look. They walked around the monument. It was roped off, so no touching.

"Did you know that the design of the stones lines up to the winter and summer solstices, and that because of the high burial rate around here, the civilization that built

Stonehenge could've used it as a graveyard or place to honor the dead?" Eamonn scrolled on his phone.

"Are you just quoting from Wikipedia?"

"I'm giving you a guided tour."

They made another loop around Stonehenge, this time with Eamonn as guide. He botched half of the terminology, but Rafe still managed to learn something new, shockingly. And as long as he kept talking in that raspy British accent of his, Rafe had no complaints.

———

"How does it feel?" Eamonn asked in the car on the way back to Guildford.

"It's just weird. I'm in the driver's seat on the left side of the road." Rafe kept thinking they were going to crash, or he was in a nightmare where he was trying to drive but he didn't have a steering wheel. He gripped his seatbelt with both hands.

But at the same time, there was something incredibly exciting and freeing. It was like he was breaking the law legally.

"Can I try?"

"You want to drive?" Eamonn asked.

"This seems like the perfect opportunity." Rafe nodded his head at the open highway that lay before them. "I have a license."

"A license that dictates you drive on the right side of the road." Eamonn glanced at Rafe, who wasn't going to give up so easily.

"Five minutes. Under the speed limit."

Eamonn quirked an eyebrow. "Deal."

He pulled to the side of the road. They switched seats. The driver setup was mostly the same as Rafe's car back home. It was just about getting over the fact he was in the passenger seat while no longer being in the passenger seat. Eamonn held onto the strap above the window. At least some things were constant between American and British driving.

Rafe pulled onto the road. *Okay. I'm doing it. I'm driving the British way.*

"Easy there," Eamonn said when Rafe began to swerve to the right side of the road.

"Sorry. Old habits die hard."

"Nobody is dying today."

The lush green of the English countryside whipped past them. Rafe waved to a car driving in the opposite direction. The world opened up to him at that point, and Rafe believed he could go anywhere and do anything on this planet. His chest rumbled with a new feeling. *Adventure.*

He opened both front windows. Wind whipped into the car and flipped their hair in all directions.

"Woo!!" He drove the speed limit while also hurtling into a new dimension.

Rafe turned on the radio, another old habit that died hard. *Hey Jude* came on. Rafe immediately switched to another station.

It was Eamonn who switched it back.

"We don't have to listen," Rafe said over Paul McCartney's soothing voice. Or was it Lennon's?

But Eamonn didn't switch the channel again. He turned it up. He gave Rafe a knowing smile, that he was ready to listen.

Rafe turned it up louder just as it hit the "na na" part. They did a telepathic countdown. *4, 3, 2, 1...*

And they each sang out the "na na" part at the top of

their lungs, with Eamonn adding the "Hey Jude" line at the end. How could you not sing along to this song? The wind rushing in the car filled their lungs and made their voices carry through the English countryside. They weren't even singing by the end. Just yelling and laughing out "na na" over and over again.

Rafe felt a hand on his thigh, not trying to calm him down, but a hand that wanted to be there with him.

He pulled to the side of the road when the song ended.

"Not bad," Eamonn said.

Rafe's lips stopped him from saying another word. The kiss was even better than the one on the soccer field. Eamonn pulled him closer as their mouths fused together. Rafe gasped for breath that would never be enough to fill his lungs.

"I'm ready to go home," Rafe said.

"Home?" Eamonn asked, a touch worried.

"To our dorm."

His chest, and more southern parts of him, rumbled with cravings for a new adventure.

Chapter 17

Eamonn

They burst into Eamonn's room mid-makeout session and fell onto his bed. Those warm, salty, American lips were his guide up the stairs and into the flat.

Eamonn's lips hovered over Rafe's mouth. He couldn't believe this. He couldn't want this any more. Every time he looked at Rafe, all the pain that had ever scuffed him up faded into the background.

"I like you," Rafe said, his eyes darting away. "I know you don't do casual, and I know I'm leaving. But I like you."

"I like you, too." Eamonn slipped his tongue inside Rafe's mouth.

He shoved a hand up Rafe's shirt and flicked his thumb over his hardened nipple, making Rafe shiver under his lips. Eamonn's fingertips skated over his skin, as measured and delicate as an Olympic figure skater.

Rafe tugged at Eamonn's shirt.

"You're so bossy," Eamonn teased. He made his wish come true and whipped off his shirt. Rafe admired his muscular chest and traced the trail that led to a very happy place.

Without thinking, like instinct had taken over, Eamonn pushed apart Rafe's legs. He reached into his underwear and stroked his cock.

Rafe shoved his head back into the pillows. His moan echoed on Eamonn's lips. Eamonn grabbed a fistful of his hair and held him in place as they kissed, his other hand busy controlling Rafe's cock. His thrust his hips up to meet Eamonn's touch.

"You're doing my job," Eamonn said.

"I..." But Rafe didn't have a retort.

"You like when I stroke your cock?"

Rafe nodded without detaching from Eamonn's mouth.

"Go faster," Rafe said.

"No," Eamonn whispered in his ear.

It's torture for both of us, mate. Eamonn's cock had never felt so hard, so heavy. It was like carrying a fucking oak tree in his boxers.

Rafe stretched his arm as far as it would go and it barely grazed the waistline of Eamonn's jeans. It was just out of reach, but the very tips of his fingers brushed against his bulge, sending a rush of heat straight to Eamonn's balls. He grabbed both his wrists with his free hand.

"You're so greedy," Eamonn said with his sarcastic sneer.

It looked like it was more than greed for Rafe. His face was a mix of pain and pleasure, as if he was going to die if he didn't get Eamonn's cock inside him soon. Nathan had never let himself lose control like this in bed. Eamonn felt that he was always holding back a part of himself. But not Rafe. He was all exposed nerve endings for Eamonn. *Fuck, you are so hot.*

Eamonn led Rafe's hands to his mound.

"Is this what you want?"

"Yes."

"What do you want?" Eamonn dragged those hands over it again, and his cock twitched in response.

"Y-your cock. I want your cock."

Eamonn had Rafe unzip him and pull his cock out. Rafe stroked it with precision, remembering everything Eamonn had told him, like a true A-student. He rubbed his thumb over the head, slicked with excitement. Eamonn held his wrists in place and fucked his hands.

"You like my cock in your hands?"

Rafe nodded feverishly. His eyes were all dilated pupils.

He moved Rafe's hands above his head so they could hold onto the headboard. Eamonn continued to clamp them at the wrists, and he caught Rafe admiring his flexed tricep. Eamonn stroked Rafe's cock, sending him moaning all over again. The tip of Rafe's underwear dampened with pre-cum. Eamonn bit his nipple through his plaid shirt. Rafe writhed in place but couldn't move.

"How does that feel?"

"Fuck!" Rafe exclaimed in pure glee.

Eamonn shoved Rafe's jeans and underwear to his ankles and finally yanked them completely off. He chucked them against the wall.

"Don't need those anymore," Eamonn said.

"You take off your pants."

"You don't get to tell me what to fucking do," he replied with a mischievous grin. Eamonn returned to kissing him and holding Rafe's wrists against the headboard.

Rafe grunted like they were on the pitch again. *I'm going to make you grunt so much tonight.* Up and down his hand went on Rafe's shaft, but Eamonn also got greedy. He traveled further down. One finger crested at the base of Rafe's firm ass, right over his pink hole. He made Rafe fucking *vibrate*. Eamonn's cock was going to tear a fucking hole in his trousers.

"You like this?" He rubbed it around the rim.

Rafe nodded manically. Rafe lifted his legs.

"Someone's eager," Eamonn said.

Eamonn bit at his bottom lip, his scruff scratching against Rafe's chin, while his finger kept circling down south. He didn't want this night to end, but still wanted it to go as fast as possible. He tried to stretch it out as much as his body would let him...and his body was running out of patience.

He unbuttoned Rafe's shirt and threw it against the wall, leaving him stark naked on his bed. Eamonn still had on his jeans, a power imbalance that seemed to turn Rafe on even more.

Eamonn smacked two fingers against his hole, as if he were a junkie trying to find a vein. Each time, Rafe cried out in pleasure.

"You don't want Heath and Louisa to hear you."

Smack.

"Or maybe you do."

Rafe let out a moan that screamed "Yeah, I fucking do!" Eamonn licked off the pre-cum pooling on Rafe's smooth, fit stomach. Rafe whimpered under his tongue.

Eamonn was officially high on lust. He threw Rafe's legs back so that his thighs hit his stomach, and before Rafe had a chance to moan, Eamonn's tongue was in his ass. Rafe held his legs close to his stomach.

"I didn't say you could move your hands."

Rafe took hold of the headboard as Eamonn went to town on his tight, pink ass, getting him nice and wet.

"Eamonn, this feels so good." Rafe covered his mouth with his ankle and let out another low moan.

Smack.

Smack.

And on the third smack, he slid two fingers into Rafe.

Rafe was practically begging for more. Not practically. Actually.

"Please please Don't stop don't stop don't stop." He was speaking in tongues. Eamonn had never had this effect on any guy. He was on the verge of soaking his boxers with come.

"You like having two fingers up your bum?" Eamonn gave that hole a spit shine. And he spanked that pale ass. How fucking dare it wiggle at the snooker table, teasing him in public view.

"You're so fucking tight." Eamonn slipped his fingers in and out in quick succession. He kissed Rafe, giving Rafe a taste of himself.

Rafe bit his leg. He was completely out of control, a plane spiraling for the ground, with the flight attendants yelling at passengers to put their heads between their knees.

"You want me to tongue your ass again?"

Rafe didn't answer. His eyes glowed in a daze. Eamonn could feel his pulse pumping under his sweaty skin. He caught his breath and seemed to be hurtled into another galaxy.

"Rafe? You doing all right, mate?"

"Fuck me."

"What?" Eamonn asked, caught off-guard.

"I want you to fuck me, Eamonn."

Rafe

Rafe had always been a well-behaved child. He was never one to throw a temper tantrum. But sometimes, words weren't enough. Sometimes, you just had to thrash and yell. He had been possessed tonight, completely taken over by Eamonn's hands and muscles and tongue and eyes, which were like black islands in the middle of the sea. Now, he wanted to be dominated by his cock.

"Fuck me, Eamonn."

Rafe liked saying his name aloud. It was a constant reminder that this was real and this guy who he found indescribably hot was all over him.

"Are you sure about this?"

"Yes." Rafe hadn't planned this. He imagined it happening the night before he left to return to America, that it would be the figurative and literal climax to his adventure.

But fuck that.

Adventures weren't meant to be planned. If there was ever a moment meant to be seized, it was this one. He felt comfortable and safe in Eamonn's arms. He knew in his bones that this was the right time and this was the right person.

"I don't know if this is relevant, but, um, I am a virgin," Rafe admitted. He didn't feel ashamed about it like he thought he would, just a little embarrassed about his timing. But when was a good time to tell a guy he was going to take your cherry?

"I kind of assumed that."

"Oh."

"And you're certain you're ready? I don't want to rush you."

"I want to have sex," he said, the answer as clear as Eamonn's crystal blue eyes. "Do you want to have sex with me?"

"More than anything." Eamonn said it more seriously than Rafe expected.

"Tell me what you want to do to me?" Rafe couldn't believe he was asking these questions, but he was dying to hear Eamonn's raspy voice.

"I want to grab you by your hair and shove my cock deep inside your throat and make you lick my balls. I want to bury your prick in my mouth. Suck you off until you're about to come. But you wouldn't. Because I still need to fuck you."

Rafe nodded for him to keep going. His shivered with a feeling of want that consumed him completely. He was a car going 100 miles per hour and shaking from the speed, no brake pedal in sight.

"But right now, what I want most is to press my warm, throbbing cock into your tight arse. When I take it out, you would scream for more." He bit Rafe's ear lobe. "You would fucking beg me for it."

It was like he had recited a Shakespearean sonnet.

Eamonn reached into his nightstand and pulled out a condom and lube. "I'll go gentle."

"Gentle's good. But not too gentle," Rafe said.

He gasped when the cold lube hit his opening. Eamonn's fingers slid back into him and he had to admit that sex prep was very unsexy. It was more like surgical prep. But he savored the sight of Eamonn shirtless, his pecs firm, his pants hung low on his hips, that happy trail teasing Rafe.

"Enjoying the show?" Eamonn asked.

"Very much so."

Eamonn dragged out the rest of his undress. His fingers pushed down his pants slowly, inch by inch (or centimeter by centimeter) revealing Eamonn's solid thighs and raging, thick cock.

"Uh uh. That's my job." Eamonn nodded at Rafe's crotch, where without realizing it, he was stroking himself. "I told you to keep your hands up."

Rafe held onto the headboard. He hated to admit that a part of him would always be teacher's pet, eager to please. Eamonn rolled on the condom and slicked himself up. This was about to happen. In a minute, he was going to have sex for the first time.

He found Eamonn's eyes through the mess of legs and sticky heat enveloping the room. They shared this look that was nothing short of cosmic.

Rafe cried out in some pleasure and some pain when Eamonn entered him. He went slowly, but it was a major breach, as his cock was thicker than his two fingers.

"Still with me?" Eamonn asked.

"Yes."

"Want me to stop?"

"No."

Eamonn slid in and out, carefully. Rafe could tell he was holding himself back. Eamonn leaned forward and kissed Rafe softly, another one of those tender moments in the heat. Electricity flickered on his lips.

Rafe reached for his cock, but Eamonn beat him to it. "I said that's my job."

Eamonn jerked him off, and that counteracted any discomfort below. It turned it into pleasure. Rafe's dick slipped between Eamonn's lubed-up fist.

Eamonn's strong build hovered above him. His pecs and biceps flexed with each thrust and jerk of Rafe's cock. He slammed into Rafe's ass, and the slapping sound was as much a turn on as the smack sound of his fingers. Each slam was another firework being lit.

"Harder," Rafe breathed out. He more he leaned into the pain, the more it turned to pleasure.

Eamonn's lips quirked up into a sly smile. "If you say so."

He jackhammered Rafe's ass, sending hard, sweaty thrusts of his cock deep inside him. Drops of sweat fell down Eamonn's head and dabbed onto Rafe's stomach. He was going so hard and fast that Rafe couldn't tell when he was in or out of him. It was firework after firework in some kind of grand medley. Rafe's body expanded to accommodate all Eamonn had to offer.

"Fuck me, Eamonn. Eamonn..." And Rafe was out of breath again. He didn't want to catch it. He wanted to lose himself completely.

And then Eamonn was out, and Rafe felt a gaping emptiness in his midsection.

"You still want this cock?"

"Yes. Please. Please keep fucking me." Rafe begged for his fucking life.

"You have to ask nice."

"I want you to drill me until my fucking legs fall off."

Or not. Eamonn's mouth dropped open. He wasn't the only one who could talk dirty.

"Right." Eamonn plunged into Rafe and grabbed his cock in his slicked-up fist, pumping him while pumping inside his hole. Rafe surrendered to this two-pronged attack. His gasped for air under Eamonn's hot, sweaty hands. Eamonn's face pinched and twisted as he edged to orgasm.

That was enough to throw Rafe over the edge himself.

"I'm...I'm..." He couldn't even get the words out. He just listened to Eamonn grunting and his balls slapping against his ass and the bed creaking.

"I want you to come. Shoot that spunk all over your fucking chest."

And Rafe did. Wave after wave of come streamed out, hitting his chest and Eamonn's forearms. A few seconds later, Eamonn let out the sexiest, most helpless moan and unloaded inside his devirginized ass.

Eamonn tossed the condom in the trash and joined Rafe on the bed. His sweaty chest glistened in the light. Rafe ran a finger down the curves of his abs. The room smelled of the saltiness and tangy smell that Rafe could only describe as sex. *The room smelled of sex, sex that I just had.*

"That was amazing," Rafe said. "I would totally give your dick five stars on Yelp."

"And I'd give your bum five stars. It's a great place for eating out."

Rafe covered his face with a pillow. Eamonn's laughter filled up the room. Rafe was half-embarrassed, and half-hard.

"Rafe."

He removed the pillow. Eamonn stared at him and all humor dissipated. He pushed hair out of Rafe's eyes, and it was like he was seeing him for the first time. Everything got pindrop quiet. All Rafe could hear was the beating of his heart.

"Yes?" Rafe asked.

But Eamonn didn't say anything. He just kept gazing at him, and Rafe wondered what he saw, perhaps parts of him he didn't know were on display.

They fell asleep, Rafe tucked inside Eamonn's arms, their fingers interlocked. Connection.

Chapter 18

EAMONN – ONE MONTH LATER

The unrelenting sunshine of the morning streamed through Eamonn's window. He tried to block it out as much as possible without getting up and closing the blinds. He didn't want to leave the bed.

He spooned Rafe tight in his arms, practically cocooning him. This past month had been nothing short of a dream. Rafe and Eamonn couldn't keep their hands off each other. Most nights after coming home from the pubs, one of them would wind up in the other's room, and both of their dicks would wind up in each other's mouths or elsewhere. Twice, they weren't able to wait until they left the pub. Rafe had gotten better at snooker, and after a heated game at Laffly's, Eamonn pulled him into a bathroom stall, yanked his jeans down, and slapped his bum.

"I do not wiggle my butt when I play," Rafe insisted.

"Oh yes you fucking do."

Eamonn slapped his arse again. The noise echoed in the bathroom, turning Rafe as hard as his butt cheek.

"Everyone heard that!" Rafe said between kisses.

"Rubbish."

Two loud bangs on the stall door said otherwise.

"Oy! Bathrooms are for pissing and shitting!" The bouncer yelled in a deep, authoritative voice.

"Sorry, mate," Eamonn yelled through the stall door.

"Take it outside." He was pretty much Paul Bunyan in the flesh, and there was no compromise here.

"We'll keep our hands off each other," Eamonn said. Rafe buttoned up his trousers, and they left the stall.

"We were just snogging," Rafe said.

The bouncer's eyes traveled south to the two huge, unmistakable boners poking at their jeans. He shook his head, like he was too old for this shit. "Get your rocks off elsewhere."

"Wait, you're seriously kicking us out a gay bar for making out?" Rafe asked.

"Seriously, mate."

"Doesn't that seem slightly homophobic? For all you know, we could be hiding from our wives."

"That's what hotel rooms are for. Out you go. Don't make me ask you again."

He ushered them out of the bathroom. Rafe and Eamonn began the walk of shame. Patrons gave them a round of applause and whistles as they made their way to the front door.

"I can't believe we got kicked out of a gay bar," Rafe said.

"It's all part of the adventure," Eamonn said. He pulled Rafe into a kiss. He would never get tired of those lips.

And now it was November. Rafe would be leaving in six weeks. Not that Eamonn was keeping count, but whenever he saw the date on his phone or passed by a calendar, that's where his thoughts instantly went. They hadn't put a definition on what they were doing. They tried to keep this casual, just very good friends with benefits. He wondered if Rafe felt the same way, but he didn't want to rock this boat.

"I'm surprised you don't smoke a cigarette after sex," Rafe had said a few nights ago. "Isn't that a thing?"

"I reckon I should give up smoking. The whole lung cancer thing." Eamonn hadn't thought about rolling a cigarette in a while. He wouldn't say he stopped for Rafe, but Rafe's smile of approval was definitely not a deterrent.

Rafe's eyes cracked open, shielding his eyes from the sunlight. "I think I smell Louisa making a grilled cheese on toast," he said.

"It's just called cheese on toast."

Rafe smiled and kissed Eamonn. He stood up, and Eamonn took in that gorgeous body in all its naked glory.

Minutes later, they were in Eamonn's shower together, soaping each other up, running their hands all over their slick chests and backs. Eamonn's hands traversed Rafe's body, skiing over every bump and curve. A waterfall cascaded over Rafe's stomach. He had abs from being naturally skinny, not because he'd spent any time at the gym. Once Eamonn's fingers skimmed over Rafe's pert ass, he knew where this was going. Although to be fair, when two people got in a shower together, everyone knew where this was going.

He picked up Rafe and pushed him against the shower wall. They kissed under the showerhead, water flooding between them, but not even close to stopping them.

"I still fucking like you," Eamonn said.

"I...you..." Rafe uttered out between kisses. Though in his defense, Eamonn had his tongue in his ear, scrambling his cognitive functionality.

Eamonn's cock pressed against Rafe's opening. He

couldn't get enough of Rafe's flesh. He wanted them to get dirty all over again.

Moments later, Rafe had his hands against the shower wall, and Eamonn had his tongue against Rafe's arse. He spanked that bouncy bum hard, and it echoed in the bathroom.

"Don't be so loud!" Rafe admonished.

"I'll be as loud as I fucking want. Heath and Louisa already know we're shagging." He went to town on that tight hole. He liked the mix of the fresh soap with Rafe's natural manly scent. He stroked his own cock, too.

As steamy as shower sex was, in reality, it was impossible. Well, impossible unless you enjoyed pain. Eamonn had learned this lesson already. Water was not the same as water-based lubricant. Water was actually the enemy of anal sex.

Eamonn swiped a condom and a bottle of lube from his nightstand and darted back into the bathroom. He carried Rafe to the bathroom counter and slicked both of them up. Rafe wrapped his legs against Eamonn once more as Eamonn pushed inside him. He gazed into Rafe's eyes with each thrust.

"Eamonn," Rafe whispered against his lips. Drops of water hung from his hair and his eyelashes. "Eamonn."

"Rafe." Eamonn's whole body shook with orgasm. He held Rafe as close to him as possible as he came.

Not to leave Rafe empty-handed, when he caught his breath, Eamonn got on his knees and took Rafe's cock in his mouth. Rafe held onto the bathroom sink and thrust his hips forward. Eamonn tasted bitter pre-cum on his tongue. Rafe grabbed onto Eamonn's hair and fucked his mouth for a few seconds.

"You drive on the left side of the road for five minutes,

and suddenly you're Mr. Bossy," Eamonn said in between licking his balls. The lusty look he gave Rafe was his full-hearted approval.

Eamonn took his cock to the base, and soon his mouth filled with Rafe's spunk. Rafe nearly collapsed shooting his load. Eamonn caught him just in time.

"I think I need some food," Rafe said.

"Let's clean ourselves off first." Eamonn pointed to the already-running shower.

"That's so convenient!"

After the shower, where they showered for real this time, Rafe put on his clothes from yesterday. In solidarity, Eamonn did the same. The smell of cheese on toast over-took his senses and compelled him and Rafe to the kitchen.

Rafe did a little spin on his way into the kitchen, as if his life was a piece of musical theater. "Louisa, I'm craving one of your cheese on toasts—"

Eamonn swung open the kitchen door and went just as silent as Rafe. Heath and Louisa sat at the table, but Rafe's seat was occupied. The familiar slinky smile and red hair looking back at him made Eamonn turn into one of those Stonehenge rocks.

"This must be the Token Yank," Nathan said. He stood up and held out his hand to Rafe. "Hiya, mate. Thanks for keeping my room warm."

Chapter 19

RAFE

Rafe shook Nathan's hand, yet despite the friendly greeting, there was a dark undercurrent beneath Nathan's words. Something about him made chills creep down Rafe's spine. Rafe stood by the door, next to Eamonn.

"Hugh Grant actually has a wicked sense of humor. He loves pranking the other actors on set." Nathan launched into an anecdote of one such Hugh Grant prank, complete with flawless impersonation. He got real quiet and hunched over the table. "And then Hugh turns to me and he says, 'Not bad for a Tuesday.'"

Heath and Louisa lost it. Rafe smiled, but couldn't pretend to laugh.

There were people who orbited and others who were orbited. Rafe was up against a guy with his own damn solar system revolving around him. It didn't help that Nathan had a fit body and wicked smile. His designer sunglasses were folded and resting in his Burberry polo front pocket. Rafe wasn't attracted to him, but there had to be plenty of other guys who were, and Nathan knew that. He seemed like a player.

Rafe squeezed Eamonn's hand to provide moral support. Eamonn didn't squeeze back. He stared down at the dirty dishes on the table and seemed to be in a different galaxy altogether.

"Hugh Grant is like fifty years old, but I'd still do him," Louisa said.

"What else is new? It's The Railway all over again," Nathan said, and the table burst out laughing. Louisa covered her face in embarrassment and playfully smacked Nathan's arm.

Rafe fake laughed, but only not to be left out.

"You told him about The Railway?" Nathan asked.

Louisa and Heath looked behind them at Rafe, who wished there was a trap door he could sail out of.

"I guess that's a no…" Nathan raised his eyes. Like Heath and Eamonn, his tone of voice made it seem like he was always being sarcastic, always mocking you. But unlike those two, Rafe got the feeling that he wasn't kidding. "Basically, Louisa tried to pull some guy who told her he was a uni student, even though he was obviously forty-something. The man had crow's feet and was balding. He walked with some kind of limp, probably from the Gout." Nathan stood up and approximated the man's walk. Rafe had to give him credit for getting into character so quickly. "We couldn't figure out if Louisa was blinded by her Midori Sours or her sheer horniness."

"Sod off, Nathan!" She smacked his arm again, and the room filled up with the boisterous laughter of inside jokes and had-to-be-there moments that Rafe didn't get. Even Eamonn couldn't resist cracking the tiniest smile. He'd never felt like more of a foreigner.

"I sometimes regret introducing you to Midori Sours," Nathan said. He patted the empty chair beside him. "E, have a seat."

"I'm good here, thanks," Eamonn said with no feeling in his voice.

Nathan cut a quick look between Rafe and Eamonn, which made Rafe's stomach turn.

"You created a Midori monster," Heath said. Rafe was surprised his flatmates were being so chummy with Nathan considering what he did to Eamonn. They were blinded by celebrity.

"Speaking of monsters, you'll never guess which famous actress is actually a complete cunt."

"Is it Judi Dench?" Heath asked. "It's Judi Dench, isn't it?"

"No. It's one of the American stars. Her British accent is pathetic. She sounds *like this*," Nathan said, taking on a Kardashian accent, before turning to Rafe. "No offense."

Rafe wanted the spotlight off him as fast as possible. He wanted to fade into the walls.

Nathan patted the empty chair beside him again. "E, seriously. You look like you're practicing to guard Buckingham Palace."

"I didn't know you were coming back," Eamonn said.

"From the sounds coming from your room earlier, you weren't holding your breath." Nathan's eyes flicked over to Rafe, who wanted nothing more than to crawl into the fridge.

Eamonn's jaw was so tight Rafe thought it was going to break off.

"The shoot wrapped early." Nathan slouched back in his chair. "My agent's been sending me tons of scripts, but I spoke about it with my dad, and I wanted to finish up uni. I only have one year left. He told me that no matter what happens, I'll always have that degree to fall back on, which is the only decent advice he's ever proffered. I don't know if I'll need it. I mean, my agent's said I'm in the mix to play James Bond."

"Are you bleeding serious?" Louisa asked.

"If they could have a blond Bond, then why not a ginger Bond?"

"Wicked," Heath said. Rafe's flatmates had been reduced to fawning. Heath was a loyal friend to Eamonn. He wondered how much of the break-up story Eamonn had told him and Louisa. Maybe he tried to leave Nathan with some character in the eyes of his friends.

"But a degree is good to have. Bond can wait. And I missed you buggers. I'm sorry for the radio silence. Filming a movie is exhausting. It's long days, seven days a week. I barely had time to check my email. No wonder celebrities check into the hospital for exhaustion." Nathan smiled at Eamonn, but it was completely one-sided. Rafe gave a silent cheer. "We only have one more year together. Let's put all the shit of the past behind us and just fucking enjoy it, right?"

His eyes shifted to Rafe and held him in place. "So tell me about yourself, Rafe. All I know about you is how loud you can moan."

Oh, hell no. Rafe felt all feeling drain from his face.

"Shut it, Nathan," Eamonn said in a low growl, which Nathan seemed to enjoy.

"Rafe is great." Louisa turned around and tugged on his sleeve. "He's here until December."

"Smashing. I'll get my old room back by January."

Hearing that put Rafe's adventure in stark lighting. It

had a finite end date. His days with everyone were numbered. Especially Eamonn.

"I'm staying up in Jones with the most annoying Americans. No offense, mate." *Actually, I do take offense. And I'm not your mate!* "But it's nowhere near as nice as these flats. We don't have lifts." He turns to Rafe again. "That means—"

"Elevators. I know."

Nathan held up his hands in defense. "Excuse me, then. He knows what lifts are."

Rafe managed a smile, and he wondered if Nathan the great actor could see through it. Nathan shot him a smile back that was anything but friendly.

"The gang's all back together." Nathan squeezed Louisa's hand.

Yes they were. And I don't belong here.

EAMONN

Nathan is back. Holy fucking shite. Eamonn was finally moving on. He didn't know what exactly he and Rafe were, but it was something dynamic.

And then there he was. His past, smiling at him at the kitchen table.

The whole day felt like a surreal dream. He remembered the tight group dynamic they all had. It was a little nice to reminisce and remember the good times. But he didn't forget about the bad times, the nights where Nathan got so smashed he spewed venom at Heath and Louisa, or when he stomped all over Eamonn's heart. Eamonn hadn't told Heath and Louisa about his race to the airport to save their relationship. He tried to respect the friendships they had with Nathan and not completely sully them. He didn't think he'd ever see Nathan again.

That night, they all went to Apothecary. This time, Eamonn pulled up a fifth chair and sat at the end of the booth. He wasn't going to let Nathan have Apothecary and his friends while he sat home stewing. And a part of him was curious to see Nathan. He wasn't proud of this part, but it was classic Eamonn. He couldn't completely cut someone out of his life. Connections were hard to break.

Rafe sat next to him, and Eamonn held his hand under the table. He could tell Rafe was uneasy about Nathan being there, but also agreed that Nathan shouldn't scare them away from living their lives.

"It's great being back here, with real people. Apothecary has really cleaned itself up," Nathan said. "I remember this place used to be a dump."

"The bathrooms were disgusting," Heath said.

Eamonn caught Nathan looking at his arm next to Rafe's, as if he had X-ray vision to see under the table.

"They weren't too dirty for us. Isn't that right, Eamonn?" Nathan asked him.

Shut up, Nathan.

"What are you talking about?" Louisa asked.

"Nothing," Eamonn said through clenched teeth.

"Oh, come on, E. You never told them?"

Rafe looked at him with such innocent eyes. "What is he talking about?"

"Nothing. It's in the past." Eamonn needed another pint, another five pints.

"Ow." Rafe jolted his hand away, and Eamonn saw he'd been squeezing it hard.

"What's the story?" Louisa asked. She was practically giddy for it.

Nathan shot Eamonn one of his classic looks that let him know trouble was around the corner. Eamonn remembered them well from times when Nathan got upset that things weren't going his way, and he was going to enjoy this.

"I can get the next round," Eamonn said.

"Oh, what is it, E? You don't want people to know that we shagged in the men's room last year? It was quite steamy." Nathan turned to Rafe, in a finishing fuck you. "We actually broke one of the stall walls."

Eamonn shot out of his chair, and it fell to the ground. He charged to the bar for another drink. Nobody was ready for another round, but he was. He would drink all of their rounds. He wished he hadn't left Rafe there. Who knew what other rubbish Nathan was spewing? This had been their relationship, he realized. Nathan pushing his buttons. Nathan hogging the spotlight. Nathan savaging any guy who dared show Eamonn any attention. It led to some fucking wild angry sex, but that couldn't compare to the sex he and Rafe had. It was wild, but also had a type of closeness that he couldn't remember having with Nathan.

The bartender poured him another Snakebite, and he drank it right on the spot. He wasn't prepared for this. Leave it to Nathan to just fucking show up without warning. He lived for the drama. Maybe he cheated just to have an interesting break-up story. Eamonn glanced back at the table, and Heath's head stuck out above the crowd. Heath gave his mate a supportive smile, and he knew Rafe wasn't alone. He wanted to go back, but he couldn't face Nathan again just yet. He couldn't face all those memories coming back.

Eamonn braved the chilly night to sit on the Apothecary's outside deck. He had a picnic table to himself, but not for long.

Nathan sat on the table, moving Eamonn's drink over. "Drinking alone now, E?"

"What are you doing here, Nathan?"

"I wanted to check up on you. You just ran off."

"That's not what I mean." Their eyes met in a moment where bullshit slipped away. "What are you doing here?"

"I told you. The shoot ended early. I wanted to come back to school."

"And you think we can all just pick up where we left off? Like what you did never happened?" Eamonn got up and stood by the fence overlooking a small thicket of trees.

"I'm sorry, Eamonn. I really am. I thought about transferring, because I hated what I did. But I wanted to come back to make things right." Nathan put his hand on Eamonn's shoulder. He flinched back.

"I can't just forget." Eamonn still remembered the smell in the air as if he could sense danger when he entered the airport terminal. Nathan's callous shrug from that night was tattooed on his brain. Nathan broke his heart, but he wasn't going to give him the satisfaction of knowing that.

"We were broken up. What you saw at the airport technically wasn't cheating."

"We had *just* broken up. Did you meet that wanker in the bloody security line?"

"I wasn't expecting to see you at my airport terminal."

"I went there because I loved you! I loved you, and you said you *appreciated* that." Eamonn caught his breath.

"I'm not asking you to forget. Or even to forgive, not just yet." Nathan slumped against the fence. "I'm not proud of myself. You may hate me, but I loathe myself."

Eamonn studied Nathan's face. Sometimes, it was so hard to tell what he was thinking, what was real and what was a story. Not like Rafe. Eamonn worried about what he was thinking right now.

"Why did you do it?"

Nathan stared at the ground for an extended moment.

For a second, he thought he saw something change in Nathan, a piece of armor fall away. When they were together, Eamonn would get the feeling that Nathan was forever putting on a performance. He would live for those glimpses backstage.

"Because I'm a fecking idiot." Nathan gave him a half-smile.

"I think you should go back to your new hall."

"E, you may not be happy to see me, but our friends are. I'm not going to quarantine myself away from them."

If the tables were reversed, he knew Nathan would make Heath and Louisa stop talking to him.

"I am back, and we're going to be seeing more of each other. I'd like us to try and rebuild what we had." Nathan stepped closer and ran his fingers down Eamonn's arm. "We have history, E. You can't just throw that away to have fun with some American twat."

Eamonn wacked his hand away. "You know all about throwing things away."

Nathan studied his face, in that way Nathan loved to do. The psychoanalyst. Eamonn hated it. "Oh, E. You were never good at casual sex. That's not you. Be careful with him. Your little cub scout isn't worth getting your heart broken over. They all leave." Nathan snapped his fingers. "Just like that."

"Fuck off, Nathan." Eamonn charged back into the bar, but he couldn't face Heath and Louisa. And he really couldn't face Rafe. Nathan had gotten under his skin like the worst kind of rash.

Chapter 20

RAFE

On top of reeling from Nathan's entrance, Rafe was dealt a rough week of classes. He faced down a physics exam and a paper on *Measure for Measure*. His Shakespeare professor had taken points off his last paper for spelling humor and color incorrectly, so Rafe had to do a "British spell check" before he turned in this one.

By Thursday afternoon, he was extra excited to go into Apothecary for his shift. Thursday afternoons at the bar were incredibly slow since most students waited until night to celebrate the weekend. But these slow shifts had given Rafe plenty of practice as a runner. At work, he didn't have to think about Eamonn or Nathan. He could just concentrate on keeping the bar in order.

Apothecary's owner, Alfie, was behind the bar today.

"Where's Sadie?" Rafe asked. Sadie was the usual barmaid during his afternoon shifts. She loved arguing with patrons about soccer teams, and she cursed more than Heath and Eamonn combined.

"She's out sick." Alfie wiped down the counter. "Or maybe she's just hungover."

"Do bartenders get hungover?" Rafe asked. "I thought being around alcohol so often made you immune or something."

Rafe took a quick glance behind the bar and picked out what needed to be restocked. He'd trained his eye not to get distracted, but to focus on his areas. Ice, well drinks, garnishes. Pay no attention to the loud patrons or the bartender's hands whipping around fixing drinks. He went into the stockroom and got more cocktail napkins and straws and replenished the bar.

"I didn't even realize we were running low. Thanks," Alfie said. He looked to be in his early forties, with thinning hair and a gut. Rafe couldn't really tell someone's age. They were either younger than him, about his age, or full-on adult age.

"It's more to prepare for tonight. At least when business really picks up, you won't run out so fast."

"Good job." Alfie put down his rag. "Rafe."

"Yes?"

"Have you ever thought about working back here?"

"Like as a bartender?"

Alfie nodded yes.

Rafe had thought about it. He imagined two scenarios: one where he was king of the bar, like a male version of Jersey in *Coyote Ugly* spinning bottles in his hands; and the other where he was messing up left and right and chaos was breaking out and the bar burned down.

"I can't stand serving these feckheads. That's one of the joys of owning a bar. I can stay in my office. Want to give it a shot?" Alfie threw him the rag.

"Seriously?"

"You've been observing the bartenders while on your shifts. I think you know what to do. There's a book behind the bar for making cocktails, but most people just want a pint. It's dead right now, so it'll be a good tryout. What do you say?"

"Yeah. That would be great!"

Rafe ventured behind the counter, and Alfie trained him quickly on how to pour, how to work the register, and how to deal with obnoxious customers. He returned to the quiet of his office. Rafe ran his hands over the bar. His bar. He was a bartender. He'd never felt cooler.

He chitchatted with the few customers he had during the rest of his shift. Sadie and Alfie were not ones to socialize with guests and ask how their day was going. Rafe figured his role was half-bartender, half-waiter. He had one patron take a picture of him mixing drinks, and he posted it to his Instagram page.

But his high from this afternoon came to a screeching halt when Nathan entered the premises. He took a seat smack in the center of the bar. He grinned in amusement as he watched Rafe serve another customer, and Rafe avoided him as long as he could.

"Look at you. This is honestly a surprise. I did not take you as a bartender."

"Well, I guess you don't know me as well as you think."

"Guess not." Nathan ordered a pint. Rafe felt his eyes on him as he poured, and not in a sexy way. Like a predator scoping out prey.

"Three dollars. I mean, pounds."

Nathan gave him a five pound note and told him to keep the change.

Rafe kept busy. He checked the well drinks and wiped

down the counter and was extra-attentive to the one other person at the bar.

"You're not the first," Nathan said.

"Excuse me?"

"You're not the first."

Rafe took the bait, regrettably so. "What do you mean?"

"Eamonn has shagged his fair share of Yanks."

Rafe rolled his eyes and let out a laugh. He knew Eamonn well enough to know how patently false that was. Anyone who met Eamonn knew that. Was this really the best he had?

"They come here every year, looking for that authentic British experience, and Eamonn gives them a royal welcome."

"Sure."

"I'm just fucking with you, mate." Nathan smiled as he drank his beer. "But you really aren't the first Yank to do this. Plenty of Americans come over here, looking for their very own Mr. Darcy to shag, who by the power of his sexy British accent can pull them out of their suburban, strip mall, moribund existence. And then they leave with a story to tell their sorority sisters back home, of how for a brief moment, their lives were interesting."

"That's a touching story, Nathan." Rafe put on a face of apathy, which took everything in him. If only he could've thrown Nathan's beer in his face. Alfie wouldn't appreciate that.

"You seem like one of those Yanks. You probably have a poster of Colin Firth hanging in your bedroom."

Maybe Alfie wouldn't *mind if I threw a drink in his face. Maybe I'd get a raise.* Rafe's heart rattled in his chest. Adrenaline flowed through his veins. But he would not give in.

That was what Nathan wanted. Then it would be easier for Rafe's flatmates to turn on him. He had to play it cool.

"You're trying to put on a brave face for me. That's cute." Nathan spun a coaster between his fingers. "I'm not trying to hit a nerve. Just making an observation. But the thing you didn't think about is that Eamonn isn't a stock character in your travelogue."

"You don't know what Eamonn is to me."

"He's a fun story for you, but those of us who really care about him see a kind soul who doesn't deserve to be treated like a piece of meat."

"I'm trying not to laugh in your face," Rafe said.

"No, I don't think you want to laugh." Nathan studied him, like he was going to play Rafe in a performance.

"You're being a hypocrite." Rafe wasn't as good as Nathan at the cutting remarks.

Nathan raised his eyebrows in amusement. "Oh, right, because you think I just ditched Eamonn. Because you know everything about what happened, and that makes you fit to comment."

"You treated him like a piece of meat. I'm sure you and Hugh Grant had a nice laugh about your ex-boyfriend watching you kiss another guy at the airport."

A dark cloud settled over Nathan's eyes. "You shouldn't talk about that which you don't understand. What Eamonn and I have is complicated. We have a real bond."

"We do, too."

Nathan burst out laughing, and it filled up the entire bar. "Keep telling yourself that, mate. Like I said, I'm trying to look out for Eamonn. If you really cared about him, you wouldn't do this to him. And I'm looking out for you, too. You don't seem like the kind of bird who shags for fun."

"I know what Eamonn and I have. I think you do, too.

But nice try with the whole intimidation thing." Rafe narrowed his eyes at Nathan like an OK Corral showdown.

Nathan finished his beer and dropped the pint glass on the floor. "You should probably clean that up, *runner*."

"Fuck you, asshole," Rafe said. After Nathan had already left.

———

HIS HANDS TREMBLED with aftershocks from his run-in with Nathan. When he returned to his room, he Facetimed Coop, who was coming back from morning classes. Coop's jacked up physique was a welcome sight and reminded him of home.

He had barely spoken to anyone since he'd been here. It was like traveling to another dimension. That reminded him to email his parents a quick update. (He listed all the boring stuff that he and Coop didn't discuss, like classes. Parents really cared about what their kids learned.) Rafe caught Coop up on his British escapades, including losing his virginity, getting a job, and Nathan.

"Congratulations, that's amazing, and Nathan's an asshole."

Coop was not one to mince words, but his certainty took Rafe a little by surprise.

"He's just very sarcastic."

"Nope. He's an asshole."

"He's a little full of himself. He's an actor. He's worked with Hugh Grant."

"Loved *About a Boy*. Still makes him an asshole."

Rafe slumped back in his desk chair. "How are you so sure of this? Maybe I'm not describing him right. I mean, Heath and Louisa are still friends with him."

Rafe knew that if Coop were here, he'd keep Nathan away from Eamonn at all times.

"Why are you defending him?" Coop asked.

Rafe shrugged. He knew that assholes existed in this world, and he knew that they attended Browerton and Stroude, and that there would be many more assholes throughout his life. But he'd never come face-to-face with one who was intent on being an asshole to him. He prided himself on not having any enemies.

Everyone liked Rafe!

"Rafe," Coop motioned him to come closer to the screen. "This is war."

"War?"

"This asshole is trying to make you look like an idiot and steal your guy."

"But is Eamonn even mine to be stolen?" Nathan was a reminder that Eamonn had a life in England well before Rafe ever dropped in, and he would continue to have that life after he left.

"The guy likes you."

"How do you know any of this? You're an ocean away. You've never met any of these people!"

"And you like him, too, Rafe. Maybe you can't see it because you're in it, but you do. So now you have to fight."

"If I fight, I'll lose. I always lose in these situations. I'm always someone's second choice." Rafe wouldn't be able to take losing him. He couldn't be Eamonn's Baxter.

"You don't know that. Eamonn seems into you."

Rafe dragged his hands desperately through his hair. "This wasn't supposed to happen. I wanted to sex myself across England. Remember what we talked about last spring?"

He was most definitely not slutting it up with Eamonn.

The sex they had was not just for fun. He hit it, and he did not want to quit it.

"I really like him, Coop."

"I can tell. I've never seen you this way."

Rafe perked up, curious to hear the assessment that came next.

"Usually, you'd be into a guy for some random, superficial reason, like he has a cute name or has nice hair. You'd obsess for a week, nothing would happen, and then you'd move onto the next one. But this feels different. You seem different."

"How so?"

"Well, it's been a lot more than a week. But...you have this added weight in your voice. And you have that same 'oh shit' look that I had when I realized I was in love with Matty."

Am I in love? Rafe wasn't sure about that, but he knew he cared for Eamonn. It would only make things harder when he got on that plane next month.

Chapter 21

Eamonn woke up on the seventh of November in usual fashion: with a phone call from his mum and sisters.

"Happy birthday!"

They broke into a rendition of "For He's a Jolly Good Fellow." It was corny, but it always made Eamonn smile. They officially celebrated his birthday last night at the house with some homemade haggis and chocolate cake. Rafe took pictures at the stove as his mum taught him how to make haggis. He had been apprehensive about attending a family event, but Eamonn wanted him there, as did his family.

"Tell your mom I loved that chocolate cake. I'm going to have some of it for breakfast. She has to give me the recipe," Rafe said. He lay in bed next to Eamonn, and there was no better sight to wake up next to.

"She'll email it to you," Eamonn said.

Rafe gave him the thumbs up. He went to the bathroom, and Eamonn continued the call.

"What are you up to tonight?" she asked.

"Heath got us all tickets to see Bloc Party in London."

"That should be fun!" his mum said.

"You have the worst taste in music, Eamonn," Olivia said.

"Did Olivia just say something, or did a cat get stuck in the dishwasher?"

"Sod off," she said.

"Oy!" Their mum yelled. "It's your brother's birthday. Be nice."

"Oh Eamonn," Olivia said, in a super chipper voice. "What terrible taste in music you have!"

"Rafe is a great *flatmate*," Mary said. No giggle this time.

"He is." Eamonn smiled to himself. These past few weeks had been one for the record books. Not even Nathan hanging around could put a damper on their relationship. Rafe was there when he went to sleep and when he woke up. His eyes, his lips, his sense of humor, it was all his.

"I'll show him how to make a gingerbread house for the holidays," his mum said.

"You'll have to swim him on Skype. He's study abroad trip ends in December." *He'll be all the way back in Arlington, Virginia by then.* The pain of time lanced his heart.

"Oh," his mum said. His sisters had no comment.

"I must go. They don't cancel classes on your birthday, unfortunately."

They said their goodbyes.

"You sound really great," his mum said, a bit serious. "When Nathan came back, I was worried. But Rafe is wonderful, even if he's..."

"It's just a birthday, mum. No need to get all mushy."

"Sod off," she said, but it overflowing with love.

Rafe came back to bed and rested against Eamonn's

chest. They stared up at the ceiling, enjoying the quiet of being together.

"I'm really excited for the concert. Thank you for going, even though you aren't a fan."

"What? I love Bloc Party!"

Eamonn wasn't buying it for a second. Rafe tried to leave his bed, but was trapped by his arms.

"As birthday boy, I compel you to stay."

"Don't you want your birthday breakfast?"

"I'd rather just eat you." He brushed Rafe's wild hair out of his face.

"But it's your favorite. Bubble and squeak."

"Shit. You're making bubble and squeak? You don't have to do all that!"

"It's your twenty-first birthday! That may not be a big deal over here, but it's huge in the states, so I couldn't let it go unnoticed."

Eamonn hugged him tight against his chest. He could stare into those brown eyes all day. He forgot how bloody sappy he got when he was in a relationship, or whatever this was, but he couldn't help himself.

"Are you ready for the first part of your birthday gift?"

"I'm hungry!"

"I wasn't talking about that."

Rafe slid his hand into Eamonn's pants and massaged his cock. "In America, we call this the Brentwood Hello."

He disappeared under the covers.

———

THAT NIGHT, the flatmates walked to the train for the concert. It was being held in Old Ticket Hall in Windsor, mere blocks from Windsor Castle, home of the royal family.

One of the homes of the royal family. Eamonn had snuck into this venue many a time before he turned eighteen to listen to bands. He was fortunate to have a lookalike older cousin who wasn't stingy with his ID.

Everything was already off to a fantastic start. All of Eamonn's favorite people were here. Heath and Louisa kept their distaste for each other on the back burner tonight for the sake of his birthday. And no Nathan, even though he knew Nathan was as much a fan of Bloc Party as himself.

"Do you think they'll play *This Modern Love*?" Heath asked him. He looked to Rafe. "It's his favorite."

"I know that. Now," Rafe said, squeezing Eamonn's hand.

"I'm keeping my fingers crossed for *So Here We Are*," Louisa said.

"It's all right," Heath said.

"I reckon it's more than all right," she said back.

Eamonn thought there was a spark of flirtation between them, but they went back to their détente. Rafe lingered when they got to the train station.

"What are you looking at?" Eamonn asked.

Rafe stared at something in the parking lot. "Do you see that jeep?"

He walked up to it and peered in the window.

"It's not yours."

"The steering wheel is on the left side." Rafe bent down in the front. "And there's an American license plate. From North Carolina. That's right by me!"

"The guy must've had it shipped over from the states. Must be a pain in the arse driving that over here," Heath said.

"I never thought I'd get all mushy at the sight of an American car." Rafe kept looking at the steering wheel like it was some national artifact. His face had a touch of melancholy. It was a brief rainstorm in the middle of this perfect day.

"Come on." Eamonn wrapped an arm around his waist and moved them to the sidewalk that led back to campus.

He rubbed Rafe's hand with his thumb, but he didn't reciprocate.

———

THE OLD TICKET Hall was an intimate space where only a railing separated performers and concertgoers. It wasn't commercialized and allowed Eamonn to feel like he was getting a private concert. His friends grabbed drinks and found a space to see the show.

Louisa took out a small cookie from her pocket. She stuck a lit match in it. It was the closest he would get to a birthday cake, which was fine because he'd rather have birthday drinks.

"Make a wish!" Louisa told him.

Eamonn locked eyes with Rafe, knowing exactly what his wish was. Rafe smiled at him, but it seemed just a touch off. It was like looking at a completed jigsaw puzzle that had one piece missing.

"I wish I had taken the train with you cunts."

Nathan joined their circle. His hair was mussed to perfection, and he wore a tight T-shirt that showed off his trim frame. Nathan had been making himself scarce since their talk at Apothecary. Perhaps he was spending time with Heath and Louisa separately, but Eamonn didn't care to find out.

"Good to see you, mate!" Heath said nervously.

"What are you doing here?" Eamonn asked. He was the only one who could ask.

"I'm a Bloc Party fan. We've gone to concerts together, listened to their music until the wee hours while we were intimate...I had a feeling you would be here, since it's your birthday and all." He threw an arm around Eamonn.

The matchstick burned into the cookie. Eamonn threw it down and stomped on it before it could catch fire. He shrugged off Nathan's arm and instantly scooped up Rafe's hand in his own.

"Who did you come here with?" Rafe asked.

"Nobody. Thank you for making me feel bad about myself, Rafe."

"We're celebrating here for Eamonn's birthday."

"You're really going to kick me out of your little circle, a circle made up of my friends? Rafe, you really need to learn to share."

Nathan began to walk away, and pissed Eamonn off to no end that he felt a sliver of guilt.

"Nathan, get the fuck back here." Eamonn was going to be the bigger person. Nathan couldn't ruin this night for him. He had his favorite band and his favorite guy in one place. Nathan was just white noise.

"Smashing. Now let's get pissed!" Heath and Louisa went up to the bar and ordered the next round. Rafe dashed off to the loo. He gave Eamonn a look wondering if he'd be okay with Nathan. Eamonn had this.

"I didn't mean to ruin your night," Nathan said, his tone now soft. "Remember when we went to Brighton last year for your birthday. We had sex on the beach and actual sex on the beach."

Sex on the beach in November was never a wise idea. They were not drunk enough for that. Eamonn found himself shaking his head.

"You do remember."

"So. I do. It's in the past."

"I know. It was a good day, though."

People up front began clapping, which spread to their area. Eamonn knew what that meant. The band was about to go on any moment. It was infectious, the energy of the venue.

"What song do you think they'll start with?" Nathan asked.

"*Only He Can Heal Me*," they both answered.

Eamonn did not find the moment cute. Most of Bloc Party's concerts started with that song. Anyone remotely familiar with the band could've answered that way.

"Relax, E. We still have something in common. It's not the apocalypse." Nathan clapped him on the shoulder. "Enjoying your final weeks with the Yank?"

Nathan knew how to hit a nerve like a nurse giving an injection.

"Rafe is the dog's bollocks." Eamonn chose his words carefully.

"I think you're falling for him, E. I warned you against this. It's only going to end in tears."

It was a truth Eamonn wasn't ready to face. He wanted to live in the present. He didn't want to think about what his life was going to be like when Rafe left, when he joined his uncle's company. Why was everyone so obsessed with the future?

"However it ends, it'll be better than finding him snogging some nobhead in the airport." Eamonn got right in Nathan's face, a face he once couldn't stop kissing and now only disgusted him. "I don't know what you're thinking, but there is no future with us. When Rafe leaves and my heart breaks, at least I'll know his is breaking, too."

"Your heart?" Nathan asked, a layer of sarcasm peeled away. "You really care about him."

"Yeah. I really fucking do." The words rushed out, but they were not untrue. It felt good to say that, to let himself admit that his feelings went deep. Even if he was headed for a downfall, he'd enjoyed the ride down with Rafe.

RAFE

"You are not going to hurt Nathan. You are not going to make a scene. You are a classy-as-fuck, peaceful individual." Rafe said this to himself as he walked back into the crowd. When he left the bathroom, he saw Eamonn and Nathan having a conversation. A pleasant-looking conversation. Nathan was being his charming, seductive, snakelike self. Eamonn was not stonewalling him. Maybe that was too much to ask, but for all Eamonn claimed he was done with Nathan, moments like this made Rafe have inklings of doubt. Like Coop said, this was war.

"Hey!" Rafe said loudly. He put an arm around Eamonn pulled him close. "I can't wait for the show to start."

"Should be any minute." Eamonn gazed into his eyes and erased most of his worry. But it was like hand sanitizer. It might kill 99.9% of germs, but you still had to watch out for that pesky 0.1%.

"I need a drink." Nathan left for the bar. Rafe didn't see him for the rest of the concert.

———

"AAAAAND IT'S OFFICIALLY NO LONGER your birthday." Rafe watched 11:59 turn to midnight on his phone. The band played their final encore and left the stage. The flatmates retreated to the bar for a final round of birthday shots.

Eamonn took his shot and the other three followed.

"Thanks for a great day," Eamonn whispered into his ear.

The night wasn't over for him. There was still one final round of birthday sex. They left Old Ticket Hall and ordered an Uber since the trains had stopped running. Everything went off without a hitch.

Which meant that something inevitably had to go wrong. It was the physics of Murphy's Law.

And that something wrong was Nathan, drunk beyond belief. He stumbled around outside the venue smoking a cigarette arguing with the bouncer. Rafe could've told him from experience that arguing with the bouncer never worked out.

"I'm fine, you fucking cunt!" Nathan yelled at the bouncer. "This is a bar. What the fuck was I supposed to do? Drink chocolate milk?"

"Oh boy," Louisa said. She, Heath, and Eamonn shared a look of familiarity.

Nathan tripped backwards into a couple leaving, making the woman drop her purse.

"Oy. Say you're sorry," the boyfriend said.

Nathan grabbed his junk. "There's my apology."

Rafe couldn't believe this was the same guy who sounded so posh, even when he insulted you.

"What's your problem?" The boyfriend launched at Nathan and was ready to pounce, if not for Eamonn intervening.

"Oy!" Eamonn kept them separated. He pulled Nathan away.

"That wanker started it!" Nathan yelled for everyone to hear. Naturally, people stopped and stared.

"I've never met you, mate." The guy said.

"Fuck you!" Nathan tried to push past Eamonn, but he was a fortress.

"I'm going to get him a glass of water." Louisa scurried back inside.

"Have a seat, mate." Heath tried to lead him to a bench, but Nathan lurched from his grip. He stormed over to Rafe. His eyes scorched with white-hot anger.

"You fucking Americans. You stick your nose where it doesn't bloody belong."

Eamonn pushed him back. "Sit down, Nathan. I'm ordering you an Uber back to Stroude with us." Something that resembled guilt flashed in Eamonn's eyes for a split-second. Or maybe it was hurt. Rafe appreciated what a good guy his boyfriend was, but he couldn't help feel a sting nonetheless.

He stuck out his hand for Nathan's phone.

"You can't," Nathan said. "Uber banned me. My drivers gave me piss poor ratings."

"Of course," Eamonn muttered to himself. "Heath, can you order an Uber? You three go together, and I'll make sure this fucker gets back."

Why couldn't Heath or Louisa go with him? Rafe was going to ask, but this was not the time. He told himself that Eamonn was doing the right thing, but Rafe couldn't help feel like he was falling right into Nathan's trap.

"Bring him back to Sweeney," Louisa said. She handed Nathan water. "I want him to stay with me to make sure he doesn't have alcohol poisoning."

"I want him to fucking apologize to my girlfriend," the

guy said. The bouncer stood in front of him to prevent a potential brawl.

"I'm sorry," Eamonn said.

Don't apologize for him.

"He's severely wasted," Heath said.

"Doesn't make what he did right," the guy said.

"I know. We're taking him," Eamonn said.

"I'm sorry. I'm so sorry," Nathan said, hand over heart. "That your girlfriend is a cunt!"

The first Uber came, and Eamonn pushed Nathan inside before the guy could wail on him. They sped off. Rafe watched their car go off into the distance.

Heath tapped his shoulder. Their Uber waited for him. "Off we go, mate."

———

WHEN THEY PULLED up to Sweeney, they found Eamonn and Nathan waiting outside.

"I forgot my swipe card," Eamonn said. He stepped aside so Rafe could open the door.

Thank you, he mouthed, his eyes full of meaning.

"Sweeney Hall is so posh. It's so much better than that pisspot Jones." Nathan gave the exterior a hug.

"Just get inside," Eamonn said. Rafe watched the exhaustion dribble down his face. He wondered how many times Nathan had done this, caused a scene to make sure the moment belonged to him.

"Rafe." Eamonn pulled him back to the door. "I'm so sorry about tonight. I couldn't leave him there to get his arse pummeled."

"I know. You did the right thing." Rafe rubbed his arm.

"Come on, you nobheads!" Nathan yelled at them at the

top of his lungs. He broke into laughter. Louisa gave him the signal to turn the volume down, but Nathan wasn't listening to anyone right now. "Are you whispering sweet nothings into each other's ears?"

"Shut up," Rafe said.

"What?" Nathan yelled.

"I said shut up." Rafe raised his voice, and though it couldn't compare to Nathan's volume level, it had a steely force all its own. "Nobody wants to listen to you anymore."

"Mate, let's go upstairs, get you some water." Heath tried to direct Nathan to the elevator, but Nathan shrugged out of his grip. His eyes were heavy and focused on one person.

"You don't want me here? Tough bullocks. Nobody wants you here, either! You're a placeholder, that's all. Something fun to play with for the fall."

"You're a cunt." The word came out of Rafe's mouth smooth as glass.

"Rafe..." Eamonn tried to play peacemaker, but Rafe was ready for war.

"What'd you call me?"

"You're a fucking cunt."

"You better watch what you say, Yank." Nathan took giant steps forward and pushed Rafe. Even in his state, he still had force. "Aren't Americans supposed to be polite?"

Eamonn stepped into the fray. "Nathan, just go upstairs."

"Alright, then." Nathan clammy palm clasped Eamonn's hand.

And that was the kick that knocked over the cauldron of fury, spilling all throughout Rafe.

"Get the fuck away from my boyfriend."

Rafe didn't move. He stared epic daggers at Nathan.

"Your boyfriend? Really?" Nathan scoffed.

Before Rafe could kick himself for such a rash declaration, Eamonn joined his side, making him feel invincible.

"You think this is going to last?" Nathan laughed like he took lessons at the Comic Villain Academy. "He's going to leave, E. He's a tourist. We're just cute exhibits to him. He doesn't want to stay here, no matter what he tells you." Each laugh was a dagger to Rafe's skin, and Eamonn's reaction hurt even more. "He's a fucking piece of American shit."

Rafe marched up to Nathan. *Thumb out. Knuckles at an angle.* Just like he and Eamonn practiced on the pitch, Rafe socked him in the jaw.

Nathan stumbled backward a little, like tripping on a shoelace. Rafe had good form, but unfortunately, he realized too late that he was too far away to truly connect.

He turned to Eamonn. He couldn't believe he just did that! He was so surprised at what he did that he couldn't heed the warning of Eamonn's bulging eyes.

The downside with Eamonn's lesson was that Eamonn never taught him to prepare for someone punching back.

Chapter 22

Rafe

Rafe braced himself for another swab of the cold cloth. He sat at the kitchen table while Louisa washed off his cut from Nathan's sucker punch. *That was a sucker punch, right? Getting attacked without looking and without warning?* The pain of the impact came back to Rafe with each brush of cold water. He could feel the nerves in his cheek send signals to his brain that this motherfucker hurt.

Eamonn filled up a bowl of more cold water at the sink. "How's it looking?" he asked Louisa.

"Colorful." Louisa smoothed the washcloth across his sore cheek.

"How're you feeling?" she asked.

"Sore. My head hurts."

"You went down. It's a good thing Eamonn caught you or else you would've smacked your head against the tile."

Rafe flicked his eyes over to Eamonn, who seemed to be reliving that memory on a loop. He set the bowl of water on the table for Louisa.

"You took the punch well," Eamonn said.

"The sucker punch," Rafe said.

"I've never seen Nathan that inebriated." Louisa pressed the washcloth on his cheek. It soothed and stung at the same time. "Usually, he's a flirty drunk."

Nathan had been taken to Louisa's room to sleep off the alcohol. But Rafe's flatmates were here, with him.

"You're smiling," Louisa noted.

"Thanks for doing this," he said to both of them.

Eamonn took washcloth duties over from Louisa. His strong hands handled it with delicacy.

"Where's Heath?" Rafe asked.

"Probably asleep, the fucker," Eamonn said.

Louisa made him a grilled cheese on toast. She took one more look at his face. "I think it should be all right. Just some black and blues, but it doesn't seem like you broke anything."

"I want to see," Rafe said.

Louisa and Eamonn traded a look. They hadn't let Rafe see the damage yet, and now he was more curious than ever. Louisa got a mirror from her bathroom and held it to Rafe's face.

"Holy shit." He was like Two Face from Batman. One side of him was normal Rafe; the other was red, blotchy, puffy, scarred.

"It'll heal," she said. "First, black and blue. Then it'll heal."

"I'm going to look so cool!"

Louisa and Eamonn traded a surprised look.

"I've never been in a fight. I've never thrown a punch or stood up for myself like that." Rafe felt power infused in his hands. "I'm kind of a bad ass."

Eamonn pointed at Rafe. "I like your attitude."

Louisa got the grilled cheese on toast from the skillet

and slid it onto a plate for Rafe. He saw she had another one on a separate skillet, too.

"I'm going to bed." She kissed Rafe's good cheek. She took the second grilled cheese on toast and left.

"That second sandwich is for Nathan," Rafe said once she was gone.

"He needs it. His stomach is a tank filled with alcohol." Eamonn pressed the washcloth to his bruised cheek. The coolness of the water and the heat of Eamonn's hand provided the perfect balm.

"What is his problem? I don't mean to be rude, but why were you guys ever friends with him? He's a dick, and not in the fun, sarcastic way."

"There are many sides to Nathan."

"He's not an octagon."

Eamonn smiled at the joke.

Rafe shook his head. He couldn't understand why people put up with guys like Nathan. He was the very definition of a toxic person, not worth the time of genuinely good people like Heath, Louisa, and especially Eamonn.

"Did you like being with him?" Rafe asked. That was probably a little intrusive, but it stung more than his bruises that a good guy like Eamonn got wrapped up with Nathan, a guy who broke his heart but was still looked after.

"Look, Nathan...he has some issues. After his mum died, his dad remarried this woman who's just as high-maintenance as Nathan. As you can imagine, they do not get along."

Rafe took his parents for granted. They might've been overprotective, but at least they cared.

"He told me how tough things were at home. His dad always takes his stepmother's side. He ran away from home when he was twelve, and his dad didn't look for him or report him missing. After five days, Nathan just went home.

"When he told me that...I remember that night I just held him. I just wanted to make things better for him. Of course, that doesn't completely excuse him for being a twat, or what he did to me."

Rafe could see it in his eyes that Eamonn still cared about Nathan, even just a little. One thread on a piece of rope that refused to snap apart. They were connected. They always would be, no matter what Eamonn felt for Rafe.

"I don't view you as a cute exhibit," Rafe said. He hated giving anything Nathan said credence, but he wanted Eamonn to hear it directly from him. "At first, I had this ideal version of events in my head, that I'd find this hot British guy, or several of them, and I'd have stories to bring back to the states. But then I met you, and I stopped caring about the story." Rafe's chest vibrated with nerves. "I'm sorry I called you my boyfriend before. I know that..."

"Don't be." Eamonn soaked the washcloth in more warm water, then returned to Rafe's bruised face. "Are you all right with that?"

"Yeah. It feels good."

"No, the boyfriend part."

"I am." Rafe wasn't sure what would happen. They were boyfriends with an expiration date, but Eamonn had burrowed his way into Rafe's heart. What they had was more than sex. It was its own kind of adventure.

Rafe leaned forward and kissed Eamonn softly on the lips.

"I can hold that." Rafe reached for the washcloth, but Eamonn wouldn't let go. Something twinkled in his eye.

"I know."

Rafe gazed into those squinty blue eyes, eyes which

could read every part of him. Their lips came together again, with more heat. But Rafe pulled away.

"Ow. Sorry." Rafe pointed at his busted cheek.

"Right."

"It kind of hurts to kiss," Rafe admitted, and hung his head.

"Then I'll just have to be more creative then." Eamonn kissed along his good cheek, then down his neck. Pleasure shot through Rafe's face, momentarily numbing his bad cheek (though he wasn't going to take chances). Eamonn's scruff scratched against Rafe's collarbone.

Eamonn ran his fingers through Rafe's hair as his rough lips dipped at Rafe's sensitive skin. "Is that hurting your cheek?"

"No."

"I should probably move further south, just to be safe."

"Just to be safe," Rafe whispered.

EAMONN

Eamonn breathed in Rafe's scent on his shirt. He motioned for Rafe to sit on the dining table so they were eye level. Eamonn had better access to his good cheek and neck. He grabbed Rafe by the hair and tugged his head back to get better access.

He felt that familiar bulge in Rafe's trousers. Rafe pulled Eamonn closer and locked him in between his knees.

"Maybe we should continue this in your room," Rafe said

"My room doesn't have a dining table in it." Eamonn kissed the tip of Rafe's bottom lip.

"There's a swinging door with no lock."

"Nobody's coming in."

"Are you sure?"

"No." Eamonn palmed Rafe's crotch, and Rafe had no choice but to gasp in pleasure.

"Eamonn."

It was hard to keep himself in check. Rafe's bruising was surprisingly sexy. Eamonn rubbed his firm hands down Rafe's chest, making circles over his nipples with his thumbs, and stopping just above his tented pants. Rafe leaned in for a kiss, but a shot of pain from his cheek nixed that plan on contact.

"It would be irresponsible as your caretaker to subject your wounded face to any potential harm," Eamonn said. With his hand spread out on Rafe's chest, he pushed Rafe on his back slowly. "Down you go."

Rafe lay prone on the dining table. Eamonn shut off the lights. Streaks of moonlight lit the room. Rafe squirmed with a repressed moan as Eamonn unbuckled his belt. The sound of Rafe's zipper echoed against the quiet walls. His vision darted to the swinging door.

"No looking," Eamonn commanded.

"But what if someone..."

His cock disappearing into Eamonn's hot mouth easily shut him up. He loved how Rafe tried to stifle his moaning. It was as if because he couldn't say anything, those moans had to come out somehow, and he writhed around on the table. They were as quiet as possible. Eamonn resisted his urge to dirty talk, which he knew Rafe couldn't resist. The silence was a turn on in its own way. Only the sounds of sex could be heard. Eamonn took Rafe to the base and felt that salty taste of pre-come on his tongue.

Eamonn snuck a peek at the door, just to be safe. The coast was still clear. He licked Rafe's balls, and dragged his tongue down further to that tight hole. (Well, a little less tight thanks to him these past few weeks.) A tiny gasp escaped Rafe's mouth when he flicked his tongue over his opening.

He ate out Rafe while stroking his cock. He wished he could've seen Rafe's face contorting, but his imagination did him well. Eamonn controlled Rafe's whole body from this angle. His tongue circled his hole, and then came back up to take his whole cock. Eamonn couldn't stop himself from devouring Rafe's tight, eager frame. He bit into his inner thigh and sucked on the sweet flesh.

"What are you doing?" Rafe gasped out.

"Leaving you a souvenir." Another mark from tonight. Eamonn's thumb smoothed over the hickey he just left. A gentleman, it was in a place nobody but him would ever see.

Eamonn pushed Rafe's legs further back, giving him a better leverage for eating that hole. He slid two fingers inside and returned to sucking his rock-hard dick. His mind was dizzy with want and lust. He remembered he had a condom in his wallet.

Eamonn stood up and faced Rafe. "Do you wanna…"

He took out the condom. The wrapper crinkled in the silence.

Rafe looked at the door, and he swore that the corners of his mouth turned up in a mischievous smile. Rafe nodded yes.

Eamonn raced to his bedroom to get lube. In the hallway, he heard moans of sex coming from Heath's room. *You and Louisa finally made up.* He felt a little bit bad that Nathan was all alone while everyone else in this flat was now having sex, but he was probably too sound asleep to notice.

Back in the kitchen, he found Rafe sitting up, fully dressed.

"Just in case," Rafe said. "I didn't want to be caught alone with my pants down."

"Like this?" And Eamonn dropped his pants to his ankles, his cock shooting straight forward, aimed at Rafe. Rafe's mouth seemed to water at the sight.

Rafe lay back on the table, and in the speed of sound, his pants were at his ankles, and his ankles were at his ears. Eamonn gave his ass one more lick before slathering on lube. He sheathed his cock in the rubber.

"Yes," Rafe whispered out in a choked voice.

"I haven't even entered you yet."

"Fuck," Rafe said once Eamonn did. Eamonn would never get enough of that warm opening.

"Fuck, your arse feels so good. I can't wait to pound the fuck out of it."

So maybe he couldn't totally lay off the dirty talk. Eamonn pulled Rafe's thighs close, slamming his thick cock all the way inside that pink hole.

"Do you want me to go slow?"

"No. Swinging door."

Eamonn complied. At first, he went a little slow until he felt Rafe unclench and get use to his cock opening him up. He pumped his meat into that opening and shook the kitchen table. He didn't care. He squeezed Rafe's nipples as he pummeled his arse. He could feel Rafe tightening around him.

He kept an eye on the swinging door, but what was the worst that could happen? One of his flatmates would see his bum for a second and shut the door? Eamonn mooned them as a first year, so it was nothing they'd never seen before. They would know that he and Rafe were shagging? No surprise there. He and Rafe were locked into a moment, and they weren't going to stop until they were spent.

Eamonn spread Rafe's ass wide with his hands and shoved his cock in deeper, down to his balls. *God, this feels so fucking good. And watching Rafe lose it without saying a word was the cherry on top.* He began jerking off Rafe, his cock hard as a fucking torch. Rafe couldn't stay still. He was a fish out of water, flopping around on dry land. Eamonn whipped his hand up and down on his shaft until his knuckles were red, as he continued slamming into that wet ass. Rafe held onto the edges of the dining table. His ass practically strangled Eamonn's cock, and it sent Eamonn over the edge. Rafe didn't have to say a word.

"Come for me, Rafe," Eamonn said in a husky whisper, one that was all bass.

Rafe fucked his hand once, twice. White streaks shot across his stomach and chest, just as Eamonn filled his rubber with hot come.

Silence continued. Eamonn didn't want to tarnish this moment with chitchat. They didn't say a word as they got themselves decent. They didn't say a word when Rafe followed him into his bedroom. They didn't say a word when they stepped into the shower together and soaped each other down. Their chests slid against each other's, and their cocks hardened into swordfighting position. But there was no round two of sex. Rafe's cheek was still sore and in no shape for kissing. So they held each other as water rained down, and Eamonn felt Rafe's heartbeat echo in his chest. Rafe tilted his head up and his question punctured the beautiful silence.

"What if I stayed?"

Chapter 23

Rafe

Rafe ignored his parents calling the next morning. Instead, he continued luxuriating in Eamonn's arms.

It had been a long night. After their shower, they laid in bed and talked about Rafe's blurted out question. It had been on his tongue for a while. First, it was just a "wouldn't it be nice if..." thought, but as his relationship with Eamonn became more serious, he realized he wasn't ready to leave. He had just found his groove in England.

"I know I can't stay here forever, but what if I tried to extend my study abroad trip for the rest of the year?" he had asked once they toweled off and got into bed.

"Would your school allow that?"

"I don't know yet. But it might be worth checking out?" Rafe phrased it as a question to gauge Eamonn's interest. He worried that he was scaring Eamonn away. He had a bad habit of coming on too strong back at Browerton with his grand romantic gesture ploys.

"You would really do that? Give up a whole year at your university to stay here?"

"I wouldn't stay here for you," Rafe added. He wouldn't put that pressure on Eamonn. "I haven't done any traveling around Europe, and there are internships I could do here. Maybe I could work at the Stonehenge museum. And I just love being in a foreign country. I'm still taking in the culture."

"And there's the legal drinking age benefit."

"That, too." Rafe studied Eamonn, trying to parse out if he was being nice, or if he wanted any part of this. "I know this came out unexpectedly, and it seems a little drastic. Please be honest with me, Eamonn, if you think this is a bad idea. I won't be offended. Maybe I've interrupted your life enough."

Eamonn kissed him. Rafe held back a wince of pain for his face.

"You haven't interrupted anything. These two months have been some of the greatest of my life."

Rafe was powerless against a statement like that. Eamonn's eyes beamed at him. He traced a finger over Rafe's eyebrow. But still, Eamonn hadn't explicitly said he wanted Rafe to stay. Rafe ignored that minor observation and began doing research on Eamonn's computer while Eamonn went to the bathroom. Browerton had an eight-point checklist for students thinking of extending their study abroad trip. That made him feel less insane. Obviously they wouldn't have this checklist ready if other kids hadn't extended their trips, and surely a percentage of those who extended did so for romantic reasons, statistically speaking. Rafe climbed back into bed just as Eamonn opened his bathroom door. They resumed their cuddling position.

Rafe's buzzing phone cut through the morning peace of laying in Eamonn's arms. His parents kept calling. He couldn't ignore them. They were number six on the checklist: *Get approval from parent/guardian.*

Eamonn didn't let him go so easily. His strong arms were like safety bars on an amusement park ride that wouldn't budge until the ride came to a complete stop.

"Tell them hello for me," Eamonn mumbled with a spritely morning wood poking into Rafe.

When they kissed, Rafe felt a jab of pain, and he touched his face. *Right, my busted face.*

Give me one minute, he texted his parents.

We're Skyping, his mom wrote back.

He tiptoed out of Eamonn's room, hoping he was already falling back asleep. When he clicked the door shut, he heard familiar sounds coming from Heath's door.

"Well, good morning Louisa."

But it wasn't Louisa.

"Hey." Allison gave him the most uncomfortable, purse-lipped smile in history. Rafe watched her leave the flat. It seemed she found something in Britain she actually liked.

Rafe darted into his room. He was so surprised by Allison that he opened Skype as instructed.

"Rafe! What happened?" his mom practically screamed.

"What?" Then he remembered his injury, which had gotten even more Two Faced overnight. "Oh. This."

His parents stared at him in horror and seemed to have one of their telepathic conversations.

"It looks much worse than it is."

"How did this happen?" His mom still had a look of death on her.

"I got in a fight. But it's fine."

"It's fine?" his dad yelled. "Rafe, you are an ocean away all bruised up. You don't want us to worry about you, yet you give us reasons to worry."

He supposed his dad had a point.

"Is this because you're American?"

"No. Not quite." Rafe wished he hadn't been so truthful. "I just woke up. Can we talk later?"

"No," his mom said firmly. "We've barely spoken to you over the past month. All we've gotten are emails about your classes and that you saw Stonehenge. I want to catch up, especially now." She was no doubt talking about his face.

"Things are good. I'm having fun."

"We know. When did you decide to become a bartender?" his mom asked. He could hear the imaginary jury gasp at the revelation.

"How did you know that?"

"You posted pictures to Instagram."

"You read my Instagram feed? But it's private." Only his friends could see his posts, and he hadn't given his parents his username. He wanted one thing of his own that he didn't have to share.

"Melody Keener's mother came up to me in the super-market and told me you were bartending and you were dating a very cute young man."

Melody Keener was one of those high school friends he pretty much lost touch with once they graduated, yet still followed each other on social media.

"Cunt," Rafe said under his breath.

"What did you say?" His dad teetered on the verge of yelling, and his mom's look of disgusted shock was no better.

"Nothing. Sorry." Rafe's head pounded as much from his bruises as from this interrogation. No amount of Advil could make this go away. "And I'm not a bartender. I'm a runner, but I got to take on a slow bartending shift once. Things seem more exaggerated on social media."

"You were able to get a job legally over there?" his dad asked.

"Yes. I looked into it. I can work up to twenty hours a week with a student visa."

His parents traded a surprised look, but they also seemed impressed at his due diligence.

"Interesting," his mom said.

"Why are you working at a bar? We wanted you to focus on your schoolwork and to enjoy being abroad," his dad said.

"Because I'm an adult, and I want to make my own money without you looking at my checking account."

"What do you want to buy that you don't want us to know about?" his mom asked. Rafe knew the subtext.

"I'm not doing drugs. I just...I want some freedom." This seemed as good a time as any to share his other news. "I'm also, well I'm thinking of maybe possibly extending my study abroad trip for the rest of the year."

"What?" his dad asked. His mom's expression seconded that.

"I'm having a great time in England. I'm just hitting my stride, and I want to stay a little longer."

"A little longer? A whole year of your college education will be spent abroad. That seems like a lot," his mom said.

"It's actually very common at Browerton. Kids extend their trips. I just have to get permission and send in the extra payment, which I will pay you back every cent."

His dad waved off the suggestion. Money was the least of their worries, something Rafe never appreciated enough. His parents unloaded a barrage of questions at him.

"Will this jeopardize your ability to graduate on time?"

"Will you be able to apply to BISHoP?"

"Does being away a whole year hurt your chances of getting in?"

"Will you come home for Christmas or spring break?"

"One of the requirements for extending my trip is getting approval from my major, so I will check with the geology department to see if this is kosher. And I will definitely look into how this impacts my BISHoP application. I'm still in the exploratory stage. I'm going to do a lot more research on what extending my trip entails and the ramifications before making a final decision, and I'll be sure to keep you in the loop every step of the way. I want to see if this is possible and give it my best shot."

Rafe gave his parents a cogent, confident answer that stressed communication. He had never sounded so mature in front of them, and for the first time, they seemed to look at him as an adult, too.

"Okay, then," his mom said with his dad nodding along.

"And if I do stay, I'll pay for my flights home to visit. Or maybe you can meet me in London?"

But she didn't seem thrilled. She still had on her concerned mom expression.

"I really do think it's wonderful that you've found this independence, and even though we're a bit blindsided, we respect your choice." She couldn't turn off the psychologist in her. "I just hope you're not doing all this to stay close to your boyfriend."

Rafe was curious how she knew, but then remembered Melody Keener's mom.

"If you really want to be independent, then you need to want to stay in England for you. Not for him."

"I know." Rafe felt his confidence shift ever-so-slightly from ironclad to house of cards.

Chapter 24

"What would you say is your greatest weakness?"

"What kind of bollocks question is that?" Eamonn gave Rafe a raised eyebrow and took a sip of his beer. Rafe stood behind the bar at Apothecary wiping down the counter.

"That's good." Rafe pointed at him drinking. "If you need a moment to think of an answer or if you're nervous, take a sip of water to pace yourself. Always accept when they offer you a beverage, but don't drink the whole thing. That makes you seem either too nervous or too comfortable."

"What if they offer a beer?"

"Ask for water instead. Your propensity for saying the c-word skyrockets the second alcohol touches your lips. Now..." Rafe gestured for him to answer the question.

Rafe's boss let him bartend during another quiet Thursday afternoon. Since the place was dead, Rafe had Eamonn come in for a quirky form of torture. The mock interview.

"Do you have all of these questions rolling around in

your head?" Eamonn asked. Rafe had no notecards, but he had been on interviews for internships and whatnot.

"Stop stalling. The interview for the management trainee program is tomorrow. Nepotism won't do you any good if you completely bomb your interview."

It was going to be a massive interview. Eamonn would sit on one side of a long conference table opposite five executives and be subjected to rapid-fire questioning. His uncle hadn't sugarcoated it for him.

"All right." Eamonn straightened his spine on the barstool and cleared his throat. "My greatest weakness is probably that I can be a bit lazy in completing things."

Rafe made a buzzer sound. "Try again."

"I am working on being a more punctual person."

Buzzer sound.

"What? I leave the toilet seat up? I give up!"

"The key is to give a weakness that isn't really a weakness. For example, 'I have a tendency to bite off more than I can chew, especially when it comes to an area I'm very passionate about. I'm hoping in this position, I can get better at delegating tasks.'"

Eamonn took out his phone and did his best to type that out from memory. "You're good. Although I don't think I can use the passionate part without laughing."

"Why not?"

"I'm not passionate about boxes, not even when used as a euphemism for fanny."

"I would hope not," Rafe said. He put down his rag. "Don't you get it, Eamonn? It's not about boxes. I doubt your uncle dreamed of working for a box company when he was a boy. This program is about management, marketing, learning the mechanics of business. That's what you have to emphasize you're passionate about. You want to bring a product to the masses and grow market share."

Eamonn got an uneasy feeling in his stomach, the same as when he tried eating paper as a boy. He knew it was a bad idea as soon as he swallowed, and he paid the consequences.

"Are you passionate about those things?" Rafe asked.

"I mean, yeah." Eamonn swirled his glass around.

"That didn't sound very convincing."

"What about you? How did you get so into rocks?"

"I used to go into the woods behind our house and try to break apart rocks. I'd learned that rocks had been around for millions of years. These same stones I was messing with could've been from prehistoric times. I managed to break open a rock by smashing it against a bigger rock, and inside was this beautiful green-and-purple crystal formation."

"Little Rafe, breaking rocks and putting them in his knapsack." Eamonn laced his fingers through Rafe's. Inside though, he felt jealousy for not having focus like Rafe did. He wasn't able to indulge his passion as a kid. He was busy helping his mum and sisters.

"I want to work for the National Parks Service or the EPA, making sure other kids can discover rocks in the future. I interviewed the head of the EPA when I was in high school for a class project. I called and emailed until I got through, even got to go to his office in D.C. and meet with him."

"They'd be idiots not to hire you." He rubbed Rafe's palm with his calloused thumb.

A customer cleared his throat a few stools down, and Rafe paused their PDA to help him. Eamonn was so proud of Rafe for his drive and direction. Over these past two weeks, he'd been diligent about checking things off his school list for extending his stay here. It seemed like every few days, he would run to Eamonn's room to celebrate getting approval from his school representative or finding out he could stay in Sweeney for the second semester. Eamonn was thrilled, truly. The thought of getting to spend an entire year with Rafe filled his heart with joy, but it would also send him a jolt of guilt. He worried that Rafe staying at Stroude might derail his future. Rafe had told him how competitive that BISHoP thing was. Even though Rafe said that he wasn't staying for Eamonn, he was afraid of what Rafe might be giving up.

"What about you?" Rafe came back and refilled Eamonn's drink. "I know you have this interview tomorrow, but have you looked up non-profits where you could apply?"

"I don't think it's for me." Rafe had brought this up before. He had found some non-profits doing amazing work, but the management trainee program was the more solid, more adult option.

"Have you heard of this company Water Water Everywhere? They're committed to bringing clean water to children around the world. It's right up your alley, and they have quite a few Brits working for them."

"I'll check it out."

Rafe didn't seem to believe him, but he didn't push it any further.

Rafe's boss came out for his hourly check of the place. The rest of the time, he was holed up in his office watching TV and reading, per Rafe's reporting. It was a sweet life.

"Hey Alfie," Rafe said.

Alfie came over and rubbed Rafe's shoulder. "Mate, have I told you how excited I am to have you here until May?"

"Multiple times." Rafe tried to act modest, but Eamonn loved watching him soak in the acclaim.

"I'm going to keep training you. By spring, you'll be bartending Friday and Saturday nights, making a lot more than you do now. Is this the boyfriend?" Alfie turned to Eamonn and shook his hand hard. "Thank you for getting him to stay!"

"Oh, no. I didn't—"

"I'm staying for a variety of reasons," Rafe said.

"Well, I'm sure having him here didn't hurt." Alfie elbowed Rafe and broke into a wheezy laugh. Rafe laughed along with him, though Eamonn could tell it was only for show.

Once he left, an awkward silence hung in the air between the boyfriends for a moment. Then it was gone, but not forgotten.

Rafe

All during medieval history class, Rafe thought about Eamonn, wishing him luck on his interview. Even if he wasn't crazy about Eamonn taking the job. Rafe had seen people he worked for in his internships miserable but unable to leave their jobs. They were stuck. Rafe didn't want that to happen to Eamonn. If only he knew how much he was truly capable of.

On his walk back to the dorm, he got a Facetime request from Coop. He waited until he was in his wifi-enabled dorm room before answering. His finger hovered over the accept button.

"Hey," Rafe said. He took deep breaths and rubbed his free palm on his jeans.

"What's up? What are you doing for Thanksgiving next week?" Coop asked.

"I'm cooking it. Or attempting to."

"Nice." Coop cocked the brim of his hat. Rafe found it adorable how this white kid from suburban New Jersey tried to act all tough.

"How's Matty?"

"He created his own version of Alexa that can turn the lights on and off and play music. I told him to name it Fuck-face so that when you ask for something, you go 'Hey Fuck-face, what's the weather outside today?'"

Rafe laughed. He missed his daily dose of Coop. They had really great roommate banter.

"I can't wait for you to play with Fuckface in January."

And here it came. The inevitable moment Rafe had been delaying. Now was time to pull the trigger. "So actually, um, the thing is...is that I'm extending my trip. I'm staying at Stroude into spring."

Coop's mouth hung open. "Oh. Like the whole year?"

"Yeah. Through May."

"So you wouldn't come back to Browerton until next fall?"

Rafe nodded yes.

"Wow."

"This is a once-in-a-lifetime opportunity to live abroad, you know? I want to take full advantage, and just going for fall semester is so short. I want to travel and keep experiencing all England has to offer."

"Yeah."

"And I'll be back junior year!" *Junior year.* He wouldn't return to Browerton until he was an upperclassmen. It sounded so much longer when he put it like that.

"Yeah," Coop said, still shell-shocked.

"And I know you're thinking I'm just staying because Eamonn is my first-ever boyfriend, but I'm not. Of course

I'm excited to spend more time with him, but he's just the free gift with purchase."

"Yeah."

"Coop, please say something else besides 'yeah.'" When Rafe got to his room, he kneeled on the floor and held the phone in front of him like he was praying to it.

"What about Dance Til You Drop?"

"Dance Til You Drop," Rafe repeated. It was a thirty-hour dance marathon that Browerton hosted every year in March to raise money for charity. He and Coop had agreed after missing out last year to do it as sophomores. They were going to dance like Charlie Brown characters for the entire time. Rafe thought of the time they practiced in their room last year.

"We can do it our junior and senior years," Rafe said.

"I guess so. Maybe I can rope Matty into doing it with me." But it wouldn't be the same. "Aw man, and you're not going to see any of my performances this year."

"Film them and put them up on YouTube."

"You're going to be missing *an entire year* of college life here. Parties and stories."

"I'll make stories here."

"But I won't know them," Coop said with a smile. Rafe thought about the games and events he would miss. Stroude didn't seem to have the same school spirit that Browerton had, or at least his flatmates had no interests in seeking it out. No tailgates or football games or festivals. No blizzards that blanketed the campus in winter or a river to rest along in spring.

There was Eamonn, though. Rafe wasn't staying just for him, but that free gift with purchase was very valuable. He had never felt this way about anyone before. He knew in his heart that what they had was more than some study abroad fling. He just hoped that Eamonn felt the same.

"Maybe I'll come out to visit you," Coop said. "I've never been to London."

"You'd like it. I'll look up British rappers we could see."

"Nice."

"So start looking up flights."

Coop gave him the captain's salute and ended the call. Browerton had never felt so far away.

Chapter 25

RAFE

Heath inhaled the aroma coming from the oven. "Rafe, my friend, you have a gift. You're like a less prickish version of Gordon Ramsey."

Rafe mashed up potatoes at the kitchen table. "I love Thanksgiving. All you have to do is eat!"

He checked his computer spreadsheet where he organized his Thanksgiving menu and created the food preparation schedule. He spent the past week watching YouTube videos and reading food blogs. This was his biggest culinary challenge, and he wasn't going to muck it up.

"What exactly is Thanksgiving?" Heath asked. "It celebrates when you Yanks committed genocide on those poor Native Americans, right?"

Rafe shot him the middle finger. "Like you Brits are so much better. The British Empire ruled the world for centuries. You think they took over colonies politely?"

"Touché." Eamonn swung into the kitchen with a bag of cranberries and two bags of white bread. "It took me three stores to find one with cranberries."

Eamonn dropped the food onto the kitchen table. He opened the oven door where the turkey cooked. "That is one sexy bird."

"Can you help me take it out? I have to baste it." Rafe pulled out the oven shelf holding the roasting pan. The bird sizzled in its juices.

"Are you meditating?" Eamonn asked.

"No. I'm smelling. Can you smell that?" Rafe asked. Heath came closer, and the three of them took another whiff.

"It smells delicious," Heath said.

"It smells like Thanksgiving." Rafe felt a tug on his heartstrings. "It smells like my grandparents' house."

Rafe was using his grandmother's recipe for the bird, but he didn't think he could actually replicate it. She had the special ingredient, one of those grandmotherly touches where she didn't have to use any measuring cups. But he was doing something right if the aromas aligned. "I can't believe I'm successfully cooking Thanksgiving dinner."

"This is going to be the best Thanksgiving meal we've ever had," Eamonn said, pointing between him and Heath.

"It's the *only* Thanksgiving meal you've ever had."

"Thus the bar is incredibly low." Eamonn kissed him, which gave Rafe an extra boost to keep on making this the best meal ever. However low Eamonn's bar might be, Rafe still wanted to impress him.

"Heath, will you begin ripping up the bread into small pieces. Next, we're going to make the stuffing!"

"Are we literally going to stuff a turkey's arse with bread crumbs?" Heath asked, seemingly disgusted and intrigued at the same time.

"No stuffing the stuffing. All of the turkey's body cavities will go unviolated. My mom told me that she and my grand-

mother never stuff the turkey." Rafe had eaten eighteen
Thanksgiving meals, but had never stepped foot in a kitchen
on Thanksgiving. The menfolk sat around the living room
TV watching football (or scrolling through Instagram on
their phones while football was on in the background in
Rafe's case). Rafe was let into a special club when his mom
divulged family recipes to him.

Rafe and Eamonn basted the turkey. He remembered
the epic Asda grocery trip to get most of these Thanksgiving
supplies. It was almost as magical as their first time there.

"Heath, when you're done, can you and Eamonn move
the table and chairs into the hallway for setting up?"

Not all guests could fit around the table in the kitchen.
The flat across the hall was letting them borrow their table
and chairs, and they were going to combine both sets in the
hallway. Thanksgiving wasn't the same without an elon-
gated dining table.

Rafe and Eamonn shoved the bird back in the oven.

"Also, I invited Allison," Rafe said, mostly to Heath.

"Cool," he said, but Rafe caught a flicker of panic in his
eyes.

"Is that okay?" Rafe asked. "All of her friends went to
Rome this weekend."

"Wait. Why would you think it wouldn't be?" Heath
asked back.

Rafe was too busy to tiptoe around this. "I know you and
Allison hooked up. Shagged. Whatever you want to call it. I
saw her leaving your room. I'm assuming Eamonn already
knows because you guys are best friends and that seems like
something you would've told him." Rafe paused to get
confirmation on this. Eamonn and Heath both nodded yes.
"Good. I couldn't not invite the only other American I know
here to Thanksgiving dinner. Are you and Allison still..."

"Shagging?" Heath asked.

"You know what? It's none of my business. I have a meal to cook." Rafe opened the fridge to get the green beans, but immediately shut it. "Like I said, it's *obviously* none of my business, and you don't have to answer—"

"We shagged twice. Both times we were perfectly pissed. We had a good laugh about it," Heath said, and Rafe breathed a sigh of relief. He didn't want to host a dinner filled with drama.

"Does Louisa know?" Rafe whispered, just in case she barged in.

"No. And she doesn't have to."

"Would she be jealous?"

Heath and Eamonn exchanged a look that said they didn't know the answer for sure.

"Let's just keep it between us," Eamonn said.

"Well, you and her were all about keeping it casual. Will it be awkward if Louisa is at dinner no matter what?" Rafe got the green beans for real this time and began snapping off the ends. "I feel like you guys have barely talked to each other for weeks. You've downgraded to acquaintances or something, particularly since she's been hanging out with Nathan more."

From what Rafe could gauge from the times they all were together, Heath and Louisa had mastered the British stiff upper lip tradition of holding in one's feelings. The détente continued. Though judging by Heath's solemn expression currently, Rafe realized that was only a one-sided agreement.

Eamonn got a beer from the fridge. He offered one to Rafe, who declined. "I need to stay sober and in the cooking zone. But you guys go on ahead. Thanksgiving isn't complete without a drunk uncle."

"What's in that?" Heath asked, taking the beer Rafe refused.

"It's an expression. There's always one relative at Thanksgiving who gets way too drunk and starts saying inappropriate, offensive, and blatantly racist things at the dinner table."

"That only happens at Thanksgiving?" Eamonn asked. "You Yanks need to drink more."

Rafe put Heath to work chopping up onion and garlic, while Eamonn was in charge of sautéing the green beans.

"Question for you, mates," Rafe said. Mate didn't really roll off the tongue for him. "Does Stroude have like a dance-a-thon event or something like that?"

"What's a dance-a-thon?" Heath asked.

"It's where you dance nonstop for a whole day or more to raise money for charity. And each hour is a different kind of music, and people dress up in costumes to dance. The whole school gets into it. Anything like that?"

Heath and Eamonn looked at each other like Rafe described something out of a science fiction novel. Like most traditions, it sounded weird for anyone who wasn't part of it.

"That sounds exhausting," Heath said. "And why would you wear costumes?"

"I don't know. To get into it. It's fun. At Browerton, they do a dance-a-thon that lasts for thirty hours."

"Sounds a bit dodgy," Heath said, wiping away an onion-induced tear.

"Yeah. I guess you have to be there." Rafe smiled to himself. He checked the weather report, and Stroude would be lucky to get an inch of snow all winter. For the first real snowfall of the year, kids at Browerton would run onto the main quad in boots and their underwear for Snow Spree.

Rafe looked up and caught Eamonn staring at him like he was trying to read his mind, but it was an inside joke he couldn't get.

Heath went to his room to wipe his eyes. That left Eamonn and Rafe, separated by more than a kitchen table at the moment.

"I'm just waiting on final word from my study abroad advisor to make sure I officially have the green light, but she says it's pretty much a go. I updated my health insurance policy to extend coverage, and that was the last step." Rafe hoped that Eamonn would scoop him up in his arms and swing him around the kitchen whilst making out. Or something like that.

"Will staying here hurt your chances of getting into that BISHoP program?" he asked.

"I can apply from here and interview via Skype."

"Will that look bad? You told me all about how every detail matters in interviews."

"No," Rafe said, although Eamonn did have a point. But why was he so concerned about BISHoP all of a sudden? Why was he bringing that up instead of celebrating? *It was crunch time, and maybe he doesn't want me here.* Rafe thought things would be different with him, but maybe Eamonn was just another guy he was scaring off.

"Shit," Rafe said, opening the fridge. "We're out of butter. I thought I got enough."

"I'll run out to the corner store and pick up some sticks."

"Thanks."

Eamonn kissed him goodbye before he left the kitchen. He was a good boyfriend, and Rafe worried that the only thing keeping them together was an expiration date.

CHAPTER 26

EAMONN

A little sprinkle turned into a steady rain that blackened the sky. It would've been pretty had Eamonn been in a mood to admire beauty. He dug his hands into his pockets and hunched down to block himself from the downpour.

Rafe had done it. He had actually fucking done it. Eamonn should be ecstatic. His boyfriend was staying! He had aced the interview at his uncle's company and was on the fast track to management! But all he felt was this sink-hole opening inside him. What was Rafe giving up to stay? Was Eamonn worth it? Rafe had all these ideas about who Eamonn could be, and as much as those ideas excited him, Eamonn doubted he could live up to them. He wasn't some globe-trotting humanitarian. He had a family that depended on him.

He wasn't impressed with the butter selection at the corner store. It sat on a dirty shelf inside a cooler whose door was frosted over with ice. He left the store and walked to the fancy market in town. Rafe deserved the most quality ingredients for his Thanksgiving meal.

Eamonn stopped at an alley a block before the market. Students at Stroude didn't frequent the pubs in town. They were a bit too dodgy for them. They would rather drink in the clean, friendly confines of Apothecary and other campus pubs. In the alley was the entrance to one of the seedier pubs, one of those places that didn't have a name, just signs for the type of beer they carried. It was an example of what this town used to be like before fancy markets began coming in. Eamonn had never stepped foot in this pub, but he heard a familiar yell wafting from the alley.

"Get your bloody hands off me! You fucking cunts!"

Two men dragged Nathan out of the pub and threw him against the brick wall. By the looks of it, they'd already had some fun with him inside. His clothes were wrinkled, and his shirt collar was ripped.

"Go home and don't ever come back!" One of the men said.

"Don't tell me what to fucking do!" Nathan, like a rabid dog, leapt up and launched at him. The man socked him in the jaw. He and his friend were about to pummel him some more, when Eamonn jumped between them and pushed them back.

"Oy! Oy!" Eamonn yelled with his hands up. He could take both of these guys, but he wasn't going to make the situation worse. "I got him."

"Keep him the fuck away from here."

"Like I would ever come back to this hellhole," Nathan said from the ground.

Eamonn stared the men down, the three of them only communicating through animal instincts. The men kept glaring at him as they walked back into the pub, their breath swabbed in ashy smoke and stale beer. One of them spat at Nathan.

He knelt down to get a good look at his ex-boyfriend. Dried blood caked his puffy face. Bruises and black-and-blues formed a patchwork over his skin. If someone had told Eamonn that Nathan had gotten run over, he wouldn't have second-guessed it.

"Nathan," he whispered out. "Y'alright?"

"Does it appear that way?" Nathan stared at the wall in front of him.

Eamonn took off his scarf and wiped away some of the blood. "What happened?"

"I got in a bit of a kerfluffle." Nathan's words slurred together. He leaned over and spat blood into the street.

"What the hell—was this because you're gay?" Eamonn's fingers locked into fists.

"No. We live in a progressive enough society where a few pricks could be all right with my homosexuality but take umbrage with me trying to punch them for claiming Arsenal is the best football team in the U.K."

"I thought you were a Manchester United fan."

"I am, but I just wanted to see their reaction. I don't know how it started. Sometime after my tenth pint, everything went into a blur."

"Ten pints?" *Jesus.* Nathan seemed hollowed out, as if everything he was saying was rehearsed. "Let's get you cleaned up."

Eamonn picked Nathan up, but as soon as he let go, Nathan wobbled backwards and fell against a trash can. He slunk to the ground and had no intention of moving.

Eamonn held out his hand. Nathan swatted it away. "Are you planning to celebrate Christmas down there?"

"What the fuck are you doing here, E?"

"I was making a grocery run, and I heard a familiar voice."

"Shopping at the bourgeois palace? My how the Yank has changed you."

Eamonn shot him a look.

"You should've just ignored me." Nathan's words jumbled together. Eamonn could barely understand him. "You should've just left me to rot in a puddle of my own piss!"

Nathan lurched out his leg in a half-assed kick. Eamonn tried to wipe a glob of blood and dribble from Nathan's mouth. Nathan smacked his arm hard, ripped the scarf out of his hand, and flung it across the alley.

"What the fuck is going on with you? What the hell are you doing drinking until your liver gives out and getting in fights with strangers?"

"I don't know," he answered, somewhat in a daze. "I drink to get rid of the pain, but then I like getting in fights so I can feel pain all over again." Nathan held his shirt sleeve to his mouth.

"Once your film comes out, you won't be able to pull shit like this anymore. People have phones. You'll wind up on the front page of *The Sun*."

"There is no film." Nathan laughed to himself.

"Bollocks. What were you doing the whole time you were gone?"

"The director fired me. Apparently, he didn't like his actors getting so wasted they couldn't remember their lines. I offered to blow him to make amends, which he *really* didn't like. He cut me loose in September, said he was going to reshoot all my scenes. There goes my Hollywood career. *Poof.*" Nathan soaked through his sleeve. Eamonn darted into the pub and grabbed a stack of napkins. He handed

Nathan a clean one, which he did not swat away. "Thank you."

Eamonn saw his ex-boyfriend clearly for the first time. His vivacity, his biting lines, they were all part of a thick coat of armor that he never took off.

"Mate, you never used to drink like this."

"Well, life happens. Life just loves to kick me in the stones," Nathan said. "I was massively excited about getting cast in the film. I really was. Then they rewrote the script and turned my character into someone who was abandoned by his mother, and it hit too close to home."

"Too close to home? Just because your mum died doesn't mean she..."

"I lied to you. One of many," Nathan said. He sat up a little bit, as if he were pulling this from deep within. "My mother didn't die. She left. She and my dad had a one-night stand, then nine months later, she showed up on his doorstep with a newborn and hightailed it the fuck out of there. My dad told me the truth on my fifteenth birthday after I came out to him, like he was trying to top my news."

"Fuck. I'm sorry."

"I had pushed that all down years ago, but the movie just sliced open these fucking...who fucking does that?"

Eamonn offered a hug. He didn't have any wise words. Nobody deserved that, and he wished he could find his mother and bring her here. Nathan burrowed himself into his chest for a moment before pulling away.

"Bugger. Now I've gone and gotten blood on your nice jumper," Nathan said

"It'll wash out." Eamonn wiped it away.

"You're the only person who knows the truth. Lucky you."

"You could've told me about getting fired."

"You were preoccupied with your Yank." Nathan stood up and winced with pain in his ribs. Eamonn checked out his stomach, which looked just as ghastly as his face.

"I think you need to go to a hospital."

"I'll be fine." Nathan held his mouth open and drank raindrops, then soaked Eamonn's scarf to clean his face. "I don't want to keep you from your *boyfriend*."

"What did you expect? You don't get to play the jealous card. I moved on. I thought you had. Right in front of my fucking face."

But Nathan held up a hand to stop him. "I know. I'm sorry for trying to fuck that up."

Eamonn made sure he heard that right.

"I am." Nathan stared up at the buzzing fluorescent signs of the pub. "I didn't even like the guy you saw me snogging. He had horrible breath."

"Where did you meet him?" Eamonn had wondered this ever since it happened.

"Grindr." Nathan let out a laugh. "We met in the Waterstones outside our terminal. He was like one of those ten pints. He got rid of the pain for a moment." Nathan cleaned his face in the rain. "It's hard to love someone when the one woman who's supposed to love you wants nothing to do with you. It doesn't really set the tone. I was scared of that happening with you. I was scared to find out if we could survive the distance, the fame. So I pushed you away. I was a total prick to you."

Eamonn never saw Nathan cry before, no matter how bad things got. It amazed him that his ex-boyfriend could be an actor where he'd have to cry on cue. Nathan didn't cry tonight, but that didn't mean his eyes were without sadness. It was worse. He was filled with it, but he couldn't let it out. Maybe one day he would.

"It's not your fault, what your mother did."

Nathan waved it off. He'd probably heard it loads before. "You don't have to do that. I'll let you get back to Rafe."

"He's cooking a big meal tonight," Eamonn said.

"*Lots of hamburgers and French fries*?" Nathan asked in his own American accent, which actually sounded American.

Beneath the joke though, there was an ocean of cold misery, one that Eamonn couldn't ignore.

"You need help, Nathan. You have a problem."

Nathan nodded in acquiescence.

"I'm going to call your father."

"Oh, he won't like this. He and the wicked stepmother are set to go on a cruise tomorrow."

"He'll come," Eamonn said firmly, even if he had to go to London and drag him out of his penthouse apartment himself.

"Thank you for coming, E. Can you please not tell anyone about this? Please," he pleaded, grabbing Eamonn's jumper. "I have a reputation as a first-rate arsehole to maintain."

"I promise."

Nathan saw his reflection in a window. "Jesus fucking Christ."

They waited in the fancy market with food from the hot bar. People gawked at Nathan, all bruised and bloodied. Once Eamonn got Nathan situated at a table with water and some food, he texted Rafe.

Am majorly delayed. Something happened with Nathan. He needed help. Can't get into it, but will be back soon – with butter! I am so sorry.

It took Nathan's dad close to an hour to meet them, and despite Nathan's prediction, his father seemed worried, not annoyed. He couldn't imagine seeing your child in this state and feeling so helpless. He took Nathan back home that night and told Eamonn that he was getting him into a rehab facility immediately.

Eamonn made the trek through the rain back to Stroude. Rafe never texted back.

CHAPTER 27

<u>RAFE</u>

Rafe's Thanksgiving meal wasn't as delectable as his grandmother's. It was missing her magic touch. But that being said, he still managed to cook edible food that tasted good, if not great. Every guest at the table complimented his culinary skills, and Rafe would have to take their word for it because he was not in the mood to eat.

Just drink.

Rafe poured himself his third, or fourth, glass of red wine. Allison had brought a bottle, and Rafe had pretty much kept it all to himself. He didn't need liquid courage. He needed a liquid therapist, something to calm his nerves about Eamonn spending his first Thanksgiving with *Nathan*. Drinking, fucking, laughing about that idiot Yank Baxter who dared to think he'd actually found a guy who wanted him but scared him away. The Baxter had gone to war, and the Baxter had lost.

What did Eamonn mean in his text that Nathan needed help? Before he hit glass number three, Rafe was concerned for both of them. Maybe there was an accident, but then wouldn't Eamonn have said as much? As the alcohol worked its way through his system, he began realizing that "help" could be another ruse Nathan pulled to get Eamonn close. Eamonn could be having second thoughts about Rafe staying—he sure seemed that way—and gladly took whatever help Nathan was giving.

"It looks like we're out of stuffing. I'll get us more stuffing!" Rafe jumped up from his chair, which fell to the floor. He swiped the empty bowl of stuffing from Heath's hands, who was scooping out the last bits, and charged into the kitchen. He kicked open the swinging door *Charlie's Angels*-style.

"I'll be right back!"

And the door swung back in his face.

"Rafe!" Louisa ran to his side.

"I really like that you got dressed up for Thanksgiving. That means a lot to me," Rafe said to the multiple Louisas in front of him.

"Up you go. On your feet."

Rafe did as she commanded, with help from her and Heath. They each hoisted him up, and he found some semblance of balance.

"Thank you," he said to both of them. "I'm fine. I need to get more stuffing for everyone."

"Do you need help?" Louisa asked.

"Nope. I can do it all, like a gay June Clever. Do you know who that is? I don't either, but my parents like talking about her." Rafe swung the door open slowly, keeping his hand on it until he made his way through.

Rafe liked to believe that Eamonn went to see Nathan with good intentions. Like maybe Nathan said he needed a kidney or something. And then bam! Nathan seduced him like a twenty-something Ian McKellen.

He wasn't so drunk as to forget putting on an oven mitt, fortunately. Rafe scooped out more stuffing from the roasting pan. He tossed some bits into his mouth since no one was looking.

He heard the kitchen door swing open, and his heart crossed its aortic fingers hoping it was Eamonn.

"Y'alright?" Louisa asked.

"I'm fine. We needed more stuffing. So I put more stuffing into this bowl." Rafe held up his accomplishment. He couldn't stand her reaction. "I'm not drunk! I'm just a little tired and anxious about everything going okay."

"Everything is smashing. You are a brilliant chef."

Louisa poured him a glass of water and handed it over. He traded it for the bowl of stuffing. He still couldn't fathom how she could drink him under the table and show zero signs of being drunk.

"He'll be here soon." She rubbed his shoulders. It felt nice, but it still couldn't get rid of the dread coating his stomach.

"That American girl you invited is really nice. She's from California, and she's giving me the whole scoop! I want to visit there so badly."

"I'm glad everyone is getting along." Rafe wished he had his wine glass with him.

"She seems friendly with Heath. Maybe he'll pull her if he's lucky," she said.

"Oh, he already has. Ow!"

Louisa's hand dug into his shoulder. "Sorry." She let go. "What do you mean?"

"They had sex. Twice." Rafe wasn't sure if that was supposed to be a secret or not. Alcohol was like a skeleton key that opened all doors.

"What?" Louisa glared at Rafe.

What did I do?

"They've shagged?"

"Yes." Rafe must've been missing something, because Louisa looked like she needed to face a punching bag. "You guys aren't together."

"We're not. I'm just surprised. She doesn't seem like his type." Louisa went back to smiling, but it still creeped Rafe out. "Will you excuse me? I'm going to have a fag outside."

"I didn't know you smoked."

"It's a new Thanksgiving tradition." She shoved open the kitchen door and the breeze it left in her wake nearly threw Rafe to the floor again.

He returned to his guests. Eamonn stood over the table, waving hello to everyone. Rafe found his beloved wine glass and poured himself another session with his fermented therapist.

Eamonn came up to him before he could take a sip. He took the glass out of his hands and kissed him on the lips. "Rafe, I am so sorry about all this."

It was a damn good kiss, one that made Rafe forget about the drama and the wine. But he couldn't shake the fact that before Eamonn gave him this earth-shattering kiss, he was with his ex-boyfriend.

"How's Nathan?" Rafe asked. "And is that blood on your sweater?"

"It's not what you might presume. Nathan was in trouble." Eamonn's damn blue eyes were wearing him down and threatened to swallow him whole.

"And you were the *only* person who could help him?"

"Yes." Eamonn said it with a surprising amount of confidence. Rafe wished he would've lied. That would've hurt less. "Can we talk in private?"

Eamonn led them into his bedroom. Rafe wanted to lie

down so badly, but he resisted the pull of Eamonn's bed. He told Rafe about finding Nathan getting the shit kicked out of him outside a bar after having way too much to drink. Rafe thought of the fight Nathan picked outside the Bloc Party concert, and it sounded like more of the same. *Nathan causes a scene to get attention, and Eamonn saves the day.*

"Why was Nathan acting like that?" Rafe asked.

"He's going through some personal stuff."

"What kind of personal stuff?"

"I can't say. It's private. I'm sorry."

Rafe couldn't get past that non-answer. He appreciated that Nathan had secrets he didn't want known. We all did. He tried his best to trust Eamonn, but this was a brutal reminder that he and Nathan had a history and a past that Rafe wasn't able to compete with.

"Great. Glad you could help him. He's lucky to have an ex-boyfriend like you." Rafe got up. The room spun again, but he pushed through it.

"Rafe, please trust me. Nothing romantic or sexual happened between us."

It was worse. There was a bond there that Rafe couldn't supersede. All of his past Baxter experiences bubbled to the surface of his mind. No matter how well he thought it was going with a guy, there was always a curveball he didn't see coming. There would come the sudden ghosting, the rejection. Rafe wondered if that ever stopped, if there was ever a point in a relationship when he could feel secure.

"I'm going to enjoy the rest of my Thanksgiving," Rafe said, feeling a flash of sobriety hit him.

Back in the hallway, the dinner table turned out to be just as tense as Eamonn's room. Louisa had come back from her cigarette break with a guy Rafe recognized from Apothecary.

"Hi. Welcome." Rafe shook his hand.

"This is Jeremy, my boyfriend," Louisa said loud and proud.

Rafe glanced at Heath, who moved his fork around his plate but seemed to have zero interest in eating. Eamonn emerged from his room and took a seat at the far end of the table. The other guests, a smattering of classmates and flat-mates, stared at their food in awkward silence.

"Welcome," Rafe said to the new guy. He sat at his end of the table. He didn't look at Eamonn.

"This is a wicked spread you made here, mate," Jeremy said. Louisa nestled into his chest, which made it difficult for him to spoon himself some cranberry sauce, but he managed.

"Here, I want to try some cranberry sauce," Louisa said. Jeremy spoon-fed her. Her face cringed when it hit her tongue. Cranberry sauce was not something meant to be eaten alone.

Rafe could feel Eamonn's eyes on him, and he wanted to look back, but he couldn't. He couldn't let himself get anymore attached than he had.

"Louisa, you're making a scene," Heath said.

"I'm sorry if you have a problem with my new boyfriend being here. Allison, have I mentioned how much I love your hair?"

Allison smiled politely.

"How long have you two been together?" Allison asked Louisa and Jeremy.

Jeremy stammered for an answer, but Louisa had one ready. "Only a few weeks," she said. "We've been in loads of classes together over the years, and...something just happened. We just felt this..." She interlocked her fingers, and it made Rafe's heart clench up.

"Connection," Eamonn said, his voice thick. He cut his eyes at Rafe.

"Right!" Louisa cocked her head at Heath. "Is something the matter?"

"Nothing at all," Heath said.

"Can we please fucking stop this?" Rafe said, making a scene at his own table but too jumbled up with his own shit to care. "How many times are you two going to go around the carousel? Heath, she's jerking you around. No matter what Louisa does to you and no matter how mad she makes you, you're still waiting for her like some fucking puppy." Rafe cut his eyes back to Eamonn.

"Fuck you, Rafe!" Louisa said.

"Fuck you right back!"

"He's right." Heath eased up, and something like clarity seemed to come over him. "I reckon that you and I never worked. We never did. It's time that I bugger off and get over you for good. If you're with someone who makes you happy, then I'm happy for you."

Louisa didn't say anything, but an eternity seemed to flash on her face.

"That's proper of you, mate," Jeremy said. He tried to spoon feed her stuffing, but she declined.

Lots of silverware clanging against plates filled the silence for the rest of the night. It was awkward. It was uncomfortable. It was Thanksgiving.

EAMONN

Once the meal was over, Heath went to Apothecary, Louisa went back to Jeremy's dorm presumably, Rafe cleaned up in the kitchen, and Eamonn returned the extra table and chairs to the neighboring flat.

When he was done, he offered to help Rafe clean up, but he firmly declined. Eamonn knew not to push. Back in his room, he lay on his bed and tried watching TV to relax him, but it didn't help. He couldn't get comfortable.

"Fuck." Eamonn sat up. He rubbed his hands wildly through his hair. Moments later, he knocked on Rafe's bedroom door. Rafe opened up, and for a second, he wished the guy would jump into his arms, and all the drama of before would be wiped from their memories.

"That was a great meal. You should be proud of yourself."

"Thanks," Rafe said. He sat in his desk chair, feet on his desk, scrolling through an article on his phone.

Eamonn shut the door. He spotted a bottle of aspirin on his nightstand, presumably for the hangover he would have tomorrow. "Do you need a glass of water?"

He pointed to one already on his desk.

"Rafe, I'm sorry about earlier. I couldn't just walk away as the shit got knocked out of him."

"I know. You did the right thing."

"There is nothing between me and Nathan."

"I know, and I realized it's not Nathan that I'm upset about."

Eamonn sat on the edge of the bed. His knees were so close to Rafe, but he could feel the distance widening.

"Do you want me to stay?" Rafe asked. His eyes were heavy and red like he'd been thinking about this for a while. "Because I thought you were excited about the prospect of me extending, but now...I don't know."

Eamonn didn't know how to answer. He wanted to be with Rafe and didn't want to lose him, but he couldn't ask this of him.

"Do you want to stay?" Eamonn asked.

"That's not an answer. I asked you first."

Eamonn had to smile at this game of chicken.

"Can we please both be completely honest with each other?" Eamonn asked. He took a deep breath. Honesty scared the shit out of him. "I do. I don't want this to end. I fucking care about you so much, but I don't want you to sacrifice your life and your future back in America, because then you'll just wind up resenting me."

"No, I wouldn't."

"We don't have snow and dance-a-thons and dining halls, and if you stay here, you might not get into that BISHoP program."

"It's just BISHoP. The P stands for program."

Eamonn cocked his head at Rafe. Now was not the time for nitpicking.

"I do miss dining hall food," Rafe admitted.

"It's probably better than the slop they serve at the first-year halls here."

"I doubt that. The company that supplies our dining halls also supplies food for prisons. I might just have low standards."

Eamonn loved being able to joke with Rafe, even now. They had a comfort level with each other that Eamonn didn't have with past boyfriends.

"Now it's your turn." Eamonn rubbed Rafe's hand with his thumb. "Do you want to stay at Stroude?"

"Yes! I want to travel and get the full abroad experience and..." Rafe dragged his fingers through his hair. The jury in his mind seemed to be arguing this out.

"Rafe."

"You. I want to be with you, Eamonn. What we have, I've been looking for since I was thirteen. I'm falling in love with you."

Eamonn squeezed his hand. "Me, too."

A tear spilled down Rafe's cheek. Eamonn's jaw tightened with emotion.

"I would be staying for you." Rafe nodded with this realization. "Fuck. I can see how that would put some undue pressure on you." He wiped the tears off his face. "But maybe it could work."

"That's a big maybe."

"Isn't it worth trying?"

Was it? That was why Eamonn liked enjoying the present rather than thinking about the future. The present had answers. He didn't have to wonder what would happen at the end of the school year. He didn't have to wonder if Rafe would go cold on him unexpectedly and leave his heart in pieces.

Rafe's eyes told him all he needed to know. They were setting themselves up for disaster if they tried to make this work. Things like this never worked.

"I'll email my advisor," Rafe said, his voice hollow.

Eamonn brought Rafe's hand up to his mouth and kissed his knuckles, the same knuckles that had punched into his palm on the football pitch, back when Rafe was just the Token Yank and nothing more.

CHAPTER 28

EAMONN

December came and finals descended upon Stroude. A week after interviewing, Eamonn had gotten word from human resources that he'd been selected for the management trainee program. She had more enthusiasm on the phone than Eamonn. His mom got choked up, which made it all worth it. He did his best to sound when he told her, but it was hard to be jazzed about anything knowing that the Yank across the hall was all packed up and ready to leave forever.

Their breakup was assumed and went unspoken. When Eamonn walked by Rafe's room and saw bare walls or overheard Rafe bequeathing Louisa his wooden spoon (the two had apparently made up), he got the idea. They hadn't had sex or slept with each other since their talk on Thanksgiving. They were cordial, friendly even, but Rafe had evidently mastered that British skill of properly holding in one's feelings.

He spent his final week of the term taking exams and writing up final papers. One more semester, and he would be done with this completely, ready to become a manager and join the real world.

Eamonn had avoided Apothecary during this time, too, for he didn't want to bump into Rafe at work. After his final class of the term, he stumbled over to Grey's, the unfettered, dive-ish bar on the opposite side of campus. It was mostly frequented by rugby and football players, who itched for a fight after a certain number of pints.

He wasn't the only one with this idea. Louisa sat alone at the bar, halfway through something that seemed much stronger than a Midori sour.

"Is this seat taken?" He pointed to the stool next to her. She signaled that it was all his.

"I'll have another," she called to the bartender.

"What is that?" Eamonn asked of her now-empty glass.

"Vodka with a splash of soda."

"Celebrating the end of the term?"

She cocked an eyebrow. Eamonn ordered the same drink. They toasted their glasses. He winced at the pure taste of vodka. That was why he stuck to beer. Louisa could always drink him under the table.

"So how's Jeremy?"

"Jeremy is no more." She swirled the straw in her glass.

"I'm sorry to hear that."

"Don't be. I cut him loose. It was never anything."

Eamonn figured that since he magically appeared at Thanksgiving dinner, and he hadn't seen Jeremy around the dormitory since.

"It's because Heath had the audacity to shag that American twat. Those damn Yanks are ruining our lives," she said.

"She didn't mean anything to him. *She* would even tell you that."

"And now I mean nothing to Heath." Louisa downed

about half her drink, and she would've chugged the rest had Eamonn not stopped her.

"I don't get it, Louisa. He's been bloody in love with you this whole time. You knew that, and you still treated him like rubbish." Eamonn would joke about the Heath and Louisa drama, but he knew how much it tortured his best mate. "You haven't been fair to him. Why did you act like that?"

"Not all of us are made for relationships." She elbowed him. "Committing to someone is scary. It's like a real fucking decision. And Heath was always just...there. Bugger. I didn't know what I wanted."

"Congratulations. Now you do."

They both drank. This time, the vodka went down much smoother.

———

HE AND LOUISA returned to Sweeney Hall. Seeing Rafe's door completely bare – no name plate, no signs, no notes tacked to the small corkboard – shot a small dose of pain to Eamonn's heart.

"Do you smell that?" Louisa asked. The savory smells of a dinner explosion spread throughout the flat. "I reckon drinking heightens all my other senses."

He followed her into the kitchen. It really was a dinner explosion. Plates of ravioli and bowls of soup covered the entire table. Heath sat at the head with a napkin tucked into his collar.

"Are you going for a world eating record, mate?" Eamonn asked him.

Rafe brought a saucepan of more ravioli to the table. "I'm making one final dinner. Oh, it's the last supper!"

"I don't think Jesus munched on Asda-brand ravioli," Heath said. He acknowledged Louisa with a nod and nothing else.

"I have all this food that I can't bring with me on the plane tomorrow, and rather than have it go to waste, I decided to cook it all. One last flat feast."

Eamonn didn't like hearing about Rafe's trip home, but the aroma of the banquet before him overpowered those thoughts. He wasn't sure if he was welcome here. He and Rafe were on very uncertain ground.

"So when is your flight?" Louisa asked, taking a seat.

"Seven-thirty in the morning. And the van from my study abroad program is picking me up at four to make sure I get checked in on time."

"Four?" Heath checked the clock. "So you're going to sleep in a half-hour then?"

"Not quite." Rafe sat at the table and poured ravioli onto his plate. "I'm going to be exhausted no matter what, so I'm going to make myself stay up. I can sleep on the plane."

Eamonn backed away to the swinging door. "Well, I'll leave you to it."

"Here." Rafe pointed to the fourth chair. "We can't all eat this by ourselves."

He checked Rafe's expression to see if it was genuine.

"There would be no dinner without you, Eamonn. I would be broke and eating scraps from the campus café. I wouldn't know what Asda is or how to use an oven." Rafe looked him square in the eye, and it froze Eamonn in place. "Thank you for everything."

"Are you sure?" Eamonn asked.

"Yes. It's my last night here. I don't want it mired in drama."

Eamonn gave him a nod filled with more than Rafe

could ever know. He took the empty seat. Louisa passed him a plate.

———

RAFE COULDN'T LEAVE Stroude without one final night at Apothecary. Eamonn led the way and kicked a bunch of wankers out of their usual booth.

"You didn't have to do that," Rafe said.

"Oh yes I fucking did. This is a special night," Eamonn said, trying not to get mushy. He was trying to enjoy this night without mentally counting down the hours until Rafe's departure.

Alfie came by and gave Rafe a free shot as a proper send-off. "I'm going to miss your smiling face around here. I'll probably never find a runner who was as excited about being a runner as you."

"Don't be so sure, Alfie."

"Since we're friends of Rafe, we get free drinks for the rest of the year, right?" Heath asked.

"Keep dreaming. I only give free drinks when somebody dies."

"Thank you for everything," Rafe said. He hugged Alfie, who didn't expect it, but seemed to warm to it quickly. How could anyone resist a Rafe hug? It was pure warmth, towels fresh out of the dryer.

A larger crowd shoved against the bar. Heath and Eamonn did their best to make inroads to the front. Heath nudged his elbow.

"Y'alright?"

"Tell me, how's the air quality up there? Are you suffering from oxygen deprivation?"

Heath shoved him, and Eamonn shoved back. He got

sad thinking that this was their last night together, until he remembered that Heath wasn't going anywhere. At least he would have Heath. Until the spring. Then they would all be going their separate directions. Eamonn's path led directly to a cubicle, a box inside a company that makes boxes.

"How are you doing?" Heath asked. He tipped his head behind them, at their table.

Eamonn shrugged. "I'm trying not to think about it. Let's just enjoy this night."

"Hey!" Rafe came up behind them. "This line is taking forever."

"Don't blame us!" Eamonn said.

"You know, this whole term, you two have insisted that you go up to get the first round. Each and every time. You forget that your Token Yank used to be gainfully employed at Apothecary and is friends with all the staff." Rafe raised his hand and waved at the bartender. The bartender smiled and waved them forward. "Which means we didn't have to wait in this bloody line."

Rafe cut between kids and marched up to the bar. Eamonn and Heath looked at each other stunned. Rafe shook his head and laughed.

"You stupid cunts," he said.

They spent the rest of the night drinking and regaling each other with stories and memories. One story led into another into another, and the fuzzy static of nonstop laughter emanated from their table. It was a perfect night where the group's chemistry fired on all cylinders, one that washed away all of the preceding drama of the term.

"I love that I now know what the hell you're all talking about!" Rafe exclaimed. He drank his Midori sour. It didn't seem to bother him anymore that Nathan had started the Midori trend.

Eamonn didn't say much. He tried to savor these final hours, as this would probably be the last time he and Rafe ever saw each other.

But he wasn't going to let a thought like that ruin this night.

"Another round?"

———

It was one of those nights where if you were a human being, you had no choice but to look up and cherish the beauty of this wondrous galaxy. Eamonn tried to hold onto this night as hard as he could. Rafe was leaving, really leaving, in six hours. But he promised himself he wouldn't get down about it until after he was gone. He wasn't going to waste the final hours they had left together.

They made their way down the sloping hill to Sweeney Hall.

"I don't need your help," Rafe said. He held his arm out for balance. "I've gone down this hill plenty of times by myself, many times after working a shift at the bar. The only reason I'm holding my arms out is just to be safe."

"And because you're pissed," Heath said.

"Oh Heath. Shut it!" Louisa said. She also hand her arms out, though in her defense, she was wearing heels.

"Not true. I am a little buzzed, but I'm mostly just tired from doing all my last minute, final packing."

"All that folding and zipping up suitcases is truly enervating work, Heath," Eamonn said. "When I went to the loo and had to unzip and rezip my trousers, I nearly passed out from exhaustion."

"Bugger off!" Rafe said. "It rained this morning, so it's a little slippery."

"Do you need a hand?" Eamonn asked. He couldn't resist.

"I do not."

"Louisa?" Eamonn extended a hand to her.

"I don't need help."

"Are you sure? You're wobbling."

"She said she doesn't need—shit!" Heath went down on his arse.

"Timber!" Eamonn yelled. Heath flipped him the bird. "Did you crack the pavement? That was like watching a building get demolished."

Eamonn was going to help his mate up, but Louisa beat him to it. She helped lift him back up, and she didn't stop holding his hand.

"I got you," she said.

They exchanged a look that neither Eamonn nor Rafe could decipher, one of those telepathic gazes built on the unique language of every relationship.

They walked down to the hall hand-in-hand, leaving Eamonn and Rafe in their wake.

Eamonn didn't think of putting his arm around Rafe's waist. It was completely a subconscious choice, and it felt like a subconscious choice that made Rafe lean into him.

"Fine," Rafe said. "Once more for old times sake."

A pang of sadness managed to squeak by and kick him in the stones. Eamonn held him close and smelled the mix of shampoo and manly scent of his hair. His hand warmed to the heat of Rafe's skin.

Rafe wrapped his arm around Eamonn's neck for balance. He rested his clean-shaven cheek against Eamonn's scruff. It was like they were slow dancing down this slope with the big moon shining down on them.

"I got you," Eamonn said. Only this time, he was going to have to let go.

Eamonn walked Rafe to his door. He thought he saw Heath go back to Louisa's room, but he wasn't sure and he didn't care because the only person that mattered at this second was standing in front of him.

"Are you all packed?" Eamonn asked.

Rafe opened the door. A suitcase stuffed to the brim sat on the floor by his bed. There were no signs of Rafe here. No posters or papers or notebooks. It amazed Eamonn how fast things could change. Just a few weeks ago, this room was bursting with life. Then just like that, it was bare, stripped of a soul.

It was the cold reality check Eamonn didn't want. Rafe was going to be gone for good, and they were never going to see each other again. Maybe they would like each other's pictures on Instagram and maybe Eamonn would send Rafe a text when he went to Asda, but it wouldn't be the same. They would be going through the motions of keeping in touch and ignoring the fire that once roared between them.

"Eamonn..." Rafe held his hand.

Eamonn was doing everything in his power not to cry, and it seemed Rafe was doing the same. They were each fortresses of stoicism.

"*It's been totally awesome, dude,*" Eamonn said one more time in his surfer accent.

"Yeah. I..." Rafe pursed his lips together in a tight dam of a smile.

"Me, too, Rafe. Me, too."

"I really wish there wasn't a fucking ocean between us."

"How long until the continental shift happens again?"

Rafe thought for a second. "A few billion years."

"I'm a patient fellow."

"Well, I might be busy then."

"Wanker." Eamonn gave him a friendly punch in the chest. Rafe caught his fist and didn't let go. A fire burned in his eyes.

Eamonn kicked the door shut before Rafe pulled him into an epic kiss.

Rafe

Rafe had pre-planned his outfit for the flight home. It was the same button-down shirt and jeans he'd worn on his flight over to England. He considered it a thoughtful bookend to his journey, and he wondered if his parents would notice.

He threw said pre-planned outfit off his bed and across the room. He lay down and Eamonn got on top of him. Rafe gladly opened his mouth for Eamonn's tongue to enter. They kissed and rolled around on the bed in a type of emotional wrestling match. They were in a cloud of sweat and tears and lust and need. All that existed was this moment, and Rafe tried to hold onto it like a firefly in his hand.

Eamonn's hot breath filled up his mouth. He wrapped him in a cocoon of his arms, strong and sinewy.

Shirts came off, then pants, then underwear. Rafe's fingers grazed down Eamonn's cut chest and abs, reading them like a book in Braille. Rafe grasped at any and all parts of Eamonn, anything he could hold onto and commit to memory.

Rafe spread his legs, letting Eamonn rest between them. His thick cock branded his inner thigh. Rafe's erection was doing the same thing back.

"Tell me what you want to do to me."

"I want to bloody devour you." The rasp in his voice gave it extra edge. He kept stroking Rafe's hair, drilling holes with his eyes.

Rafe fetched his bottle of lube and a condom from his toiletries bag, which was of course buried at the bottom of the suitcase. He didn't care if his clothes got wrinkled. He'd deal with that back in America.

He stood at the edge of the bed. "Actually, there's something I want to do."

Eamonn cocked an eyebrow.

"I want to...well, rim you."

Eamonn's mouth perked up in the hottest smile, which was such a relief to Rafe.

"You are so cheeky."

He flipped onto his stomach and arched his back. Rafe had long admired Eamonn's ass. He's watched it walk away from him in the bathroom or get covered with boxer-briefs when Eamonn got dressed. Now it was in front of him in its smooth, muscular glory. Rafe got on the bed and spread Eamonn apart, finding his pink hole. He pressed his tongue against the opening.

"Fuck. Eat that fucking ass, mate." Even on all fours, Eamonn still had control of the situation.

Rafe rimmed Eamonn, feeling those firm cheeks in his hand and the taste of musk and sweat in his mouth. Eamonn moaned his approval. His balls and cock hung heavy just below. Rafe licked those, too.

"That's right. Tongue those balls."

Rafe pushed through the ring of muscle and played with his tight hole. With a free hand, he stroked Eamonn's hard cock. Eamonn let out a string of expletives, all positive.

"You taste fucking amazing," Rafe said.

Eamonn sat up and turned around, putting his cock

right in Rafe's face. Rafe was so horned up from the rimming that right away, he took Eamonn to his base. He gagged, and Eamonn had to pull out after a second, but it was worth it.

"Take that prick," Eamonn commanded with a lusty drawl.

Rafe sucked and stroked his uncut cock, remembering their lessons. Eamonn lightly threaded his fingers through his hair, knowing exactly how much pressure to give. They both felt a sense of time evaporating and need desperately pulling them together. The time for foreplay was over. He deep-throated Eamonn one last time and savored the final taste of his dick filling up his mouth.

He lay on the bed, and Rafe straddled him. His thick cock rubbed against Rafe's hole. Rafe ran his hands over his chest. Rafe felt some power being on top, king of the mountain.

Eamonn plunged two lubed-up fingers inside him.

"Eamonn," Rafe said, trying to mask the want and hurt strangling his throat as the Brit entered him.

"No tears."

They made love that night in a fever dream of longing and fear. Eamonn didn't let Rafe go, not even when he fucked him. He grabbed his thighs, then sat up and hugged him close. His arms were bungee cords around Rafe, holding him tight against his sweaty chest as he thrust into his opening. Eamonn's hair fell in his eyes, and he had this intense, almost wounded look etched in his face.

"Fuck me harder," Rafe said. He wanted Eamonn deep inside him, filling him up completely, digging his hard fingers into his back.

Eamonn fucked the life out of Rafe, pounding his ass

and giving him the cock he so badly wanted. He rested his forehead against Rafe's.

"Rafe." He thought it was sweat that glistened on Eamonn's face, but it was salty tears.

He threw Rafe on his back and hovered over him. Their slicked-up chests slid over one another. He didn't look away from Rafe. His stare was a tractor beam Rafe couldn't wiggle free from.

Rafe knew when Eamonn was coming. He knew the shocks and shifts of his body tensing up, of the pained moans he emitted. Rafe wasn't far behind, grunting as his balls drew up, ready for release.

Eamonn interlocked his fingers with Rafe's as they came. *Connected.*

———

AFTER THEY SHOWERED TOGETHER one final time, they spent the rest of the night, or rather early morning, watching old episodes of *The I.T. Crowd* on Eamonn's bed, since his monitor was still set up. Just as Rafe was about to fall asleep in Eamonn's arms, his phone alarm went off.

Time's up.

"It's four already?" Eamonn asked.

"Unfortunately."

Rafe shrugged. What was he supposed to say in this moment? *I'll see ya?* Nope, he wouldn't. *See you around?* Not that either. *Have a great Christmas and New Year's?* Who gave a fuck about those holidays right now when Rafe's heart was getting squashed?

The best goodbye was not saying goodbye at all.

"Why don't you come with me to the airport? We can at

least have a little bit more time in the van together," Rafe
said.

"All right."

Rafe thought he'd be more into the idea.

"I'm going to get my stuff together and brush my teeth.
I'll meet you in the hallway in a few minutes."

Eamonn gave him a thumbs up.

He raced back to his room and did a thorough, final
search of his dorm room. He left no stone unturned in his
quest to find anything he forgot to pack. Under his desk, by
the power outlet, was a Stonehenge brochure he'd gotten on
their excursion. He rubbed it between his fingers and stored
it in his backpack.

Rafe saw the van drive up outside his dorm. He waved to
the driver and gave the "one minute" signal. He recognized
him as Joseph from the original drive to Stroude. That
seemed like five million years ago. Five million Rafes ago.

"Eamonn, you ready?" he whispered. Rafe tapped lightly
at his door so as not to wake his flatmates. "Eamonn? Don't
tell me you fell asleep."

He was not asleep. Nor was he dressed or wearing shoes.

"The van's here."

"I'm...I don't think I'm going to go with you." Eamonn's
eyes were all bloodshot, his skin paler than usual. "I can't."

"Oh."

"We should just say goodbye here."

Rafe went in for a kiss, but Eamonn gave him a tight hug
instead.

"Get home safe."

"We'll definitely keep in touch. Email. Skype for sure. I
want to hear that British accent again."

Eamonn gave what could barely be considered a nod.

"Maybe this doesn't have to end. We live in a global

village. We can try to do long distance. Lots of people do it. And with technology, it's so easy. I can come back for the summer, or you can come to America after you graduate. You could telecommute for your uncle's company." Rafe grasped at any rope he could find. He couldn't let this be the end. "Tonight was so great. We can make this work."

He thought his suggestions would be romantic, but said aloud, without Eamonn nodding his head in agreement, they sounded chock full of desperation.

Eamonn shook his head no, which might as well been one of his fists to Rafe's face. "We both know that's not going to happen," he croaked out.

Rafe's phone rang. "Hello?"

"Are you coming down?" Joseph asked. "I have to pick up other kids and get you to Heathrow on time."

"I'll be right down." Rafe hung up.

This was it.

"Okay, then." Rafe gave Eamonn one final hug, and Eamonn pulled him close for a second before releasing.

Rafe wheeled his luggage to the door and stopped. "Eamonn." He figured out his goodbye. "You changed my life, and I love you."

Eamonn's hand gripped his doorknob. He was trying so hard to be stoic that his face might break. "Cheers, mate."

His voice cracked at *mate*, and before he could say anything else, Eamonn went into his room and shut the door. The relationship, or whatever this was, ended as quickly as it began. *Just like that*, Rafe thought.

Outside, the sky was as black as it'd been earlier this evening, but without the mystique. The moon continued to shine, but now it was a spotlight on a solitary Rafe.

"Ready to go?" Joseph asked once they loaded up his luggage.

"Yeah."

Joseph looked at him through the rearview mirror. "I didn't get a chance to thank you, mate. It worked!"

"What?" Rafe asked, mostly out of it.

"Your plan for Janine. The heart made of candles and roses outside her balcony. We're about to celebrate our three-month anniversary." He was downright giddy for this ungodly hour.

"That's great."

"You told me to go big, and it worked."

At last it works for someone.

The engine roared to life, and they drove away. Rafe peered out the back window once more at Sweeney Hall. His eyes traveled up to his floor. His old floor now. Through his tears, he thought he saw someone watching him from the kitchen window, though it may have been wishful thinking.

CHAPTER 29

R<small>AFE</small>

"So, how was England?" his dad asked in the car ride home from the airport.

What a question.

Rafe rested his head against the window, drained from the long flight and his general heartbreak. His body was on a five-second delay, weighed down by sandbags of exhaustion.

His mom handed him a bagel from Dunkin Donuts. "Welcome home!"

He stared at the bagel as if it were an alien. He had zero appetite, and he wouldn't tell his parents that he declined both meals offered on his flight.

"I'll bet it was nice to see the American flag and regular signs once you got off." She was way too perky for first thing in the morning.

"Yeah."

"You look exhausted," she said. "Did you sleep on the flight?"

"How was the flight? Were you in a window or aisle seat?"

"And what kind of food did they serve? You never get meals on airplanes anymore, but I think it's different for international flights. They had to at least have given you breakfast and a snack."

"I didn't really get much sleep on the plane," Rafe said. Every time he tried to shut his eyes, he kept seeing montages from his time at Stroude. Flashes of hanging out at Apothecary and cooking dinner in his flat and waking up next to Eamonn. Hearing Eamonn say "cheers, mate" and shut the door. The montages never ended on a high note. His time abroad felt like he had entered a new dimension. Alice went down the rabbit hole and nobody would believe her tales.

"How does the jetlag hit you coming back?" his dad wondered aloud. "You should probably be more awake since it's afternoon for you."

"But then he's going to be more tired tonight because it will feel like midnight at dinnertime."

"He should probably fight to stay up until his regular bedtime."

"Can you guys stop talking about me like I'm not even here?" Rafe's voice had a cat-like scratchiness in his throat. "It's kind of rude."

"We didn't know if you were sleeping back there," his dad said.

"Well, I'm not. I'll try my best to stay up until tonight." Rafe was afraid of going to sleep. He didn't want any more montages and their down endings.

"Rafe, are you all right?" his mom asked him through the rearview mirror.

Y'alright?

Rafe felt a tear forming just above his cheek.

"He's just," his dad started before looking into the rearview mirror. "You're just tired, right?"

He glanced out the window. They were driving on the right side of the road. He saw all the familiar green highway markers, all the familiar billboards with their familiar stores and prices listed in their familiar dollar signs. It was good ole Virginia. No more adventure here.

"Yeah."

"Was it hard to say goodbye?" his dad asked, and he was not referring to the campus. It took Rafe by surprise.

"It was."

His mom turned around in her seat, her face full of motherly concern. "Are you two going to keep in touch? It's so easy nowadays!"

Keeping in touching sounded so trifling for him and Eamonn, as if they'd met at a networking event. And Eamonn had already given him an answer. A door in his face. No need dragging out the slow death of their relationship. All those times he'd been the Baxter or his grand romantic gestures failed, he had bounced back. Because it wasn't serious. It wasn't deep. He had given it the old college try and nothing more. But with Eamonn, he was invested. He had given himself completely and came up short. Being heartbroken was so much worse than being rejected. His heart wasn't even broken. It had been ripped apart, and he could feel every tear.

As he stared out the window, he thought that maybe there was a still of version of himself back there in England, one who stood on his own two feet. And they were connected.

"I was thinking about it, and when I go back to school,

I'm going to get a part-time job. Maybe as a waiter or runner or something."

"Rafe, I wouldn't do that. I mean, how many hours are you talking about? You don't want it to interfere with your course load." His dad pinched his face and seesawed his head, and usually, Rafe would heed that warning. His father always knew best. But not this time. He was tired of following his parents' good ideas.

"I'll be fine."

"Working at a restaurant, you'll be exhausted from being on your feet. You'll have to work at all hours, and you won't even come home with that much," his mom said.

"I don't need your permission to get a job," Rafe said with an eerie calm. His mom was surprised at his reaction, and he hoped that maybe for the first time, she saw her son as a man. "Also, I'm going to apply for my own credit card. It's about time I have one that's solely mine. To build up credit."

"Oh, okay," his mom said.

His dad gave a small smile in the mirror. "We're proud of you, Rafe."

"You're growing up!"

He realized that his parents, despite being overprotective, always meant well. He was grateful to have them, grateful that they loved him unconditionally. He didn't realize that he had missed them until he was home. "I love you guys."

His dad reached behind him and squeezed Rafe's knee. "Love you more."

EAMONN

Eamonn chundered.

He barely got "Cheers, mate" out before rushing into his room and hurling into the bloody toilet. The pain and hurt barreled through him and had to get out.

The next day, there was no vomiting, but his body still felt like a bag of shite. He packed up for winter holiday and tried not to think about Rafe.

You did the right thing cutting it off. This was never going to work.

He shoved his clothes into his bag extra hard, not caring if they came out stretched or wrinkled. Doing the right thing wasn't easy. Holy fuck, was it not easy. It was for the best that he put a firm end on their relationship in the flat. The truth was Eamonn couldn't go with Rafe to Heathrow. He couldn't bear seeing another man he loved get on another airplane.

He felt sick all over again. Back to the loo he went.

Doing the right thing was bollocks.

THE FEELING PERSISTED THROUGHOUT HOLIDAY. Eamonn attended the box company's office Christmas party, and he couldn't even get in the festive mood despite the abundance of free food and alcohol. His future co-workers treated him like a full part of the team. They summoned him to the Xerox room to take shots. His two team leaders were in their forties, but they downed those shots like it was one quid drinks night at Apothecary. He liked all of his future co-workers. None of them took what they did too seriously. "At the end of the day, we're just making boxes," his boss had told him between shots.

Eamonn went shot for shot with his co-workers, but his heart just wasn't in it. Uncle George came up behind him and swung an arm around his shoulders. They clinked glasses.

"Hiya. Having a good time?" Uncle George asked.

"Yeah. It's a great party."

"After a year of full-time work, you'll come to truly appreciate a party like this." Uncle George led him to where his cubicle would be. It had been decorated with red and green streamers like the rest of them. "I have big plans for you here. You have a very bright future ahead."

Eamonn smiled and nodded, appreciative of what his uncle was saying, but unable to muster any genuine excitement.

Uncle George slapped him on the back. "You seem so serious! Loosen up. You're at a party!"

"I guess I just need more to drink."

"Don't go overboard. These will be your co-workers and you still have to work with them." His uncle left him to join some of the higher-ups for a cocktail.

Eamonn looked out at the party, wishing he could feel an iota of the merriment that surrounded him.

He left a few minutes later and met up with Heath at a pub in Guildford, not too far from his mum's house. He instantly felt a bit better when that gangly Eiffel Tower of a man sat down next to him.

"Happy Christmas," Heath said.

They ordered drinks, though Eamonn also asked for a glass of water. He didn't feel like getting drunk. He wanted to be somewhat present.

Eamonn told him about the Christmas party.

"Sounds fun!"

Eamonn shrugged. "Wasn't my scene."

"Well, it will be."

"It's a good place to work, but…it's all right." Eamonn didn't even feel like talking about it. "It's a job."

Heath held up his glass, and they clinked to something. Eamonn couldn't remember. "I got offered a job at the Tate working in their business affairs department. I'll be surrounded by great works at the office."

"Cheers, mate!" Eamonn saluted him with his drink.

"Can't believe we're all moving on. Even Louisa is scheduling job interviews for January."

Eamonn cocked an eyebrow. "Back on, then?"

Heath blushed. It was amazing how goofy his face could look when he was smitten. "I think this time it's going to stick. That night when I fell, we went back to her room and just talked the whole night, about everything. We've been doing loads of talking about what went wrong in the past. It feels different now."

"Different is good."

"And if it all blows up in my face, you can happily tell me you were right."

He clapped his tall friend on the shoulder, while a pang of jealousy hit his stomach. Heath's good news was just a dash of salt on an open wound.

"That's really great, mate," Eamonn said. He took a long sip of his drink and happily let the alcohol burn his chest. "Really great."

Heath stared at him for a long second, then shook his head. "What?"

"You look like complete shit," Heath said.

"Bugger off. I just came from a party filled with free top shelf liquor and food."

"That's not what I mean."

"What? Is there a stain on my shirt or something?"

Heath rolled his eyes. "Don't take this the wrong way, but you are a complete sodding cunt of an idiot."

"What is the right way to take that?"

"I can't stand looking at you."

"Fuck you." Eamonn stood up and pushed Heath. Heath stumbled off his bar stool. He came back at Eamonn and shoved him hard with his tree limb arms. Eamonn hit a chair on his way to the floor.

Heath stood over him. "You hate your new job. You don't want to work there. Yet you're just going to give up and take the safe route instead actually trying for something great."

Eamonn jumped up. He was never one to give up in a fight, not when his opponent was spewing lies about him. He charged at Heath, and they both fell backwards into another table and chairs. Salt and pepper shakers shattered on the floor.

"You don't know a bloody thing about me!" Eamonn said.

"Right. Cause I've only known you for the past three years and roomed with you. You're a complete stranger!"

They rolled around on the floor. Eamonn kept pushing Heath off him, but his friend wouldn't let go.

"*I'm* supposed to be the puff here!"

"I can't take watching you act like a prize fucking idiot." Heath sneezed. He let go of Eamonn to cover another one.

Eamonn was going to say something, but sneezed also. The pepper was all over the floor, and they'd rolled around in it.

"So what if I want a job that allows me to support myself and *achoo* help out my mum and sisters?"

"There are loads of jobs that do that, ones you could like. Rafe redid your C.V. and looked for jobs for you, but you did nothing. *Achoo!* And I don't think your family wants you being miserable on their behalf. You're not a martyr. So get off your cross and shove it up your *achoo!*"

Heath elbowed Eamonn in the stomach. He sank to the floor and crouched into a fetal position. Heath went to stand up, but Eamonn grabbed his foot and dragged him back down.

"Oy!" The bartender swatted at them with his broom until they separated.

Eamonn punched Heath in the back, the only place where his fist could connect.

"You punched me in the fucking kidney, you twat!"

"You fucking deserved it!"

Pub patrons pulled the friends apart. Heath glared at Eamonn so sharply it could cut glass. Heath was not one to get angry, and never at Eamonn.

"What the hell has gotten into you?" Eamonn asked.

"I can't stand watching your life turn to day-old shit. Rafe was the best thing that ever happened to you, and you just let him go!"

"I didn't let him go! He left. He was always going to leave." Eamonn tried to squirm free. Another patron came over to restrain him.

"Rafe busted his arse to find a way to stay in England. He wanted to stay for *you* because for some reason, he fucking cares about you and believes you're capable of more than settling for a future you don't want and never wanted. And what did you do? Nothing! You just sat back, too scared to make a real effort, because at least this way, you could blame someone else."

"What was I supposed to do?"

"There are loads of American companies that sponsor employee visas. Maybe if you'd come to one of those job fairs with me, you would know that."

"I can't do that."

"Why?" Heath held up his hand before Eamonn could remind him that he had a fucking family he couldn't just abandon. "And don't use your family as an excuse."

"It's not an excuse." Eamonn kicked pepper at Heath's shoes. "I'm not going to walk out on them like my dad did."

"This is not the same thing! But as long as it keeps you from having to make a fucking choice, you're happy to use it as an excuse."

Heath signaled for the patrons to let him go, that he was no longer a threat. They did the same for Eamonn. Heath grabbed his jacket from the coat rack.

"You're just walking away?" Eamonn asked, itching for another fight.

Heath got right in his face, and his intensity hit Eamonn at his core. "I've *never* seen you so happy as you were with Rafe. Fuck, it was like I got my old mate back. He *made* you come alive, and you just gave that all up. You didn't try to hold onto it."

"The last time I tried, I got my heart broken."

"Yeah, it's a good thing you didn't try this time around. You *definitely* didn't get your heart broken." Heath put on his jacket and threw a few extra quid on the bar. "Happy Christmas."

CHAPTER 30

RAFE

Rafe went back to Browerton a few days before winter quarter started up. He wanted to get into campus mode. Christmas with his parents had been a nice time, but he was ready to be on his own again, ready to be his working, independent self here in America.

He walked through the Browerton campus, and it was the same buildings and same pathways. Nothing had changed except for that one new residence hall they'd finished building, but it still felt different. Or maybe he was the one who was different.

Rafe signed up for winter quarter classes and got all of his textbooks. His friend Coop was renting an apartment off campus sophomore year, and Rafe crashed with him a few days. He contacted local businesses about finding a part-time job. This cupcake place called Dollop said they might have an opening and to contact them again in mid-January. He tried to put in an application at the one gay bar in town, Cherry Stem, but the owner said he didn't like to hire people under twenty-one because of liability issues. Even though it was legal, which Rafe reminded him of, he'd had a bad experience with a runner drinking out of customers' glasses.

"It was like the first second these kids get anywhere near liquor, they lose their minds!" the owner said. "I think they need to lower the drinking age to eighteen. This will make kids less prone to binge drinking and better at handling their alcohol. It's eighteen in England, and everyone there can hold their liquor. Well, you should know."

Rafe did. The memories of his time at Stroude glowed in his mind, but like the brightest ray of sunshine, they were followed by a dark cloud. There was one Brit in particular he couldn't get out of his mind. He hoped it would get easier, and he hoped that a new year at Browerton older and wiser would snap him out of this funk.

On New Year's Eve, Coop took Rafe to a house party a few blocks away. It was a bitterly cold night, the kind of cold England never got.

"When does Matty get into town?" Rafe asked.

"Sunday night. He likes to maximize family time, and it's still eighty degrees in Dallas. I can understand him not wanting to come back so soon," Coop said of his boyfriend.

The party took place in an old house that had been rented out entirely to college students. The windows glowed with festivities indoors. A wall of steam hit them when they entered. Coop whipped off his sweater. He took any opportunity to walk around in a tank top. Though if Rafe was that jacked, he'd probably do the same.

"What do you want to drink?" Coop asked him. Since he had the muscles, he would push through to the bar—or rather, the kitchen table that housed all the alcohol.

"Do they have Midori Sours?" Rafe asked with a nostalgia-tinged smile. Could one have nostalgia for something that happened only a few weeks ago?

"What are those?"

"Or maybe a Snakebite."

"I think it's just the usual. Cheap beer and jungle juice."

"Cheap beer then."

Coop maneuvered his way into the mishmash of thirsty coeds. Rafe watched him go, almost expecting to see Heath's head poking out from above the crowd.

Kids clumped together in nearly every room. Somebody's grandmother's furniture decorated the living room. It could've been a set piece for a period play were it not for the huge flatscreen TV hanging on the wall. Times Square went nuts on screen, with the evening's hosts narrating from a booth high above the masses.

Do they have the ball drop in England? It was already the new year there. People were probably hard at work on their resolutions and turning over new leaves. Maybe Eamonn was at a pub with Heath and Louisa. Or maybe he was babysitting his sisters, which he would claim he was forced to do even though he secretly loved it.

"Those people are crazy." A guy sidled up to Rafe, wearing a Browerton T-shirt and jeans. He wore black, thick-framed glasses that were in style. "I know it's Times Square and all, but they're freezing, hungry, and most of them probably have to go to the bathroom but they don't want to lose their spot. That's not how I want to spend my New Year's."

"I don't know. It seems fun. Yeah, it's inconvenient and probably uncomfortable, but it's an experience." Rafe found himself jealous of the revelers on TV, until he remembered how he almost froze on the way over here.

"I'm Alvin." He wiped beer foam off his thumb and shook hands.

"Like the chipmunk?"

"You know it. I don't think my parents really thought this through." He had a nice smile. That was something Rafe liked to notice in people. A genuine smile was one of the few times when we let our guard down.

"Rafe." He pointed to himself.

"Do you want something to drink, Rafe?"

"Someone's already waiting in line for me."

"Like a boyfriend someone?"

Rafe shook his head no. Alvin nodded with delight.

What this actually happening? It might've been the first time in recorded history that a guy came up and started flirting with Rafe. He was not the initiator.

Correction: the first time on American soil.

Perhaps he had this post-European aura to him. It was a major milestone for Rafe, but he had no interest in celebrating.

"What year are you?" Alvin asked. Poor, sweet Alvin, who was definitely Rafe's type, but did not stand a chance.

"Sophomore." Rafe pointed at him.

"Junior. What are you studying?"

"Geology."

"Political science." Alvin leaned forward and curved his lips into a flirty smile, a smile Rafe had given to plenty of guys in the past. "You have really nice eyes."

"Thanks." He wanted to give Alvin something. A reference for future dates. A participation trophy.

Alvin seemed to get whatever anti-vibes Rafe was putting out.

"You're not into this, are you?" He sounded firm, which Rafe knew was masking a feeling much more tender.

"I'm sorry. You're—"

Alvin stopped him. "Don't worry about it."

"Wait," Rafe said as walked away. He caught up to him in the hallway leading to the bathroom. "It's not you. Really. It's isn't. I'm getting over someone."

"It's fine." Alvin continued walking.

Rafe jumped in front of him, making Alvin lurch back and spill some beer on the floor.

"Look, I've been in your shoes before. Many, many times before. I hated it. But there is someone out there for you. I promise you, there is. Don't lose hope. Don't try to shut down that part of yourself like I did, because it doesn't work. And you don't *want* it to work." Rafe searched Alvin's face for a trace of proof that he got through. He wanted to impart this wisdom so badly.

He got an eyeroll instead.

"Jesus, I was just hoping we could make out at midnight, maybe give each other hand jobs in the bathroom. Chill out, dude." Alvin stormed off, but stopped at the end of the hallway. "Would you still be up for making out at midnight?"

"No."

Alvin raised his eyebrows in a question and mimed jerking off.

Rafe gave him the finger and motioned for him to run along.

———

THE PARTY ROLLED ON. Rafe only had the one beer. Not just because it was gross. He wasn't in the mood to drink and be merry. He would've been a depressive drunk, and nobody needed to ring in the new year with someone like that.

As it got closer to midnight, more people paired off.

They all revealed themselves to be as desperate as Alvin. Rafe used to be the same way, spending the latter half of parties searching for someone to make the whole night a success. But he was in no mood to kiss anyone, not when his heart was still mending.

Coop found them a spot on the carpet in front of the TV at eleven-thirty. Coop FaceTimed with Matty. They planned to do a long distance kiss.

Rafe noted all the couples and soon-to-be couples that surrounded them. Coop seemed to read his mind. He rubbed Rafe's shoulder.

"It's going to be a new year in a few minutes. A fresh start."

Rafe turned to his friend. "What if I don't want a fresh start?"

It was a question that didn't come with an easy answer, or any answer for that matter.

"I'm going to get some air," Rafe said. He got up and went to the front porch, but it was full of party spillover. One kid set up an iPad that livestreamed the ball drop.

He returned inside the house and squeezed through the crowd to the back porch. An ashtray overflowing with cigarette butts sat on the porch railing. The lingering smell of smoke hung in the air. But at least it was deserted.

All except for one smoker.

One very familiar smoker.

"Hiya."

EAMONN

Rafe gave him a look that brought Eamonn back to life, or at least helped him push back against the wicked jetlag he was experiencing. Eamonn wanted to pull him against his chest and smother him with a kiss, but he didn't know where they were at. Rafe was in shock. He was in shock.

"I'm not out here smoking." Eamonn showed him his empty hands. "None of those butts are mine."

"You're here," Rafe said, still in a daze.

"I coordinated with Coop. I landed in *Pittsburgh*." He said it with an American accent, the only proper way to say Pittsburgh. "Then I took a shared van all the way to wherever we are."

"Duncannon, Pennsylvania." Rafe ran a hand through his hair.

Bleeding Christ. His hand felt so good. He missed all these details of Rafe that he'd taken for granted. The crease of his brow. The curve of his neck.

"You flew all the way here. You hate to fly."

"I'm still not a fan. Our plane slammed into the runway when we landed. And the food was one level above dogshit."

That hadn't been the worst part about traveling. When Eamonn had arrived at Heathrow Airport, he couldn't go in. He stood outside the automatic doors, his heart trembling, bad memories searing his brain from the last time there. It took both Heath and Louisa literally shoving him inside.

He went through the same security line that he'd been in when chasing after Nathan. That meant the same terminal. The scene of the crime. His gate happened to be one over from where Nathan had taken off from. God loved to fuck with him. He wanted to turn back. His stomach crinkled like foil. But his love for Rafe, his need to hold that Token Yank in his arms, it was stronger than all the sad stories of his past, all of his fears and doubts, and it would continue to make him a stronger man.

"I had to come back," Eamonn said. "I had to give you this." He removed Rafe's mobile from his pocket.

"My phone! Did Scotland Yard find it?" Rafe turned it on and marveled at the home screen.

"No. The bouncer at Laffly's did. He found it behind the toilet. I think when we were in the loo...not using the loo, it slipped out."

"That's what we get for not using the bathroom for its intended purpose." Rafe looked at his phone one more time. The screen lit up his beautiful face, then he put it in his pocket. "So you came all this way just to bring me my phone?"

"I am a gentleman."

The moment was too big for witty banter.

"Eamonn..."

Their lips met in a heat that could've melted all the snow around them. Eamonn cupped Rafe's cheeks and savored the taste of his lips. He felt a part of himself get put back together.

"So what do Yanks do on New Year's Eve?"

"We count down. And we watch the ball drop."

"Whose balls drop?"

Rafe heaved out a laugh that was a cloud of air in his face. "The ball. It's in Times Square in New York City. It's all Waterford crystals or something like that. Then we sing *Auld Lang Syne*."

"You'll have to teach me." He kissed Rafe again. And again.

"What do they do in England for New Year's?"

"Where my mum is from, right before midnight, you say 'black rabbit' a few times. And then right after midnight, you say 'white rabbit.' And we also light off fireworks."

"Like on the Fourth of July?"

"You Americans, always trying to upstage us." Eamonn dragged his lips along his neck, smelling the Rafe scent that was imprinted on his brain. Rafe dug his hands into his back. He wasn't letting go. *Neither am I.*

"I can't believe you're here. When do you go back?" Rafe asked.

"Tomorrow night. But it's only temporary."

"What?"

"I've never been to America. I want to see all this great country has to offer."

Rafe stepped back, another wave of shock lighting up his face.

"I applied to Water Water Everywhere."

"You did."

"Don't celebrate just yet. I have a first interview in January, so nothing is a done deal. But I've been doing some research and there are loads of companies and non-profits that sponsor work visas, particularly for recent college graduates. I even found summer camps that hire Brits as counselors."

The chatter from the party got louder as it got closer to midnight, but he and Rafe were in their own bubble.

"What about your job at the box company?"

"I turned it down. They're not short of applicants, so they'll find someone else to fill my position. I'm going to work part-time in the warehouse until I graduate, so at least I'll have money saved."

He was surprised at how cool his uncle was about the whole thing. He understood that Eamonn wanted to explore what was out there. He himself had backpacked across Europe for a good six months before settling down into his first job. He even offered to connect Eamonn with colleagues who do business with American companies.

"Until then, we'll have ample amounts of phone sex," Rafe said.

"And sexting."

"And Skype sex."

"And I'll write you dirty handwritten letters."

"And I'll commission an oil painting of me reading them while touching myself." Rafe rested his head on Eamonn's shoulder, right where it belonged.

"We'll figure it out. Winter holiday has been bloody awful, thinking I was never going to see you again. But we're only getting started."

They joined in a kiss that turned into a long embrace. Rafe nestled against him, warming Eamonn all throughout his body. They swayed to nonexistent music, just the buzz and chatter inside.

"I'm no expert on phone sex," Eamonn said, itching at his scruff. "but I reckon we'll need experience to draw upon, to make sure our calls are technically accurate."

"That's a valid point. What do you think we should do?"

Eamonn leaned in and whispered in Rafe's ear: "I'm going to drill your arse until your fucking legs fall off."

Rafe wrapped his arms around Eamonn's neck and kissed him. "That's the sweetest thing anyone has ever said to me."

"You said it first."

"That's right! I did!" Rafe shook his head with realization. "I am such a bad ass."

Minutes later, Eamonn had Rafe up against the side of the house. His legs fastened themselves around Eamonn's sturdy hips. His pants bunched up just below his ass as Eamonn reamed his thick uncut cock inside Rafe's opening. Eamonn hoped nobody came outside and saw his bare bum pumping into his boyfriend. Americans could be squeamish like that, and he didn't want to make a bad impression in this new land, one he looked forward to knowing better.

Need pulled them together, and they held on so tight that Rafe was going to rip Eamonn's coat sleeves.

Their mouths bounced around trying to find each other in the heat. Snowflakes fluttered out of the black sky. Rafe's face clenched up.

"Is something wrong?" Eamonn asked. They had had to improvise with spit.

"Nothing. Nothing at all." Rafe was a vision of peace. "As you were."

Eamonn wanted to hold onto this moment, but he didn't worry. He knew there would be more. Many more.

Inside the house, people began the countdown. Their voices carried through the house. From all the houses on the block, they heard the countdown. Eamonn didn't know what the new year would bring for them. He was scared, but that was what made all adventures worth it.

"I love you," Eamonn said. "I should've said it when you left. I bloody love you so much."

"I love you, too."

6...5...4...

"We'll figure it out."

"We will," Rafe said.

They held each other's vision, neither one looking away.

3...2...1...

CHAPTER 31

RAFE

"Eamonn, do you have your passport?"

"Yes." Eamonn patted the front pocket of his backpack.

"Why is it loose in your backpack?" Rafe rubbed his forehead as Eamonn cocked his head at him. "Your passport is the most important document you have in your possession..."

Eamonn silenced him with a kiss for the whole Pittsburgh Airport to see. Rafe realized the familiarity of this conversation. Even though his parents could be annoying, they did have a point. Pickpockets probably had a field day with student travelers.

"Do you have a window, aisle, or middle seat?"

Eamonn shrugged his shoulders. "I got the last seat on the flight. I'm probably sitting on the drink cart."

"Will they let you drink on international flights since you're under twenty-one?" It was one of many complicated questions Rafe looked forward solving with his international romance.

"My mum told me not to get drunk on the plane. She

didn't want to see a news story about me being dragged through Heathrow in handcuffs."

"How is she about all this?" Rafe asked. He thought about Eamonn's family more than he should. And that photo of little Eamonn dressed up as Harry Styles.

"She's all right. She's going to miss me in the states, but she's glad that I'll be here with you. She trusts you to make sure I don't cock up. My sisters want me to get Jennifer Lawrence's autograph. Because *that* won't be a problem." Eamonn glanced at Rafe sheepishly. "So, when do I get to meet your parents?"

"Are you nervous?"

"They sound somewhat intense."

"Nah. You can handle 'em." Rafe's parents always called him just after midnight to wish him a good new year. This time, he didn't pick up since he was in the middle of getting his brains fucked out. Thank goodness nobody came outside! When he finally called them back, flush with after-glow and a full heart, he told them all about his night—minus the sex part—and the plan he and Eamonn drafted. They talked about the challenges that would come with this relationship, ones Rafe admitted up front. But they didn't tell him what to do. That was all Rafe.

"You'll meet them this summer," Rafe said.

They hung around just before the security checkpoint. Rafe kept looking at the departure board, hoping that Eamonn's flight would be delayed and they would have just a little more time. He tried to stretch out the minutes and seconds as far as they would go.

Eamonn seemed to sense this. "This isn't the last time we'll be together. No bloody way."

"When are we seeing each other next?" Rafe asked. "I was thinking I could fly to Europe for spring break. I was in

England for almost four months, and I never traveled. There are so many countries I want to see."

"*Spring break, dude,*" Eamonn said in his American accent.

A pair of actual California dudes, complete with flowing blond hair and wearing flip flops despite it being January 2nd in the Northeast, walked by.

"Can't wait for spring break, dude!" One of them said to Eamonn.

"Totally!" said the other.

"*It's gonna be so rad,*" Eamonn said. It shocked Rafe how spot-on his accent really was.

They each hi-fived Eamonn and entered the security line.

"I reckon I'm going to like this country."

Even though Eamonn had smiled at Rafe countless times, it still made him swoon. Those sparkling blue eyes, his bed head and scruff. But mostly it was the heart underneath, the heart that cared so much for people he loved.

They spent the next ten minutes chatting about nothing important, but using that time just to be with each other.

And then it was time to go.

Eamonn hoisted his backpack over his shoulder, but dropped it right after to hold and kiss Rafe one more time.

"Don't forget Skype sex," Rafe said, a single tear pooling in his left eye. "Lots of fucking Skype sex."

Eamonn wiped it away. "*Hey Rafe. Don't be afraid...*" he sang, the familiar melody of *Hey Jude* filling Rafe's ears.

"*Take a sad song...*" Rafe rested his head on his firm chest. They swayed to the song in their head.

One more explosive kiss and slip of Eamonn's tongue in his mouth, and then it really was time to go. Eamonn headed to the TSA agent.

"I know you like to wear your wallet in your back pocket, but maybe you should wear it in front," Rafe said.

Eamonn made a small production of putting his wallet in his front pocket for Rafe. He showed off the new bulge proudly. It was Rafe's second-favorite bulge on him.

"I'm your boyfriend. It's my job to worry about you."

"I like it."

Eamonn faded into the crowd of travelers, but before he went through the body scanner and disappeared into the terminal, his eyes found Rafe. He interlocked his fingers together.

Rafe did the same.

Connected.

CHAPTER 32

EAMONN – THREE MONTHS LATER

"What's your favorite ice cream flavor?" Rafe asked as they walked in the park just beneath the Eiffel Tower. Kids and families scurried all around them on this crisp day.

"I'm not a fan of ice cream," Eamonn said. "I prefer gelato."

"Then what's your favorite gelato flavor?"

"Coffee."

"But you don't drink coffee."

"Coffee by itself is gross." Eamonn extended his arm, letting Rafe go in front of him as they headed inside the Eiffel Tower. "What's your favorite ice cream flavor?"

"Vanilla."

"Are you serious? Out of all the flavors available, you would choose vanilla?"

They climbed inside the crowded elevator that creaked up the tower. They had only been together for eight hours, but to Eamonn, they hadn't missed a beat. All the emails, texts, calls, FaceTimes, and Skypes really did add up. They even mailed each other a worn T-shirt to see if they could smell each other. Not really, but that didn't stop Eamonn from wanking it many a time with the shirt balled up in his fist. Rafe said the key was not waiting for big events to contact one another. They had to keep each other abreast of the little, inconsequential events of their day, too.

Although no matter how much Skype sex they had, it couldn't hold a candle to the real thing. As soon as Rafe landed, Eamonn picked him up from the Charles de Gaulle Airport. They went to the hostel just to drop off Rafe's suitcase, but within seconds were clawing at each other's clothes, even though they were in a shared room. Eamonn put his tongue on pretty much every spot of Rafe's body. It was unstoppable, inevitable. Eamonn was going to take advantage of all their alone time.

They ascended higher and higher over Paris. Rafe was about to make a point, something he had clearly thought about for a while.

"When somebody gives me vanilla ice cream, there's so much I can do with it. I can put it in a sundae under hot fudge. I can smother it in whipped cream. I can plop it on top of a brownie. I can eat it in an ice cream sandwich or Klondike bar. Vanilla enhances the flavors of the food around it. Try having an ice cream sundae with rocky road or butter pecan. It's weird. Because you want to taste the ice cream, but you're also trying to taste the toppings. Not so with vanilla. You can taste both without feeling you're missing out on anything. Vanilla is the ultimate team player."

It was moments like these when Eamonn wanted to smother Rafe with a kiss. He would forever be curious as to how Rafe's mind worked.

"How did you come to this realization?"

"Years of practice and research."

They stared out the elevator window as they rose above Paris. The scope and size of the city hit Eamonn more than he expected. He hadn't wanted to do such a touristy activity, but he found himself awed by the Eiffel Tower. He held Rafe's hand. It was instinctual, like he had to process this with another human being or else he was going to implode in a cloud of dust.

They stepped out onto the landing. The air felt different up here, like they were in their own private universe.

"This really is a beautiful city," Rafe said. "I can't believe I'm here. I am on top of the Eiffel Tower. It's like next stop world domination."

"With a spot in BISHoP, you're on your way."

"Almost. I only filled out the application."

"Your professors this term said you had a great shot."

Rafe nodded modestly. "I'm not going to jinx it."

"Fair enough." Eamonn would just silently root for his boyfriend then.

They looked out at the twinkling lights in the night sky.

"I'm trying to hold onto this moment as long as I can," he said.

"Me, too," Rafe said. "But it's only going to be one of many."

Eamonn didn't know how long they stood there, watching the City of Love twinkling in the darkness. It wasn't long enough.

"I can't believe you don't like ice cream," Rafe said on the way back down.

"I like gelato, which is a million times better."

"I doubt it."

"Have you ever had gelato?"

"I can't say I have."

"We have to get some," Eamonn said.

"Is anyplace still open?"

Eamonn raised his eyebrow. "I've heard Spain has some of the best gelato in the world."

Rafe

The next day, they were in Barcelona, strolling down Las Ramblas, the main strip of the city. Rafe had counted at least five gelato places so far. He and Eamonn had hit up three, and they'd only been in the city for seven hours. He couldn't believe how easy it was to travel from country to country by train. It was like the DC Metro system, but instead of different neighborhood stops, they were in different countries. When Eamonn had proposed a spontaneous trip through Europe, he really meant it!

It was warmer here than it had been back at Browerton, and the sun shone down on them, making it very appropriate to be eating gelato.

Rafe was not disappointed. He shoveled coffee gelato into his mouth faster than his mouth could shallow it.

"This is freaking amazing," he said.

"What did I tell you? You refused to believe me."

"What's the difference between ice cream and gelato anyway?"

"One is the best dessert in the world, and the other is ice cream." Eamonn held his hands and gave him one of those deep gazes that locked Rafe in place, even when it was through a computer or phone screen.

A girl walked by carrying a Water Water Everywhere-branded Nalgene bottle. Rafe instantly glared at it.

"They suck," he said to Eamonn.

"They are helping millions of people get access to clean water. They do not suck just because they didn't hire me."

Eamonn had been particularly disappointed about not getting the job and the form email their human resources rep had sent him. It had been like a cold rejection to him. As someone very familiar with rejection, Rafe told him to get used to it. It just meant that job wasn't the right one, something Rafe also knew much about.

"Heath's cousin works for the British embassy. He's gotten in touch with some humanitarian organizations that work with ambassadors, and long story short, I got an email this morning about a second interview with this one called Food Planet. They're focused on hunger initiatives. They have an opening for an assistant project manager that starts this summer."

"That's great! Look at you networking. Where are they located?"

"Washington, D.C."

"That's right by me! You can have dinner with me and my parents every night," Rafe said, hoping Eamonn found the humor in that. Eamonn had met Rafe's parents in a group Skype session last month, and he told Rafe afterward how he couldn't get over all the questions they asked him.

"Just wait," Rafe had said.

"I really hope I get it," Eamonn said of the job. "There are millions of people who need our help."

"And you're just the one to help them."

Rafe yawned with the last remnants of jetlag. He wouldn't let it take over him, not for this precious week. It didn't help that he'd just completed a five-hour shift at Dollop before racing to the airport to catch his flight. He didn't think standing behind a counter serving cupcakes could be exhausting, but it was, especially when they hosted kids' birthday parties. Those things were like surviving battle. But at least it came with a paycheck. Rafe didn't tell

Eamonn that he was saving up for a flight back to England for Eamonn's graduation.

On Las Ramblas, music played while people dined and drank outside. It was like a tourist advertisement come to life. He dug the relaxed vibe of Spain. It chilled him automatically. They found a spot to order sangria. Rafe took all the fruit. He didn't know why he never tried soaking fruit in alcohol before. It was best of both worlds.

"So you've conquered gelato and sangria. What's next on your culinary bucket list?" Eamonn asked.

"Honestly?"

"No, I'd prefer a lie."

Rafe cocked an eyebrow at him. "I've always wanted to smoke pot."

"They don't have weed back in the States?"

"They do. But my friends never did it, so I didn't either. At college, same thing. I just never found the people who smoked."

Eamonn laughed, and the laugh got bigger and bigger. Rafe sized him up.

"What's so funny?"

"Well, you know where we have to go next."

————

THE SIGHTS and sounds of Amsterdam were very bright but also very dark for Rafe and he felt like he'd been here for two weeks already but when he asked Eamonn how long they'd been out tonight, he said it'd only been two hours and forty-seven minutes. And when Rafe asked him how he could be so specific, Eamonn replied that Rafe had been asking him how long they'd been out every minute on the minute. Rafe pictured a minute on top of a minute. Could time stack on itself like that? Maybe it already was. Maybe our whole perception of time was all wrong, and we were just one of infinite parallel universes all balanced precariously on a single minute, and if there was the slightest shift in any of the infinite worlds, then we would all tip off the minute hand and fall into an abyss. But was there really anything like an abyss? Could an abyss even be possible because you couldn't have nothingness. There always had to be something in the nothingness, and the realization struck Rafe like a shovel to the head, and his mind was incredibly clear as he had this amazing breakthrough and how could nobody else in this whole world have realized this it was so amazing.

"Eamonn, I've figured out the universe. I know what's it about."

"No more weed for you." Eamonn removed the joint from Rafe's hand.

"We are in a coffee shop, but we did not drink coffee."

Eamonn laughed, and his laugh was the loudest it had ever been. It sounded like a Mozart symphony echoing in the grandest concert hall in all the world. The Sydney Opera house, like from *Finding Nemo*.

"Let's go to Sydney, Eamonn."

Eamonn just laughed again. What if he was so high that he lost the ability to talk and Rafe didn't know Dutch and he couldn't get Eamonn to a hospital and he would never be able to speak again.

"Eamonn, please say something that is word length."

"You are so bloody high, mate."

People walked around them. They all looked so normal in their coats and their hats. Were they all high? Rafe wondered if people ever went low when they smoked, like if they sunk into the ground because we were all on quicksand technically. The earth that we think is the earth is just another layer and underneath are fossils and ancient cities. There were cities and worlds beneath their feet. How could people dig up ancient remains underneath without the cities above them collapsing in the hole? And rocks have been around for millions of years. The pebble Rafe just kicked could've been kicked by a dinosaur. Rafe wondered how those layers came into existence and became strong enough to hold skyscrapers. And would this road they were standing on be underground one day, beneath even bigger skyscrapers?

"We are blips, blips of history. There was a whole history before us, and there's a whole history after us. We are just tiny cogs in human history. There are ancient cities under sinkholes, many of which were formed during the Pleistocene Era. The sinkholes, not the cities."

Eamonn kept on laughing.

A few hours later, Eamonn pulled him into a hug. All of Rafe's skin was extra sensitive like he'd just been sunburned, and it was that moment after you shower when you realize *holy shit I'm sunburnt and my skin hurts*. Why did that only happen after showering?

"Rafe, I don't know if you'll remember this, but I'm going to say it anyway," Eamonn whispered in his ear. "I've never been happier than I am with you. You have filled my heart completely."

The statement punctured Rafe's high for a second, and it sent a wave of calm throughout his languorous body. No matter how high he was, and no matter if he remembered any of this or not, things would be all right.

"Eamonn, how long have we been out here?"

"Two hours and forty-eight minutes."

THE END

Want to be the first to get details on my next book? Become an Outsider. Outsiders always get the first scoop on my new titles, new covers, and sneak peeks, plus members-only contests and other cool goodies via my newsletter.

Join the Outsiders today and instantly receive a free short story called "The Road Trip."

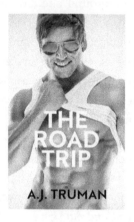

Get in with the Out crowd today at www. ajtruman.com/outsiders.

Please consider leaving an honest review on the book's Amazon page or on Goodreads. Reviews are crucial in helping other readers find new books.

Say "Hi" at www.ajtruman.com or on Facebook, and you can also follow me at Bookbub and my Amazon page to be alerted to new releases.

And then there's email. I love hearing from readers! Send me a note anytime at info@ajtruman.com. I always respond.

Can't get enough Rafe? He was introduced in *Out of My Mind* and kinda stole the show in *Out for the Night*.

Can't get enough of Nathan? This bad boy finds redemption in the next book, *Outside Looking In*. Turn the page to learn more.

Thanks for reading!

OUTSIDE LOOKING IN

Trust fund kid Nathan learned years ago that he's patently unlovable. He dulls his loneliness with casual sex, acid wit, and lots of booze. That way, no one else can abandon him like his mother, or ignore him like his father. Fresh out of yet another stint at rehab, Nathan stumbles onto a clue that leads him to his late mother's whereabouts. His search takes him halfway around the world to New Zealand to solve the mystery of why she left--and connect him to the family he never knew existed.

Liam would rather deal with sheep than people. After catching his girlfriend and BFF cheating, he moves back to his family's farm to connect with his roots and help his widower brother raise his kids. His other brothers want him to sell the farm so they can all make a big profit, but Liam needs one more year to prove he can succeed. When a handsome Brit wheeling designer luggage wanders onto his field claiming to be the farmhand he advertised for, Liam is suspicious, but he can't make it through lambing season by himself.

As Liam helps Nathan transform from Posh Spice to Old Macdonald, they realize they're the perfect salve for each other's tattered souls. But the longer Nathan holds off on telling the truth of what brought him to New Zealand, the harder it becomes for him to come clean. Because if he admits who he really is, it could shatter not only Liam's family--but also Nathan's one true shot at love.

OUTSIDE LOOKING IN is a slow burn, opposites attract M/M romance about lonely hearts finding redemption--and sheep. Lots of sheep. It follows Nathan from OUT OF THIS WORLD, but can be read as a standalone.

Available now on Amazon (and free on KU)

ALSO BY A.J. TRUMAN

The Browerton University series follows witty college boys falling into bed and falling in love, usually in that order. All books are free for Kindle Unlimited members. Each book can be read as a standalone, so jump in anywhere!

Browerton University Series

#1 - Out in the Open

#2 - Out on a Limb

#3 - Out of My Mind

#4 - Out for the Night

#5 - Out of This World

#6 - Outside Looking In

Short Stories

A Week by the Lake (starring Greg and Ethan from *Out in the Open*)

You Got Scrooged

Hot Mall Santa

ABOUT THE AUTHOR

A.J. Truman remembers his college days like it was yesterday, even though it was definitely not yesterday. He writes books with **humor, heart, and hot guys.** What else does a story need? He loves spending time with his cats and his husband and sneaking off for an afternoon movie. You can find him on Facebook or email him at info [at] ajtruman [dot] com.

www.ajtruman.com

CPSIA information can be obtained
at www.ICGtesting.com
Printed in the USA
LVHW051103040819
626449LV00002B/711